EMBRACING
the
DRAGON

Works by K.L. Bone

Rise of the Temple Gods Series
Rise of the Temple Gods: Heir to Kale
Rise of the Temple Gods: Heir to Koloso
Rise of the Temple Gods: Heir to the Defendants
Rise of the Temple Gods: Heir to the Prophecy (coming soon)

The Black Rose Series
Black Rose
Heart of the Rose
Blood Rose
Shadow of the Rose
Silver Rose
Princess of the Rose
Daughters of the Rose (coming soon)

The Flames of Kalleen
Embracing the Dragon
Releasing the Dragon (coming soon)

Other Works
The Indoctrination

See www.klbone.com for more.

EMBRACING *the* DRAGON

K.L. BONE

DEDICATION

This novel is dedicated to Stacey R.
for her patience while I was writing this story
and her never-ending friendship.

Also to my family
for supporting me through every step
of this journey.

CHAPTER I

ASH FELL FROM THE SKY, blanketing the charred ground like cascading snow. Amelia stretched out her fingers, finding the burnt residue cool against her pale skin, lacking the heat responsible for the land's horrific transformation. As she searched the valley for the conflagration's source, or any living being, toxic particles coated her lungs with each labored breath.

Normally this lush region would have been filled with the merry songs of chittering birds, and the scattering rustle of creatures hidden amid the tall grass. As she walked the field, the only sounds were the crunch of charred vegetation, and her occasional cough as her chest attempted to expel the smoke-laden air.

She scanned the horizon, seeking flames. Gloomy air surrounded her, with smoke so thick she couldn't even discern the fire's glow through its suffocating layers.

Amelia pushed forward, drawing shallow breaths as more particles lined her throat, turning coughs to occasional gags as she reached what should have been the forest's edge. In place of towering trees, she found blackened stumps. Her heart skipped at the sight, her mind rejecting the ruined vision of the land she had loved.

"What happened?" she asked the desolate terrain. "What, by the gods, took place here?"

She had cherished this land with its lush shrubbery, thick enough to hide even her darkest secrets. A place all were once welcomed to enjoy shaded comfort, perfumed by the sweet scent of fresh grass and wildflowers. Now, only cooling embers remained.

When she reached the clearing's center, a pitiful squeak drew her attention. She knelt, brushing her hand through ash and soot to find a bird chirping meekly between desperate gasps. Gently cradling the suffering creature between her hands, Amelia closed her eyes.

As though anticipating her intentions, the wren remained motionless against her palms, and its labored breathing eased.

Settling her mind upon the bird, soft-blue light emanated from between her fingers, bathing the unremarkable brown feathers in cerulean light. As Amelia's power drew out the toxins poisoning the delicate creature, it first flapped its wings, and then flew from Amelia's hands.

"Fly away," she urged. "The air remains poisonous."

The bird chirped in thanks before fluttering away, though Amelia was uncertain as to the safety of its chosen direction.

She resumed her survey of the ruined forest, helping a struggling squirrel in the same manner she had the bird. As it scampered away, Amelia stood and attempted to brush the soot from her hands, but only managed to smudge the fine black powder.

Without audible warning, orange flames surged toward her, forcing Amelia to jump to her left, rolling through the fire's debris, hands and knees stinging as they encountered hidden rocks.

A roar resounded, shattering the unnatural silence as Amelia glanced toward the sky to face a looming figure.

Above, darker than the choking smoke, hovered an immense beast, its wingspan casting a wide shadow over her curled form. The deep purple wings had a feathered appearance, glowing with what appeared to be golden flames, though they did not burn. Instead the menacing creature's wings fanned hotter, reminding Amelia of a forge fire amplified by a blacksmith's bellow. From an ebony body, its back feet were hooved, but its front arms had claws similar to a bird's, while larger talons protruded from the outer tips of both wings. A terrifying creature of utter destruction.

The dragon stared down with glinting silver eyes, glowing nostrils framing the fire within. With each methodical beat of its wings, Amelia's blonde tresses were alternately tugged and blown back in the wash of hot air.

Fear consumed her, stole her breath, and froze every thought. She briefly considered running, but knew she would never escape the creature's wrath.

Shakily, Amelia climbed to her feet, her blue eyes wide as she waited for her inevitable fate. The dragon's jaws opened, flames spilling to engulf the girl below before she could even utter a scream.

CHAPTER II

THE FOREST SHE LOVED—DESTROYED. The unknown dragon whose fury knew no bounds. The flames as inescapable as the recurring nightmare.

Rising quietly from silken sheets so as to not wake her love, Amelia grabbed her discarded robe, slipping it around her bare shoulders. Grasping the satin belt held in thick loops, Amelia secured the garment around her, pulling her blonde locks outside of the material before cinching it around her slender waist. Grateful the glass doors slid in near silence, she stepped onto the balcony.

Ancient stone cold against her bare feet, Amelia welcomed the chill as she walked to the terrace's edge. Cracks and chips dotted the gray wall, worn from centuries of use by the dragon shifters who called the ancient keep, hidden in the ice-tipped mountains of Kalleen, their home. The sun glowed with the promise of a new day behind the distant horizon, traces of color distorting the dark sheet blanketing the land. A cold breeze blew, only a few degrees above freezing, yet she welcomed it, lifting her chin to the sky. The icy touch soothed her heated flesh, the frigid air barely containing the fire within.

Tonight, she thought, grateful for the momentary solitude. *She'll be crowned, and everything will be as it should.*

The castle and surrounding grounds, usually a quiet oasis, had been transformed to a bustling labyrinth, with people coming from near and far for the new dragon queen's coronation. As a younger sibling of the destined sovereign, protocol demanded Amelia support her sister's preparations, and greet various high-ranking visitors. Both tasks Amelia detested.

Only as she crawled into her lover's arms had she found any sense of normalcy since the first dignitaries had arrived. Having spent centuries struggling to find her place as the former dragon queen's youngest child, the spare princess had never known contentment until she met Stephen, whose persistence and patience had pierced her strong walls to find a place in both her bed and heart.

And so she embraced the morning breeze, this one in particular, grateful her sister's crowning would be complete tonight, and she would again be free to return to quiet pastimes.

The sliding door alerted her to another's presence. Amelia did not turn, but kept her gaze on the snow-tipped mountains. When a hand touched her left shoulder, she relaxed, leaning until her back pressed against her lover's chest.

"You were restless last night," Stephen observed. "You always are, when you don't get to fly."

Though most of her kind preferred to embrace their fiery form with the light of the sun, Amelia favored the quiet, cool night. Each evening at sunset she would escape to the balcony, shedding her simple garments to take flight. She used to fly alone, but for many moons now, Stephen had flown with her. They enjoyed the quiet heights, the rushing wind muting all thoughts as they danced through clear skies, or whimsical clouds.

But these past few days she had returned from various duties so exhausted she could not enjoy the freedom her heart craved.

Turning from the mountains at last, Amelia wrapped her arms around Stephen's neck and pulled him close for a kiss. Pressing her cheek to the side of his neck, she snuggled against his warmth. "One more day, right? Then all of this will be over."

"Would seem so. None have challenged her right to the throne thus far."

"I didn't expect anyone to," Amelia answered, before pulling back enough to meet his golden eyes. "Unless you were considering doing so yourself?" She gave a teasing smile.

"Challenge your sister?" He issued a gruff laugh. "Have you seen her when she's angry? She'd feed me my own wings for breakfast."

"True. I'm relieved others seem to be aware of this fact as well. Though I have no doubt she would defeat any challenger, having to defend her right to the throne would place her in a rather foul mood."

"So I'm not the only one who's noticed she's had an especially short temper this week?"

"It's only because of the visitors. I'm guessing we're not the only ones who have been denied our daily flights."

Stephen nodded toward the icy peaks, now bathed in streaks of light. "Do you think we have time?"

Amelia sighed. "I would love nothing more. Alas, I promised to give a castle tour to the son of Lord Richardson and his new wife. He would find it insulting if one of lower rank did so in my place."

"Ah, yes. Must keep the nobles happy."

"Only until the coronation, thank goodness."

Stephen nodded. "One more day."

Amelia drew a deep breath, inviting the cold air to push back the flames. "One more day."

CHAPTER III

AMELIA SPENT THE DAY MUCH as she had the tedious one before. Guiding visitors to carefully assigned rooms based on their rank, and showing them around the castle grounds, had left her exhausted. Managing to steal an hour's rest around sunset, she woke to a curt knock at her door.

Slightly taller than her younger sister, the future queen entered without being invited. Normally Kaliyah's golden tresses, a few shades deeper than Amelia's sun-kissed blonde, would fall freely down her back, but tonight they were gathered in an elegant upsweep, baring her neck for placement of the silver pendant she would wear upon official pronouncement as queen.

"Amelia," her sister scolded, "you should be dressed by now. You weren't out late flying again, were you?"

"No." Amelia shook her head. "Sorry, I didn't sleep well last night." She ran a finger along her left eye, clearing specks from the corners and lashes as she attempted to fully awaken.

"The ceremony begins in two hours," her sister warned. "I expect you to be on time and presentable."

"I'm always presentable," Amelia countered with a tired smile.

The future queen did not rise to her teasing tone, instead glaring and walking to the closet to retrieve the gown she had insisted Amelia wear for the event. The floor-length dress required multiple layers of petticoats to fit properly. A shade of deep sapphire, the gown matched the eyes of her human form, and was adorned with a row of sequins, which spiraled down the satin to glisten in flickering light.

"Is this really necessary?" Amelia asked, preferring the less elaborate garments she generally wore. "Couldn't I simply swear fealty now and go back to sleep? You know how uncomfortable these gatherings make me."

Kaliyah's emerald eyes narrowed to slender flames. "You are my sister," she spoke sharply. "You will attend the coronation, and ball, and you will be properly attired for both events, even if you have to be tied down to get you into this dress."

"May I do the tying?" Stephen's voice entered the room unexpectedly as he stepped forward with a twinkle in his eyes. "Then again, if I do, we both might end up being quite late."

"You will *both* be there on time!"

Stephen put up his hands, fingers splayed in a sign of surrender. "Only teasing," he soothed. "I was coming to wake her."

The future queen did not join in their mirth, instead walking past Stephen to the door, her chin firmly forward.

Amelia turned and eyed the deep blue gown with a heavy sigh. "I don't see why I have to wear an outfit that's so elaborate; I'm going to have to strip it off for the ceremonial flight after the crowning anyway."

"To appease your sister," Stephen replied as he stepped forward and pulled Amelia into his arms. "Besides, I want to see you in the gown as well."

"You just want me to dress so you can enjoy taking it off later."

"You know me so well," he laughed. "You could test your sister's patience, and attend nude, but doing so might steal attention from the queen-to-be."

Amelia could not prevent a smile. "I suppose it would be unfair to steal the court's attention on her big night."

He gazed down and leaned forward, drawing her into a slow, sensual kiss, his hands reaching around her to unlace the simple white garment she currently wore.

"What about getting us there on time?"

"We will," he assured. "But if we're there at the last minute?" He offered a coy smile.

She lightly smacked his arm when he pulled her closer. In response, he peeled the straps of her gown from her shoulders as she melted into his caress. He pushed the material down, and she shrugged, allowing it to pool on the floor, revealing her to be completely naked underneath.

Amelia whimpered as Stephen buried his face in the side of her neck, nipping lightly at her exposed skin as he moved down her throat, his left hand sliding to the side of her bare breast. A sigh escaped, transforming to an appreciative moan as his lips moved down, Stephen dropping to his knees so he could press his mouth against her right nipple.

She shivered as his hands slipped back around her, pulling her closer, allowing him to engulf more of her sensitive flesh. Closing her eyes, Amelia savored the warm sensation of his tongue flicking against her skin. With a pained moan, she knelt before him, wrapping her arms around his neck as she pulled him close for a passionate kiss.

When she leaned back for breath, she met his golden eyes, the flames of his passion clearly visible. Amelia gave him a smile tinged with regret. "You know we have to get ready, right?"

Stephen's pupils narrowed, transforming to elongated slits before expanding back to their round, human shape. Pressing his cheek against her bare shoulder, he groaned in frustration.

"Trust me, love, I would much rather fall into the sheets with you."

Stephen sighed as he pulled away, pushing back a strand of her blonde hair to place a kiss upon her lips before he rose. "I'll leave you to it." He gazed down longingly at her kneeling form, and considered the sapphire gown. "You'll look lovely tonight."

"Come back in an hour?"

"Absolutely," he replied with a soft smile, before turning to leave the room.

CHAPTER IV

DRESSING TOOK CLOSER TO TWO hours than the predicted one. Several maids came in to assist Amelia in donning the impossible gown, lacing her into a boned corset and layers of itchy skirts, before finally pulling the deep blue gown over her form. Uncomfortable, the confining material and corset restricted her to short, pained gasps. They fussed with her hair, curling her straight locks into dozens of ringlets running down her back, to stand in contrast to her sister's elegant upsweep.

A touch of rouge and deep red lipstick completed the elegant transformation, and as much as she would have loved to deny it, Amelia could not argue the gown accented her best attributes, showcasing her hourglass figure before rising up to pull tight across her breasts, displaying the top of her ample cleavage. She considered adding a scarf to the strapless gown to create a more modest look, but the heat in Stephen's eyes when he arrived caused her to abandon the additional material.

"You look wonderful," she complimented him as she took time to appreciate the classic black suit, his shoulder-length blond hair pulled securely into a low ponytail.

"And you are stunning," he answered with a wink. "Though I must say you were correct. I prefer the outfit you wore earlier."

Amelia rolled her eyes as she stepped forward, her golden heels giving her a few extra inches, but did not make her as tall as her evening's escort.

Holding out his arm in a formal gesture, Stephen bowed his head before asking, "Will you allow me to accompany you to the great hall, Your Highness?"

"Certainly, my lord," she curtsied, before allowing him to lead her from the room.

The castle was a vast stone fortress; a maze of expansive halls and grand rooms. Though ancient, the building was well-maintained, benefitting from constant repairs and renovations.

Transformation came upon most during their fifteenth year, and was difficult to control initially. It took years to learn how to fully master the beast within, and even among those who had learned such forms of control, there was always the danger of turning in a heightened emotional state. As such, most of the rooms had been built to allow shifters to transform, while not comfortably, at least without the danger of damaging the ancient keep or harming themselves.

Amelia's heels echoed against the stone, swallowing Stephen's quieter footsteps as they glided down the corridors before emerging into a vast room filled with visiting lords and ladies also dressed in splendid regalia. Uncomfortable in larger crowds, Amelia was grateful for Stephen's firm grip upon her arm as those gathered greeted the sister of their future queen. Faces blurred in a sea of bows and curtsies, leaving Amelia exhausted before the night had officially begun.

Soft music filtered into the room, from an orchestra on the far side, helping to lessen the murmur of voices with the sweet sounds of the violin and soft drums. Delivering her near the wall, Stephen left momentarily, allowing the princess to scan the crowd, taking in the abundance of colorful gowns, sequins, and sparkling jewels.

Warm, late sunlight filtered into the room, but the majority of the chamber was lit by firelight, from large torches burning in even intervals along the walls, and candles in massive chandeliers. Shadows twisted, flickering between guests as they celebrated this rare gathering.

So enthralled was she in her quiet observance, she jumped when Stephen appeared to hand her a crystal flute of gold champagne. She accepted the glass gratefully, indulging in a sip of the bubbly liquid, enjoying the hint of fruit and slightly bitter finish.

Stephen leaned forward, slipping an arm around her waist. She welcomed the embrace, leaning against him, appreciative of his attempt to ease her discomfort.

"Would you like something to eat?" he asked.

"No," she answered. "I can barely breathe in this gown, let alone eat."

"Well, it's only for a few hours. I promise to be most diligent in helping you take it off."

"Stop it!" Amelia scolded, but could not keep the laughter from her voice. She turned to meet his golden eyes. "How did I get so lucky?"

"I don't know," he answered slyly. "Being a princess probably helped."

She tilted her head, her gaze challenging his words in the playful spirit she knew they had been intended. "You, sir, are supposed to be charming."

"I am," he replied with a matching smirk.

"Says who?"

"You," he answered, drawing her close for a kiss.

She returned the caress, when another voice interrupted, "Forgive me, Your Highness. Your sister commands your presence."

Amelia pulled back, downing the remainder of champagne before handing the empty glass to Stephen. "Duty calls," she said, with a trace of regret. "Wait for me?"

"Always," he replied, as she turned to follow the messenger across the room, and into a corridor, before being led through a wooden door leading to a chamber beside the banquet hall.

Surrounded by a select group of elders, and a few younger advisors, Kaliyah stood near the far wall wrapped in a shimmering silver sheath. Unlike Amelia's dress, worn over layers of petticoats, Kaliyah's gown clung to her like a second skin, the silver lined with rows of sparkling jewels, including down the long train, which dazzled with even the smallest motion.

"You look stunning," Amelia complimented her sister.

"Could say the same of you," Kaliyah replied with a tight-lipped smile before reaching to push back a stray strand of her sister's golden hair. "Blue suits you."

"Thank you for selecting this dress. I've never had your eye for fashion."

"True," Kaliyah answered. "Then again, you've had less experience attending these formal occasions."

"For which I am grateful, sister. You know how I feel about parties."

"I do. Which is why I appreciate all you have done over these past few weeks, to entertain our guests, and make arrangements for the event tonight. It has been rather taxing."

"I'm happy to help. Though, next time, if someone else could give Lord Richardson his tour, I'd be indebted."

Kaliyah failed to stifle laughter. "Is he still attempting to convince you his son would make a suitable companion?"

She shook her head. "I'm surprised he hasn't tried to force the kid on you instead."

"Who says he didn't try?"

Amelia laughed before switching to a more serious tone. "Have you considered a suitable consort? I mean, as queen, that's one of the things they are going to expect you to announce."

Kaliyah's smile dimmed. "Let's deal with one issue at a time. Tonight, the coronation. Tomorrow, the business of ruling."

"As you wish."

The smile returned to Kaliyah's face as she leaned down and softly kissed Amelia's cheek. "What do you say we get this event started?"

"Sounds good." Amelia dropped to a curtsey and added, "Your Majesty."

Her sister straightened at the acknowledgment of the higher rank she would soon hold, and proceeded to walk toward the door, pausing to converse quietly with the eldest of her advisors, Lord Rowland.

The woman in charge of the ceremony approached the princess. "Your Royal Highness," she began, "you will follow immediately behind your sister to the ceremony. You must attempt to remain precisely three paces behind her, never more or less. During the crowning, you shall stand on the left side of the throne, as heir apparent."

"The procedure has already been explained," Amelia replied.

"Yes, but were you listening as instructions were given?"

Amelia raised an eyebrow, pupils narrowing, but the elder woman ignored the shift in her demeanor.

"This is a sacred, time-honored tradition, which has been upheld by the ruling families for thousands of years. I'm aware of your rebellious spirit, Amelia. I will not have tradition disrupted by—"

"I'll behave," Amelia interrupted. "I promise."

The woman looked unconvinced, but dropped the remainder of the lecture, and moved around the room, issuing instructions to the party's subsequent members.

It took another half-hour, but eventually everyone was in place, and the group began the prolonged procession. The crowd had been moved from the banquet hall into the grand throne room, where those of highest rank sat closest to the throne on elegant benches of carved dragon shapes. Stained glass windows, illuminated by flickering lights, occasionally offered a glimpse of flames, and winged creatures represented in the colorful images.

Amelia's eyes did not take in the beauty of the normally forbidden chamber, instead focused intently on remaining the instructed three paces behind the train of her sister's elegant gown.

Only when they reached the steps leading to the throne did Amelia pause, glancing in an attempt to find Stephen. He was exactly where she'd expected, standing beside his younger brother in the second pew.

She flashed a quick smile, which Stephen returned, before turning to follow her sister's ascension.

Heels striking polished marble, she reached the steps on the left side while the high priestess of Kalleen moved to the right, and Kaliyah to the center. Other leaders and dignitaries lined the steps up to this trio.

All seemed to hold their breath as the priestess turned to address those gathered. "Sons and daughters of Kamar, great goddess who melds flesh and flame within our blood, we ask you to be with us now for the coronation of our new queen.

"A full year has passed since the death of our previous and beloved monarch, Queen Eliana. Now, our time of traditional mourning has ended.

Claiming the throne tonight is the eldest child of our late queen, Princess Kaliyah.

"Before I can begin the ceremony, I am required, by the goddess we serve, to ask if anyone claims the right to challenge Kaliyah's assent to this most honored and sacred throne?"

As one, the room seemed to take a breath, heads remaining as still as possible, yet eyes swept the room nonetheless. No challenge was expected, but once the crown was placed upon Kaliyah's head, and the necklace of Kamar secured around her neck, none would be permitted to challenge, nor to question her command, for the following six years. And even then, only one of royal blood would be permitted to do so. Rational, or not, Amelia's greatest fear was that someone would challenge her sister. One of the high-ranking nobles perhaps, or the son of one seeking to prove themselves.

The uneasy room remained silent.

The priestess drew an audible breath of relief, as though she too had feared an alternative claim, and continued, "Since none hath offered objections, I shall proceed with the coronation. First, I shall administer, and the queen will take, her sacred oath, after which I'll adorn her with the jewels of Kamar."

She turned to Kaliyah bowing her head, a gesture which Kaliyah returned before kneeling down in front of the silver throne she would soon occupy.

Standing in golden robes, the priestess began, "Princess Kaliyah, do you vow to protect this land, and the people who dwell upon it, with the grace of the gods you serve? To guard those who follow you from all who would seek to cause harm? To defend this kingdom from foreign and internal threats alike? To trust your people, and govern in a manner benefitting all, from the highest to the lowest of ranks, mortal and immortal alike, from this moment until your last?"

"I do so vow," Kaliyah answered solemnly.

"Do you pledge yourself to the goddess? That you will allow Kamar to guide you in her great wisdom, and aim to lead in her grace?"

"I do."

"With the power bestowed upon me, by she who blesses our people and guides our kingdom in all ways, I name you Queen of Kalleen, and grant you the gifts of both crown and sacred amulet."

The priestess turned, motioning for a young woman standing behind her to step forward. The girl carried a large pillow, upon which lay the mentioned adornments. Reaching first for the necklace, the priestess grasped the ends, displaying the thick silver carved into the shape of two dragons, each with blue-diamond eyes. As the clasp was fastened behind Kaliyah's pale neck, Amelia's breath caught at the memory of her mother wearing the same symbol.

The priestess reached for the silver crown, holding it high before laying it to rest upon Kaliyah's brow, where by design it tucked perfectly into her coiled hairstyle.

"I give unto you, Kaliyah of Kalleen, the jewels granted to our ancestors when the first dragon was born among us. Protect these sacred treasures with the same care you have vowed to exercise over this kingdom and its people."

The priestess turned from Kaliyah to face the gathered crowd. "My lords and ladies of Kalleen, your queen."

The pronouncement shattered the expectant silence, those gathered giving a cheer as Kaliyah rose to face her people, a princess no longer.

As she seated herself upon the silver throne, the cheering transformed to a distinctive chant.

"Long live the queen!"

CHAPTER V

THE REVELRY LASTED ALL NIGHT, people celebrating the crowning of their new ruler with joy and mirth. Together, the citizens of Kalleen danced ancient steps under swirling firelight, transforming the room to an elaborate gala of bows, twirls, and laughter. The party culminated with the rising sun. Dragons, one and all, shed their shimmering garments and took wing, filling the sky with a display that left those below in awe.

Amelia dutifully flew a few wingspans behind her sister, her blue scales cool in the frigid air, though the fire within kept her from feeling the cold. Her sister, and now queen, took the form of a silver dragon, eyes transforming to vivid blue. With her shimmering, reflective hide, she could vanish amongst the fluffy clouds, brushing aside the formed crystals that clung to her wings with each powerful beat.

Beside Amelia, and much larger with scales nearly pure white, flew Stephen. What she lacked in size though, she made up for with her blue flames, which burned with more heat than the golden fire the majority of dragons possessed.

Not that she had ever, thankfully, needed to test this ability for combative use. Her mother, the late queen, had been a powerful ruler, who reigned during a time of peace. Their people flourished under her leadership, and it had been a deep loss to all when she at last submitted to death's eternal embrace, having ruled the land over six hundred years.

Amelia had been only twenty-three at the time of her passing, and envied her sister's near century with the woman they alone had called Mother. A year later, she found herself longing anew to hear the voice that had guided her through so many confusing nights as she struggled to come to terms with the transformation demanded by their goddess.

She had been fifteen the first time she had felt the call, the transformation not painful so much as frightening. The crunch of shifting bones while scales rose to blanket her stretching skin. Once complete, she had stood in her room, a young dragon for the first time.

Amelia presumed she would have to be taught to fly, yet discovered that once in her winged shape, her body seemed to intuitively know how to respond, even if she did not. More startling, she was no longer alone in her own head. Not exactly a second conscious, for the dragon rarely spoke. Its presence more of a primal beast that pressed against her mind.

One's first transformation was always the worst. The fear of the change, and lack of physical control, emerged with the fury of a creature who had spent a lifetime suppressed under its meager human form. Most dragons transformed early in the morning, drawn to the light of a rising sun. Amelia, though, had transformed at dusk, where her blue scales glowed under a darkening sky. She recalled little of her first flight. The dragon had taken over, reducing Amelia to a prisoner in her own mind.

She had awoken the following morning back in her usual form, exhausted from the night's flight, with her mother by her bedside. Confused, she had sprung from the bed, jerking back the sleeves of a white gown she did not remember wearing the previous night. Expecting to find blue scales, she had let out a sigh of relief as she found soft, pale skin. She touched her arm, looking for any sign of the dragon.

"Your gown was shredded," her mother had explained calmly. "I dressed you after your return to human form."

"What happened?"

"You received the blessing of Kamar. 'Tis a great honor to be chosen; not all are, as you are aware."

She had referred to Amelia's best friend, Kelsie, who had passed her nineteenth summer without transformation. Though Kelsie had been a few years older than Amelia, the princess had been devastated when she learned her friend had failed to gain the favor of the goddess, and heartbroken when Kelsie was removed from the palace to live amongst the mortal population.

Amelia now recalled her first transformation. How she had clawed at her arms as the itchy scales spread, covering her smooth skin. The ground appeared smaller as she rose into the crisp air, driven by a compulsion she had never experience. A glimpse of blue flame.

"I don't understand." Amelia had shaken her head. "Why did I transform at night? Dragons are creatures of sun and fire."

"Most are," her mother had answered. "But occasionally, special dragons are blessed by the goddess of moonlight. The blue coloring of your dragon form marks you as one of these selected few. You will be sensitive to the pull of moonlight as others are called to the sun."

Amelia's face had fallen. "Does this mean I'll never fly with the other dragons?"

"Not at all." Her mother had given a gentle smile. "You will be most comfortable among moonlight, and for these first months, the transformation shall come upon you at nightfall. Do not worry; eventually you'll learn to control the change, and tame the beast within. In time, you'll be able to transform at will, as do all dragons."

The compassionate understanding had eased Amelia's fears, and offered a comfort no other had been able to match, until she had found Stephen. Having met him prior to her mother's death, he had proven a comfort in her grief, without which she would have floundered after the unimaginable loss.

Her mother had not been especially old by dragon standards. Members of powerful families commonly survived two, or in rare cases even three, thousand years before old age claimed them. However, during Amelia's nineteenth year, her mother had succumbed to an illness, which none seemed able to cure.

The realization this joyous occasion was also the anniversary of her mother's death placed a fresh pang in Amelia's heart. This processional flight, allowing the dragon within to push back the heartache, was a blessing. After all, only humans could cry for their loved ones; dragon eyes remained eternally dry.

Amelia pushed these thoughts from her human mind. Her dragon form had continued the formational flight even as her mind wandered. She appreciated the jagged mountains and rolling valleys from her view among the clouds. From this vantage, everything below seemed serene, peaceful. The powerful beat of her wings cut through the air, carrying her with ease as she followed her sister, hints of ice melting against her fire-laden wingtips.

When the group landed, they did so on various balconies, festivities officially concluded with the end of the ceremonial flight.

Amelia immediately transformed back to human form. The shifting of bones was always disturbing, though thankfully painless as her wings retreated into her back. The blue scales also receded, as though absorbed by her skin, causing an itching sensation that tested her self-control not to scratch.Transition complete, Amelia headed immediately toward her chambers where a hot bath would be waiting, having been drawn by one of the castle's many servants. Grateful to see the steaming water, Amelia sank down immediately into the tub, reaching for a bristled brush.

"May I help?"

Stephen's voice brought a smile as she stared up to meet his eyes before allowing her gaze to slide down his body, his pale skin unblemished by the change. His chiseled chest and flat stomach featured a thin line of black hair, drawing her eyes down. As she stared at the hard flesh between his thighs, her lower stomach tightened.

Stepping closer to the side of the tub, he leaned down and took the brush from her hand. "With your permission, my lady?"

"Please," she answered, sliding forward in the expansive basin as he climbed in behind her, warm water sloshing.

Once settled, he buffed her flushed skin, easing the itch.

"Thank you," she practically purred, basking in the relief granted by the soft bristles against her skin. She leaned into his embrace, pressing her back to his chest, the tips of her golden hair dipping into the water as she relaxed.

His hands came around her, encircling her slender waist before rising higher, cupping the underside of her creamy breasts.

"I'm so tired," she spoke softly, only to gasp as his hands closed lightly over her.

His fingers traced circles before running his thumbs over her nipples, which tightened under his touch.

Amelia raised her arms, tilting back her head enough to draw Stephen's lips to her own for a passionate kiss, his tongue sliding along hers as she gave into his touch. She turned, water splashing outside the tub as she faced him, rising to her knees to press her breasts to his lips, inviting desire to replace exhaustion.

Obliging, he suckled gently, then more aggressively, applying enough pressure with his teeth to leave imprints on her skin.

The pain of the bite drew another gasp from Amelia's lips, which turned into a moan as Stephen's hand pressed between her thighs, stroking. Her hands moved to his broad shoulders to steady herself.

Stephen moved his lips, licking across her chest to her other breast, pressing his teeth down, stopping just shy of breaking skin. The mix of pleasure and pain played to her inner beast, drawing the creature forth enough to change her eyes from blue to reptilian green.

"Stephen," she panted his name on a heated exclamation. Understanding her warning, he released her breast, and focused on stroking the place between her legs, where a patch of blonde curls matched the wet locks flowing down her back.

He slipped a finger inside her, and she moaned, the sound and hungry shift of her hips calling to his own beast. Stephen immediately stood, pulling Amelia from the water. She wrapped her legs around his waist, and her arms around his chest, as he carried her from the bath, through the door to deposit her on the bed.

Stephen did not spend time on additional foreplay, instead falling on top of the soaked princess, pushing her legs wide as he crawled between them. He glanced at the woman beneath him, glistening with remnants of the warm water, her damp hair splayed around her. The tips of her breasts were tight, flushed skin marked with an imprint of his teeth where he had staked his claim.

Unwilling to wait further, he leaned over her, pressing his lips to hers as he thrust his hips. She gasped at the rough intrusion.

Once fully embedded, he did not pause for her to adjust, instead pulling back until he was barely within her, before thrusting immediately back inside. Full-length, demanding strokes. He liked her this way, somewhere between passion and pain, pushing her limits. The thrill of seeing the royal dragon's flames peeking from her glowing eyes as he forced his way inside her. Stephen had never had a taste for gentle lovemaking. He delighted in the knowledge he alone could count himself among her lovers, having taken the virgin princess to bed shortly after the passing of her royal mother.

To hasten her pleasure, he reached down to stroke the delicate nerves above where their bodies connected. He paused, buried deep inside, and rubbed with his thumb long enough to feel her moisten slightly before continuing his rough intrusion, plunging in and out until his body tightened. He groaned his pleasure as he spilled himself inside her.

When he was finished, he collapsed, selfishly reluctant to withdraw from the princess who had given her heart far too easily.

Chapter VI

AWAKING HOURS LATER, AMELIA REALIZED she had overslept. She reached for Stephen, but found herself alone on the bed, with the covers pulled tight. Stephen must have moved her into the blankets at some point, though in her exhaustion, she had no recollection of him doing so.

Stretching, Amelia rose groggily. Selecting a simple black gown from the closet, she slipped the garment over her head, grateful the clothing required none of the multiple layers of undergarments that had been necessary the previous evening. Running a brush swiftly through her golden locks, she coiled the strands into a bun as neatly as she could manage, and went in search of her sister.

As many of the nobles had planned to leave in the mid-afternoon, the hallways were eerily quiet, save for the sound of her footsteps against the stone floor. The silence a welcome relief, but she hoped her absence had not been taken as an offense to any of the departing lords and ladies.

She walked into her sister's primary living quarters, and found her seated at a rectangular table reading over a stack of scrolls, several advisors standing nearby.

"Ah, Amelia," the new queen greeted. "Good of you to finally join us."

"Sorry," she apologized. "You know I'm more of a night person."

"A child of blessed moonlight," she mockingly applied the term her mother had used with such endearment.

Amelia ignored the tone. "Would you prefer me to come back later?"

"No," Kaliyah answered. "Stay. I have some important matters which we must discuss."

"Oh?"

"Take a seat while I finish with Lord Salvar." She motioned to the older man on her left.

Amelia obediently sat across from Kaliyah, losing herself to private thoughts as her sister spoke of the treasury status, which had been drained to pay for the coronation, and additional matters that Amelia found equally boring. As the voices droned on, she absentmindedly spun her mother's ruby ring—the only item she possessed from the late queen—and was thankful she had been the second born.

Utterly engrossed in her own thoughts, the queen's voice finally broke through. "Amelia, are you listening?"

"What?"

"Clearly not."

"Sorry! What were you asking?"

Kaliyah sighed. "I wish to speak with you, sister."

"Sure."

Kaliyah raised a hand, motioning for her advisors to depart upon whatever tasks Amelia had been too bored to follow.

The queen waited until the room had cleared, then pushed the chair beside her from the table. "Come closer, Amelia. I have a lot to talk to you about."

Amelia stood and turned the indicated seat to more easily meet Kaliyah's gaze. "What is going on? Did I upset the departing lords by not being present? I really didn't mean to sleep so late. You could have woken me if—"

"It's not that." Kaliyah shook her head. "Though a few were saddened to leave without bidding you goodbye. Those who mentioned you also expressed they understood, as they themselves were rather exhausted from the night's festivities."

Tension left her shoulders. "I'm relieved to hear I didn't upset anyone too much."

"Not at all."

"Okay. What are we discussing?"

Kaliyah stood, moving a few paces before turning to gaze down on her sister. "Amelia, there is something you must accept."

Her sister's tone caused the hairs to stand up on Amelia's arms. She straightened against the chair, more directly meeting her sister's eyes. "What?" she asked, concern filtering through her voice. "What's wrong?"

"You're aware, when a new queen is crowned, there are traditions I am required to fulfill and honor. A sacred charge passed down from queen to queen."

"What does this have to do with me?"

"As I am now queen, this leaves a question as to your position."

"My position?"

Kaliyah nodded.

"I don't understand."

"No, I suspect you don't."

"Well then, explain. Do you wish for me serve in a new advisory capacity, or…"

"In a way, yes."

A relieved smile curved Amelia's lips. "I'm happy to serve in any way you require."

"I appreciate your loyalty," Kaliyah answered. "Which is why this is so difficult."

"Difficult?"

"Upon taking the throne, there are many positions which must be filled. Lord Salvar, for example, has been promoted to head of treasury for both the kingdom, and my personal household. Lady Paulette will help to govern several of the smaller provinces in the eastern kingdom."

"What does this have to do with me?"

"One of the positions, which must be filled as part of the requirements to secure favor from the goddess, is to appoint a junior high priestess."

Amelia blinked uncomprehendingly.

"The junior priestess trains in the temples, to eventually become the high priestess of the land. A new junior priestess is selected with the coronation of each rising queen, with the expectation that one day the two will work together in harmony. The person chosen must be from among the purest of shifter bloodlines, and hold high rank in our society. I have considered several candidates for this greatest of positions, but after much contemplation and prayer, have decided you, Amelia, shall be the one to have this honor."

"Me?" Amelia clenched her hands together. The point of her mother's pear-shaped ruby cut into her palm, serving as evidence she wasn't dreaming.

Kaliyah nodded. "Who better than my own sister? And what better offering to give the goddess than a princess of Kalleen?"

Amelia stared, mouth agape, as her mind refused to process her words. "You want me to…"

"Become the next high priestess."

"I…"

"This is not what you expected, and therefore I can understand your initial shock. However, once you take time to consider my words, I'm certain you will find this is best for the kingdom."

"For the kingdom…You want me to…" Amelia stood from the chair as shock gave way to anger. "Priestesses are—"

"Among the most powerful and honored women in the kingdom."

"They are taken to the temples and locked away!" Amelia found her words with instant venom. "They are prisoners. Brides of gods they'll never see!"

"Prisoners? No, but it is essential they remain in seclusion, in order to hear and interpret the voice of the gods."

"I don't want to be a priestess."

"I believe, given time—"

"No!" The word was sharp. "I won't!"

Kaliyah sighed. "I was afraid you would be difficult about this."

"Difficult? You want to take my life away, and lock me up in the middle of nowhere. Why? Children are customarily chosen from birth to enter the temple. They spend their lives pure and virtuous, of which I am neither. Why would you choose me for this? I don't understand."

"Normally, yes, those selected for priestesshood are taken younger than you. However, when selecting the future *high* priestess, this is the traditional method."

"Find yourself another candidate. I will not consent to this. I love Stephen. You can't force me to leave him, and you can't force me to enter the temple."

Kaliyah's emerald eyes took on a bluer shade, pupils narrowing to reptilian form. "I am afraid, sister, you have no choice in the matter. You shall be taken to the temple by force, if necessary."

Amelia looked incredulously at Kaliyah, unable to hide her disbelief. "You can't be serious."

Kaliyah's voice grew cold as she said, "You will find I am perfectly serious. The matter has already been discussed at length with the high lords, and temple leadership. You will be escorted from the palace at sunrise, and taken to the temples to begin your training."

"No! Please, Kaliyah, why are you doing this?" she pleaded. "I can't go to the temple. Stephen—"

"Will be informed of my decision."

"I don't…" She searched her sister's eyes, but found only the beast within. "I love him. Please, I…I love him with all my heart. Please, don't do this."

Her sister's eyes remained cold. "I'm sorry," she spoke without a hint of sincerity. "You will leave him in the morning, abandoning all possessions and thoughts of any future but the one I have seen fit to bestow."

"I won't," she protested, but her heart sank as her sister called for the guardsmen stationed outside the door.

"Escort the princess to one of the castle's inner sanctums, away from any balcony or window. Ensure she remains there."

Her dragon stirred, but as the physically superior guards closed in, she found herself grasped securely in their power, two of the men grabbing her arms while another pressed a hand on her shoulder, pushing her toward the door.

"No!" she protested, courage failing as the words transformed to a scream. "Wait! Please!"

Kaliyah did not respond, instead watching with unnatural eyes as the men dragged Amelia from the royal chambers, unmoved by her sister's anguish.

CHAPTER VII

AMELIA PACED THE SMALL CHAMBER, anger inviting her beast to lurk just below the surface. "How can she do this?" she asked the empty room. "Why?"

Her heart screamed for Stephen. Surely by now he would have begun to wonder where she was. Had Kaliyah informed him of her fate? How had he responded to the queen's decree? Had he attempted to see her? Or was he, like her, a prisoner?

She flopped onto the plain bed with a groan of frustration, smacking her hand onto the mattress, the sting of her palm a distraction against overwhelming mental anguish.

That night was the longest she had known since her mother's death, as she endlessly reviewed and dismissed her options.

The queen's rule was considered to be absolute, sealed the night prior when the crown had been placed upon her brow. *Had Kaliyah been planning this the entire time?* She must have, as she wasted no time in making the pronouncement. Amelia could fight, but even in her dragon form, she would be outnumbered by the guards, who also were shifters.

Had she access to a window, escape might have been possible. However, as she waited, trapped in the center of the palace, surrounded by thick, stone walls, Kaliyah had effectively secured her inside. Finally, Amelia attempted to sleep, hoping to gain a few precious hours of rest so she'd be cognizant the following morning.

When she awoke, she kept her eyes closed, drawing several breaths in hopes the previous day had been a terrible nightmare, but as her eyes opened to reveal the unfamiliar surroundings of her confinement, she knew it to be real. She sat on the bed seething until the door eventually opened and three men entered.

"Forgive me, Princess," a tall man addressed her. "The queen has ordered us to immediately transport you to the temple."

"Where's Stephen?" she demanded. "You cannot expect me to go without seeing him."

The man's dark eyes caught her gaze with what appeared to be genuine sympathy. "I'm sorry, Your Highness. I am afraid you have been forbidden from seeing anyone."

Anger gave way to a numb fear as Amelia stared at the lord. "Gwain, isn't it?"

"Yes, my lady."

"Have you ever loved someone?"

Gwain nodded.

"And if this were your last time seeing her, Gwain?" Amelia's voice was softer than she would have liked, revealing pain the anger was no longer able to mask.

"Were it up to me, Princess, I would allow you to do so. Alas, 'tis not. The queen has given orders." He took a step toward her, compassion in his eyes. "I would ask, my lady, for you to turn and place your hands behind you."

"My hands?"

"I have been ordered to chain you, to prevent escape. I'd prefer to do so peacefully."

Amelia stared at him in disbelief. "You intend to drag me from the castle in chains?"

"I'll provide a cloak, so the people will not know, if you wish."

Amelia stared as Gwain approached. When he reached for her left arm, she jerked away. "How dare you touch me!"

"I have no choice in the matter, Your Highness. Please, don't make this more difficult than it already is."

When he again reached for her, Amelia stepped to the right and rushed toward the door. Grabbing the metal handle, she threw open the thick wooden panel, only to be met by additional men stationed on the other side. The guardsmen grabbed her, forcing her back into the room and yanking her arms behind her, holding her tight as Gwain slipped the thick, silver manacles around her wrists, before placing an additional chain across her upper chest.

The binding made it not only difficult to escape, but nearly impossible to shift as well. The chains would cut into expanding wings, damaging both her human and dragon forms.

Once secured, Gwain stepped in front of her and again met her gaze. "Would you like a cloak, Princess?"

"Please let me see Stephen."

Gwain ignored her plea. "Cloak or no?"

She trembled, heart racing, harsh reality washing over her with the same strength of the chains around her wrist. She stared at the floor, the world shifting as her heart pounded, hammering in her ears.

"Princess…"

"No," she answered on a harsh breath. "If you are going to drag me out of the palace in chains, let the entire court see what she has ordered."

Gwain nodded. "As you wish, my lady. Will you walk from here on your own accord?"

A tremor ran up Amelia's spine, but she managed to nod, not wanting to invite these men to put their hands on her.

She was escorted out of the room where more men waited, making it a total of eight guards charged with ensuring her safe arrival at the temple. Having traveled there once before with her mother, Amelia knew the journey to be a long road, requiring several weeks.

As she moved down the palace halls, and into the courtyard, several people stopped and stared, some walking by before turning to take a second glance, disbelieving. She searched the faces for her love, but he was nowhere to be found.

Her heart crumbled with each step that brought her closer to the castle gates. When they reached them, multiple stable hands stood, holding the reins of several horses, rations tied to the saddles.

"I'm afraid, my lady, you will not be permitted to ride by yourself. I would welcome you to ride with me, but understand if you would prefer another." He motioned to the additional men. "Your choice, Princess Amelia."

She swept the faces, recognizing none of her captors by more than a vague knowledge of their family origins. More pieces of her heart chipped away, and all traces of bravado vanished as tears rose. "Please," she begged. "Let me see him. You're taking away my life."

Gwain's expression softened, her pain pulling at the strings of his heart in a way her anger had failed to do. His regret rang true. "I'm sorry, Your Highness. Truly."

"Please." A tear spilled from her eye.

Shifting his gaze to the ground, he repeated, "I'm sorry. The queen has forbidden it."

Amelia's eyes squeezed tight, chains preventing her from being able to wipe away her tears.

"Will you consent to ride with me, Princess?" Gwain repeated the earlier invitation, but avoided her direct gaze.

She did not verbalize her answer, but merely nodded in defeat.

Hand gently on her elbow, he walked her over to a waiting horse and stroked along its ebony mane. "Hey, Gabriel," he spoke to the familiar mount. "You're going to have an extra passenger. No mischief. Be nice to her."

The horse gave a short huff in acknowledgment before Gwain turned back to the princess. "With your permission?"

Again, the princess merely nodded, allowing Gwain to lift her onto the saddle before mounting behind her, maneuvering his arms to grasp the reigns. "Forgive the proximity, my lady," he apologized.

Glancing behind, confirming the other men were mounted, he commanded, "Let's go," before pulling lightly on the reins to direct Gabriel from the courtyard and out the castle gates.

And thus the princess was removed from the only world she'd known, unable to wipe away the tears coursing down her face.

CHAPTER VIII

THE PRINCESS DID NOT SPEAK during the first day's ride, remaining silent in her misery. When they stopped to make camp, the captain set up a tent for her before pulling rations from his saddlebag.

As he arranged the simple meal of bread, cheese, and dried meat, the princess asked, "Are you going to untie me, or must I suffer the further indignity of being fed from your hands?"

"I'll unchain you to eat, my lady. But I require your word that you'll not attempt to escape, at least until the meal is finished."

Amelia's eyes narrowed. "Only until the meal is done?"

"I would be a fool to expect you to offer a vow extending beyond a limited time period. I imagine you would rather surrender your dignity in allowing me to feed you, than agree to an oath you cannot keep."

"And what makes you believe I wouldn't lie?"

"Because I served your mother," Gwain answered. "She never directly broke her word once given. I trust I can expect no less from her daughter."

Amelia wanted to call him a fool, but he was correct. The word of a royal must be trusted at all costs, lest all future promises be deemed worthless. Amelia considered refusing, but as she caught scent of the cheese, her stomach grumbled.

"I won't run for the duration of the meal," she promised.

"That's all I ask. Now turn around so I can unlock the chains."

She did as he asked, remaining still as he removed the heavy chain from below her shoulders before unlocking the cuffs. Once freed, she grabbed her wrists, rubbing alternate sides where the metal had chafed her skin, leaving it raw. She had a deeper cut in her left wrist, from when she had initially fought being bound.

Noting the discoloration and open wound, Gwain called for bandages. Amelia considered refusing his assistance, but relented, allowing him to apply a soothing salve before wrapping the injured wrist.

"Should help it heal," Gwain informed her. "And ease the pain."

"Pain you caused."

"For which I hold deep regret."

"Why are you doing this?"

"The queen's command," he answered simply. "Though I wish it were not."

"Does Stephen know? Did you stop him from coming to me?"

"I'm afraid these are questions I cannot answer. I was told only to escort you to the temple, which is the duty I am carrying out."

"Why me? I don't understand. There are many who desire this *honor*. I'm not one."

Gwain sighed. "Again, my lady, I have no answer. It came as much of a surprise to the guard as it did to you."

Prolonged silence followed before Amelia reached for her food, eating several pieces ravenously before forcing herself to slow, not wishing to upset her stomach by eating too fast.

A half-hour later, with the remainder of the camp set up, Amelia was escorted to her private tent, and re-chained, but in a modified way intended to allow her to sleep. Gwain left to give instructions on how shifts should be split for the night's watch.

Alone, Amelia settled herself onto the narrow cot. She thought sleep might not come, and had planned to plot her escape, yet as soon as she relaxed, her eyes began to close.

CHAPTER IX

AMELIA WALKED ACROSS THE GRASSY *field, the smell of smoke filling her nostrils. She coughed, struggling to breathe the toxic air. What had once been a lush, green forest now stood as a skeletal structure. Trees, previously covered in foliage, now husks of blackened bark. Formerly soft grass now crunched beneath her feet.*

Fear gripped her as she continued forward, wanting to run from the thickening smoke, yet compelled by a force she couldn't name. Breathing grew more difficult as she walked, the smoke stinging her eyes and throat as white ash fell, covering her clothes and tangling in the strands of her golden hair.

"What happened?" she asked the question that was never answered.

A loud crack drew her attention. She squinted, attempting to seek the sound's source, yet could see nothing through the thick gray air.

"Is someone there?" Cautiously she walked in the direction of the sound, yet saw no movement.

A roar filled the air, forcing Amelia to raise her gaze toward the sky. Staring back through silver, reptilian slits, she met the eyes of the furious beast responsible for the devastation. Expansive purple wings, textured more like a bird than a dragon's, with feathers glowing as though burning from within.

The creature gave another roar, which shook the ground where Amelia stood, his short snout revealing jagged teeth and a forked tongue.

Amelia's heart leapt to her throat, shaking in the face of this creature's wrath. She should fight, should move. Yet she remained frozen, gazing into silver eyes encasing a rage she did not understand. Staring helpless, she watched as the dragon parted his lips and drew a breath, fire visibly gathering in its open throat before he rained flames upon her.

CHAPTER X

AMELIA JERKED AWAKE, FALLING FROM the cot onto the hard ground. Waking to the jarring discovery of her unfamiliar confinement, she was unable to suppress a scream as her mind struggled to sort dream from reality.

Normally, in the dream, she at least avoided the first blast from the mysterious creature who haunted her nights. But this time, she had simply stood there, frozen.

The sound of her scream had alerted the guard, who threw open the flap of her tent. "Princess!" one of them exclaimed. "What happened?"

Amelia shook her head, pulling her knees to her chest and wrapping her arms around them before she lowered her head. She shook, overcome by the stress of the repetitive nightmare clashing with her life.

For two weeks they had been traveling, and were now two days' ride from the temples, where the men were destined to leave her in the hands of her new captors. Over the journey, she had formed an uneasy alliance with Gwain, in spite of the fact she had made two failed escape attempts, being brought back both times by men sworn to obey her sister's command.

Gwain arrived to find Amelia kneeling on the ground, refusing to face any of the men. "She screamed," one of them explained their reason for intruding on the princess' only sanctuary.

"I heard," he answered as he knelt, leaving a few paces between himself and the princess. "I'll take it from here, gentlemen. Thank you for your diligence."

The two men nodded before stepping back, allowing the thin piece of fabric to fall into place, creating the illusion of privacy.

"My lady." Gwain moved to the side and lit a group of candles, providing limited light. "Are you injured?"

"No," she whispered miserably.

"My lady."

Amelia kept her face buried in her sleeves, tightening her grip.

"Princess," he tried again, "I cannot leave until I'm certain you're unharmed."

"Unharmed?" The word delivered in bitter challenge. "You truly think forcing me into a life I do not wish isn't harming me?"

"This is not the first time you have had nightmares."

"You know nothing about me!"

"Teach me."

"Why? You're dragging me to this fate, against my will, on orders of your sworn queen. What does it matter if dreams plague me? Soon we will be at the temples, and you will be rid of me."

"My lady—"

"What should I dream of, Captain?" she asked with venom. "With what you're doing to me?"

"Your dreams began long before this journey, Princess."

Amelia's eyes widened.

"In guarding your mother, I've watched you for many years. You've woken in the night from these dreams long before now, my lady."

She looked at him, heart raging as she contemplated his words. Ashamed of her fear, Amelia had told no one of her dreams. Not even the man she loved. A man who slumbered so deeply, her tossing and turning rarely woke him, a fact for which she had always been thankful. Now this stranger claimed to know her better than the one who had slept beside her each night. It both entranced and infuriated her. She found herself unable to pull her eyes from his.

"What do you dream of, my lady?"

Against her better judgement, she answered, "A burning forest."

"Burning?"

Her voice dimmed to a haunted whisper. "The one in the valley, closest to the castle. It's burnt to near nothing. A ghost covered in soot and ash. And a dragon."

"What dragon?"

"One I've never seen before." She shook her head. "I've never seen anyone transform in such a way. It…"

"What do you mean?"

"The dragon is…"

"Someone you don't know?"

Amelia shook her head. "It's a dragon. But…it's different than us."

"How so?"

"It looks like our forms in the main body, and the same hide, but the wings are different. More like a bird, with feathers."

"A dragon with feathers?"

"It sounds crazy."

"Describe it to me."

She raised a hand to push back a stray strand of hair. "It's so dark of a purple that it's almost black. The darkest coloring I've ever seen. The wings appear like feathers, but a few of them glow, revealing the flames within."

"Like a phoenix?"

Amelia shook her head. "A phoenix has wings of solid flame, not encased within feathers. And not every plume shows the fire—only a few."

"A dragon with wings of a bird."

"Yes."

"A dragon with…"

At Gwain's trailing words, Amelia finally tried to meet his gaze. His eyes seemed distant, focused on the spot beside her instead of on her.

"The creature is immense. The largest I've seen. And he burns the forest with a terrifying rage that radiates from silver eyes like a heat against my skin. I don't understand."

"And how…" Gwain's words again trailed, forcing him to draw a breath. "How often have you had this dream, Princess?"

"Since my mother became ill," she answered, shaking herself. "I sound crazy. A dragon with feathered wings. No wonder my sister chose to send me away."

"Again, my lady, I'm sorry." But his words seemed distant, his gaze focused on something she could not see.

A dragon, but with wings of a bird, the terrified voice rose from Gwain's memory. *I'm frightened.*

He turned back to the princess. "Do you think you can sleep?"

"Yes," she assured, mainly wanting to return to the limited solitude she'd been granted.

He nodded, but never really looked at her as he departed.

He thinks I'm insane, she thought before returning to her cot, arm aching from her tumble.

Adjusting herself as comfortably as she could, Amelia lay down and attempted to return to the realm of dreams.

CHAPTER XI

"GWAIN!" THE TINY VOICE HAD pulled him from slumber. "Gwain, please!"

He had sat up, wiping sleep from his eyes as his sister had climbed on the bed. "Gwen, what is it?"

"Dragon with bird's wings," his sister had whispered in a hushed tone. "He did bad things."

"What?"

"It burned the trees."

"Burned?"

She had nodded as he reached down and moved her more securely onto the bed before rising to take a knee beside her.

"It burned everything," she had insisted. "Trees. Forest animals. The flowers. Then it tried to burn me."

"Are you saying…" He had stared into his sister's frightened expression, tucking his covers around her tiny frame. "You had a bad dream?"

Her blue eyes had brimmed with tears. "The dragon, he tried to burn me too."

"Oh, Gwen." Gwain had offered a smile, and took her tiny hand in his larger one. "You had a nightmare. Nothing bad is going to happen."

"But the dream so real. The dragon had wings, and I could see the fire inside. Bird wings. Daddy doesn't have wings like that. Are they more dangerous if they have bird wings?"

"Gwen, there are no dragons with bird wings, nor wings where fire can be seen on the outside. You had a dream. You have nothing to be scared of."

She had sniffled as he reached a hand and wiped her tears using a corner of his blanket. "It's all right. You're safe."

"Promise?"

Her young voice had pulled at his heart, prompting a reassuring smile. "I promise, Gwen. Nothing is going to hurt you."

The reassurance had stopped the last of her tears. She had stared at her brother briefly before throwing her arms around his neck.

Gwain had returned the embrace, running a hand gently down his sister's back. "I'll always take care of you."

"I know," she had answered with a half-sniffle before pulling back and gifting him a lovely smile. "Can I stay here?"

"Sure," he had answered, pulling down the blankets and allowing her to crawl under them before tucking her in. Seating himself on the bed, he had asked, "Would you like me to tell you a story?"

"Please."

Her smile had brightened as he began one of the ancient tales passed down by their grandfather. He continued speaking until her eyes closed. Leaning against the headboard, he had settled himself as comfortably as he could before closing his own eyes.

HE HAD BEEN FIFTEEN. HIS sister, only four. Over and over again, she had experienced the same dream, their compounding effect becoming more vicious as time went by. With his father often traveling for political reasons, and a mother who cared more for the status bearing heirs granted her than the children themselves, Gwain had been the one to soothe his sister's fears.

The siblings, though years apart, had birthdays within days of each other, and often celebrated together with a joint gathering. Most assumed he would be jealous, sharing with his younger sister, but Gwain had never minded, having been enchanted with being an elder brother from when his mother had allowed him to hold his sister for the first time.

On his seventeenth name day, and his sister's sixth, everything changed.

Having successfully transformed to a dragon at fourteen, and having little interest in following his father into politics, Gwain decided to begin knight training. From a highly influential family, Gwain was given his choice of training locations, and was excited to be embarking upon his new path.

He had paused his initiation, wanting to spend a last celebration with his sister. She had awoken excited, as he had promised to take her on a special trip for the day, waking him with the first rays of the rising sun.

After saddling his favorite horse, Gwain had taken his sister along a series of pathways up the mountains, eventually arriving at a thicket of wild roses. "I was going to cut some blossoms for you," he had explained, "but the roses were so lovely, I knew you would enjoy them more where they are."

"They're alive this way." She had grinned at her brother. "I wouldn't want them to die. It would be sad."

He had smiled at his sweet-hearted sibling. "That's why I brought you here instead."

"I love them!" she had exclaimed, as her brother dismounted and carefully assisted her in doing the same. She ran to the green vines and leaned down to inhale the flowers' sweet aroma.

"Careful of the thorns," he had cautioned, watching her flop down into the green grass. She turned on her back, staring up at the crimson flowers. "This isn't quite the grand gala you may have been expecting."

"I love the flowers, and time with you. Thank you, brother."

They had stayed there for a long time, his sister playing in the field under his watchful eye, when she had asked, "Gwain, what's it like?"

"It?"

"To be a dragon. To fly and look down at the clouds."

He had sat on the grass beside her, staring into her blue eyes. "Well," he began, "it's scary at first."

"Scary?"

"A little," he had answered honestly. "But not too scary. You see, once you transform, the dragon becomes a part of you. It's like…meeting a new friend, only the friend speaks in your head, instead of your ears."

"Your head?"

He had nodded. "And if you're nice to the voice, she will help you. She'll take you flying, protect you when you're scared."

"Like you help me when I'm afraid?"

"Exactly." He had smiled. "One day, when you meet your own dragon, she will protect you as well. She'll teach you to be strong and confident."

"Do you think I'll make a good dragon?"

"I think you'll be a wonderful dragon, Gwen. Almost as good as you are a sister."

The flattery had drawn a laugh as she lay back and stared to the sky, gazing up. "I wish I could fly now. I would love to touch the clouds."

"You will one day," he had assured gently. "And when you do, I'll come back so we can play in the sky together. How's that sound?"

"It sounds beautiful!" she had exclaimed, rising up to give him an enthusiastic hug.

Hours later they had returned to the manor they called home. Gwen had chattered away, excited to tell their mother of her day as her brother pulled a few blades of grass from her golden locks.

When they emerged into the grand dining room, where Gwain had expected a special cake awaited them, he found instead a gathering of men and women he had never seen before. His mother, Lady Lila, spoke earnestly with another woman on the far side of the room.

Surprised at the unexpected visitors, Gwain had wondered why his mother had invited unknown nobles for what was usually a private celebration. "Mum?"

At the sound of Gwain's voice, their mother had glanced up. "Ah, there you are."

"Is this the child?" the woman beside their mother had inquired, motioning behind Gwain toward his sister.

"Yes," Lila had answered.

"Bring her forth."

"What's going on?" Gwain had asked. "Is this about her name day?"

"Gwain," his mother had said, "this is Lady Viviana. She is here to see Gwen."

Gwen had come forward as requested, but instead of walking to her mother, she stopped at Gwain's side.

Viviana had moved closer, prompting Gwain to instinctively take his sister's hand in his, glancing from the advancing woman back to his mother.

"Come, my child," Viviana had encouraged. "Let's have a look at you."

Glancing up at her brother, after Gwain gave an encouraging smile, Gwen had moved to meet the woman.

Moving a hand to her chin, the woman had forced the child to meet her gaze, golden eyes assessing the child's blue. As the older woman had run her hand down Gwen's arms, the young girl attempted to turn her head, when the woman had corrected, "Look at me, child."

Gwen had done as Viviana bid, again meeting her gaze, the golden pupils narrowing as though moved by an unnatural power.

"Yes." The woman had turned Gwen in a circle, as her eyes scanned over the child. "She is the one."

The words had come low and sharp, prompting Gwen to jerk away and run back to her brother, grasping his hand with both of hers.

"What is going on?" Gwain had asked, anger filtering through his words at the woman's rough treatment of his sibling.

"It is good news," Lila had told her son.

"What is?"

"Viviana is a priestess of Kamar. She had a vision of a child who was destined to join her order, and one day speak for the goddess." Lila had moved her hands in a sweeping gesture, a smile lifting the corners of her lips. "Gwen is the child they seek."

"Gwen?"

His mother had nodded, smile widening. "Isn't it wonderful?"

"I don't understand." Gwain had shaken his head.

"She has been chosen," his mother had explained.

"For what?"

"To join the temples and become a priestess of Kamar."

"To join the—"

"She has been blessed," Priestess Viviana had explained. "The goddess of fire has chosen your sister to become her vessel."

"Vessel?" Gwain had questioned, his sense of unease increasing with every word spoken by the woman draped in golden robes. "I don't understand."

"She will be trained to become a priestess, and be given all the blessings of one granted such an esteemed status."

"She's only a child."

"Yes," Viviana had answered. "A blessed child." The woman had knelt, lowering herself closer to Gwen's height. "Come with me, my dear. You shall know wonders few shall ever witness."

"No." Gwen had pushed closer to her brother, who reached down and gathered her into his arms. "I don't want to leave."

"It can be scary," Viviana had acknowledged as she straightened her robes. "But you'll see this is for the best."

"No!" Gwen's arms tightened around her brother, who had turned toward his mother, unease growing to anger.

"Does Father know of this?" he had demanded.

"Of course."

"And he's content to simply hand her over to some stranger?"

"This woman is a priestess of Kamar," Lila had scolded. "It's a high honor to be chosen to serve any deity, let alone the goddess of flame herself."

Gwain shifted his sister in his arms, struggling to contain his frustration as he had lowered her back to the ground. "Gwen, will you do something for me?" he had asked as gently as he could.

Her eyes were wide, but Gwen had managed to nod.

"Will you go to my room, Gwen? And wait there for me. I have to speak with Mother. Get this sorted out."

"Please?" she had pleaded.

"It will be all right. Go to my room."

Gwen had nodded and, trusting her brother implicitly, ran from the room.

With her departure, Gwain had turned to face his mother. "She's not old enough to leave home, nor to know what path she wishes to take. You cannot send her away."

"It is not my doing, Gwain. 'Tis the will of the goddess."

"You're lying," Gwain challenged.

"I don't like your tone, young man."

"I don't care. You've never enjoyed caring for her. You were happy enough with a single child to secure your line, but Gwen?" He had shaken his head. "You never wanted a second child, let alone a daughter."

"A lie!" his mother spat.

"It's the truth. If you don't want her, fine. I'll take care of her myself."

Lila's eyes had narrowed. "You are training to be a knight. You cannot possibly do so taking care of a child."

"I'll choose another profession."

"Out of the question!"

"I will—"

"And besides," his mother had interrupted, "the choice is out of both our hands. Your sister has been named a future priestess of Kamar. Her fate cannot be altered."

"You think I am simply going to allow you to take her?"

"Yes!" his mother had exclaimed. "You have no choice."

"Young man." Vivian had walked toward him with an unnatural grace, as though she glided through the air, footsteps silent in spite of the stone floor. She had stopped a pace from him, golden eyes causing his skin to crawl under her piercing gaze. "Do not fear, for your sister shall be well taken care of. She'll enjoy all the luxuries and education of one befitting her station and high status. But...she must come."

Gwain had parted his lips to argue, when Viviana added, "Many have gathered in order to escort her back to the temples. If you resist, her last memory will be of you in chains as we take her away. She is sure to be nervous going under the best of circumstances. Do not make her more frightened than necessary."

"She's a child. Don't force her from all she knows. Not yet."

"I'm sorry," the woman had said, without a trace of empathy. "We must collect her now."

"Now?" Blood had drained from his face as he heard his sister scream his name. He turned, rushing from the room toward her cries, reaching a hallway where he found two men forcing his sister toward the outer castle grounds.

"Stop!" he had screamed, only to find himself pushed against the wall by two men he hadn't seen, his vision having narrowed to only his sister.

"Gwain!" Gwen had screamed, struggling to escape the man pulling her forward.

"Let her go!" Gwain had fought against the men, but they were stronger, easily holding him against the cold stone wall.

He had watched the men pulling his sister along in slow motion when a cold, feminine voice commanded, "Stop!"

When everyone paused, she had added, "Let the boy say his goodbyes."

The men holding Gwain had stepped back.

He had drawn a breath, heart racing as the man holding his sister released her arm, allowing her to rush to him. She had wrapped her arms around his legs before he knelt down, numbness washing over him as he had pulled his sister to his chest. He would never forget how her entire body had trembled as he took her in his arms.

"Gwain help me," she pleaded. "Please, I want to stay with you."

The entreaty had broken his heart to infinite shards, mainly because gazing at the gathered men, he realized he could do nothing to prevent them from taking her. Moving his gaze to the priestess, he silently begged for mercy, but instead found pitiless indifference.

He had struggled to find reasonable words. "Gwen." His voice had shaken and he drew a breath to steady it. "Listen to me."

"Please," she implored, shivering in his arms.

"Gwen, I spoke to Mum."

"Mum?" She pulled back enough to see her brother's eyes.

"You know how I am to become a knight?"

Gwen had looked uncertain, but nodded.

"And you know how excited I am to have been accepted for training?" She had nodded again.

"Well, you see, becoming a priestess is a lot like becoming a knight. It's a great honor to be chosen. They'll teach you lots of fun lessons. You'll get to learn about history, read lots of books, and even learn about magic."

"Magic?"

"Yep." He had forced a smile. "It's very exciting. When I was your age, I would have loved to have been selected to learn spells and magic."

"You would have?"

"Of course!" he had spoken the comforting lie with as much enthusiasm as he could muster. "But I wasn't chosen. Only the most special of all children get to be chosen. Like you."

"Me?"

"Yes, Gwen. You, sister, are the most special of all. Far more than me. Which is why you get to go with this nice lady and learn all you can. The same way I am going to go learn to be a knight."

She had looked at him, tears slowing as she considered. "But...I'm afraid."

"Yes, it can be scary. But it can also be exciting, if you let it. To be a knight, you have to be very brave. The same is true to become a priestess." He had reached forward and wiped the tears from her cheeks, drying her face on the back of his sleeve. "Do you think you can do that for me, Gwen?"

It took several deep breaths, but Gwen had managed to smile. A trembling, tear-streaked attempt, but a smile all the same. A trusting expression that had pierced his heart for his treachery, and inability to protect this child he adored.

"I'm going to hug you, and then you'll go to this nice woman. You'll learn all you can, and have a wonderful time. You'll become so smart being with the priestesses who will teach you."

"But…"

"I'll write to you, Gwen. Every day. And any time you're scared, you can write to me as well. I promise to read every word, and it will be like you're telling me everything, even if we're far away."

At her courageous nod, Gwain had felt his own tears gather. He pulled her close, hugging her tight so she would not see his pain. Once he managed to restrain his emotions enough not to scare her, Gwain pulled back and kissed her cheek. "Every day, Gwen. I promise."

"I'll try to be brave."

"You already are," he answered. "I love you, little sister."

"Love you too, brother."

Gwain had stood and, walking her to Viviana, had transferred his sister's tiny fingers from his hand to those of the priestess, who smiled down at the child.

"Your brother is right," she had assured. "You will learn a great deal at the temples, and become a fine priestess for the goddess. Now come, we must depart immediately."

And with that, Viviana had pulled Gwen from his sight.

CHAPTER XII

"CAPTAIN," A VOICE CALLED THROUGH his dream.

"Gwen!" He woke, jerking to his knees.

"Forgive me, Captain. You said to wake you at sunrise."

"Oh, yes," he answered, but his heart pounded faster than he would have preferred, memories blending with dreams the closer they moved toward the temples.

How long had it been since he'd awoken calling his sister's name? *Years.* The memories, painful. Of all his failures, Gwen, by far, was his greatest.

As the guard left him to rise and pack the provisions he carried, Gwain attempted to push the past from his mind.

She's a princess, he reminded himself. *Set to be a future high priestess. What happened to Gwen won't...*

Despite the reassuring mantra, with each passing day he grew more uncertain. His sister had been highborn. Their father, a powerful man from a prestigious bloodline. All of which had aligned to condemn, not save, the little girl he had promised to protect from all harm. Now here he was, ordered again to hand a girl in his charge over to the same temples who'd torn his frightened sister from his arms.

Heart heavy, Gwain finished packing and offered a few extra oats to Gabriel before saddling the horse. Leading the stallion to the princess, Gwain assisted her onto the horse before mounting behind her. Now only two days' ride from the temple, Amelia's pleas for him to change his mind had ceased, the fire in her eyes dimming to resignation.

That evening, his men suggested, if they could stand riding a few more hours, they could reach the temple grounds that night. Gwain rejected the idea, ordering his men to bed down.

Sometime in the night, he heard a shout. He had dreamed of her again, his sister, her child-like plea transforming to the deeper tones of the man calling his name.

"Captain Gwain!" the shout came again, drawing him from troubled dreams to a far more dangerous reality.

"Gwain, get up!"

He jerked awake, panic in the call bringing him to instant awareness. Reaching for the sword beside him, Gwain removed the blade from its leather sheath and rose in a single, fluid motion.

Astride matching black horses, seven men approached, garbed in gray cloaks, silver swords in their hands.

"Who goes there?" Gwain demanded, his men gathering to form a wall between the intruders and the princess, who had crawled from her tent at the commotion.

"What's going on?" she asked quietly, but no one paid her any attention. The guards kept their eyes forward.

When they reached the clearing where the guard had made camp, the advancing men stopped, save for one who rode forth into the firelight. Features highlighted, Gwain looked up at the man in confusion.

"Lord Yarin?" he asked the high-ranking aristocrat. "What brings you here?"

"A change of plans," Yarin answered. "The queen has reconsidered her sister's placement in the temples. I am to personally escort her back."

"Personally escort her?" Gwain stared at him with instant distrust. "Why would the queen choose your men to return her, over her own knights, who have seen her safely through this journey?"

"She requests you continue on and deliver the letter she prepared for the high priestess."

"There are eight of us. It only takes one to deliver a letter."

"It's a missive of great importance, and after your long journey—"

"No longer than yours, my lord."

"We flew the majority of the way, and journeyed only from a nearby estate. You could not fly, with the princess in chains."

Amelia's heart leapt at Yarin's words. Her sister had come to her senses! Amelia's lips split into a smile as she walked toward her savior, but Gwain held out his arm, blocking her steps.

"It's all right," Amelia said, relief audible in her words. "She's changed her mind."

Gwain turned and met her eyes. Only then did she notice his tense body, the too-straight line of his back, and the tight grip on his sword. He shook his head, a slight movement meant for Amelia alone.

"Come, Princess," Yarin beckoned, moving closer. "I'll take you home."

Amelia looked again from Gwain to the man on the horse. He had a thin appearance, with a narrow nose and thin, pronounced cheeks. Pulling his mount to a complete stop, he stared across the firelight, but his eyes were only for the princess. His piercing gaze, even from across the campfire's slender flames, and possessive expression caused Amelia to step closer to Gwain.

Turning back to face Yarin, Gwain politely inquired, "I assume you bring sealed orders to verify your claim?"

"Are you questioning my honor?"

"Not your honor, my lord. Duty dictates I must insist on seeing the sealed orders."

"You should know better than to question your superiors, guardsman."

"Captain," he corrected, with a deceptively easy smile, "charged with protecting the royal family from all possible threats. No matter what their rank."

"Protect them?" Yarin gave a crude laugh. "You are taking this lovely creature at your side to the temples. You, of all people, Gwain, know what is done to beautiful women behind those *sacred* walls."

A harsh silence fell, prompting Amelia to turn toward Gwain. "What is he talking about?"

The captain did not answer, but maintained his gaze on the men across the shadowed field.

"Gwain?" she asked again. "What does he mean?"

"Ah, so the good captain hasn't told you what's entailed in being trained as a priestess? Though, given you were ordered there by the queen, I suppose warning you would have been a moot point." Yarin dismounted, lightly holding his horse's reins as he stepped closer, both arms out in a non-threatening gesture. "Come, Princess. Don't you want to be safe? Come to me and all will be well."

Amelia's skin crawled, though she was uncertain as to why.

"Your written orders?" Gwain repeated his previous demand.

"Here." Yarin reached into an inner pocket of his cloak to withdraw a tied scroll. One of the men to Amelia's left took the offered proof and brought it to Gwain, who sheathed his sword to remove the ribbon. The seal appeared official, the recognizable imprint of the queen's ring standing against the wax. Gwain broke the seal, opening the parchment to find Yarin's statement mirrored by the inscription within, and signed by the newly crowned queen.

"This seems to be in—"

"Gwain." His words ceased when the princess said his name and stepped closer. Whispering into his left ear, Amelia continued, "That's not her signature."

His eyes went to the bottom where the seal had again been pressed into the parchment. The queen's personal seal. "Are you certain?"

"My sister did not sign this order."

50

Gwain nodded and raised his hand. "I'm afraid, my lord, these orders do not meet protocol. I am happy to escort the princess back to the palace, but I cannot release her to you, or any other. She is royal."

"You intend to surrender her to the temples, revoking her royal status."

"But these orders change that, do they not, Lord Yarin? If the princess is to be returned to the palace, she falls under the protection of the royal guardsmen. My men are happy to escort the princess back to her sister."

"This is not what the queen has ordered. You'll surrender her to our care, and you shall do so now." Anger filled Yarin's voice, making Amelia grateful to have Gwain standing between her and the strange lord, in spite of her captive status.

"Surely such a transfer could wait until morning?" Gwain attempted a different tact.

"No," Yarin insisted. "You will hand over the princess and continue your errand, per the queen's orders."

"The letter is a lie," Gwain cut pretense.

"It most certainly is not."

"That's not Queen Kaliyah's signature," Amelia inserted herself into the conversation.

The declaration surprised Yarin, who turned toward one of the men behind him. "You said the letter was a perfect match!"

"I thought it—"

"I don't know how you forged her seal," Amelia said, "but she did not write this letter."

"Yarin," Gwain challenged, "what's this about?"

"I would think it would be obvious," Yarin answered. "You have a princess of Kalleen. Do you think the other nobles would have stood for having her hauled to the temples, had the queen given time to offer objection?"

"Her sister is crowned. This one has no ambitions for the throne."

"Ah, but she could. Or her children could."

"I don't understand. What do you want?" Amelia again cut in.

"Why, you, Princess," Yarin answered. "Once you enter service to the temples, surrender all titles and status. Any possible claim to the throne. Why do you think your sister ordered you there in the first place, if not to remove you from the potential line of succession? After she was crowned, you, and those of your direct line, alone have the power to challenge her throne."

"Challenge her throne?" Amelia shook her head. "I've never wanted anything to do with it."

Pulling his sword from its sheath, Gwain focused on Amelia's sapphire gaze. "What he means, Princess, is if you were to marry and have a child, your own desires would not matter."

"What?"

"Tradition dictates, if you marry and bear an heir, your husband would have the right to challenge for the throne, in the name of fighting for your child's right to succession. Were he to succeed, he would rule as regent, until said child came of an age to rule on their own."

Amelia shook her head. "I don't understand."

"He wants you for his bed, Princess."

Amelia jerked to look at the lord, her eyes meeting his in newfound fear.

"Come now, Princess. Surely my bed would be better than anything you will find in the temples. I'm a skilled lover, as many ladies have attested. I promise to make it good for you. And should you not enjoy my company, it need only be until you produce my child."

"Produce your child?" She stepped back, ice filling the veins which had held warm blood moments before. "No."

"You have no choice, and I tire of this discussion." Yarin refocused his attention on Gwain. "Hand over the princess, and this will end peacefully. Or refuse, and we shall take her by force."

You have no choice, Gwain's mother echoed.

Followed by his sister's screams.

Jarred by the memory, he took a step toward the noble, hand flexing on the grip of his blade. "You are not taking her anywhere."

"Yes." Yarin motioned, and his men encroached upon the camp. "I am."

With a flick of Yarin's wrist, the standoff shattered as men raised swords to the ring of clashing steel. Gwain did not rush to engage though, instead grabbing Amelia's arm and dragging her back toward the horses, which had thankfully been tethered on the far side of the field, placing the other seven knights between the advancing men and their princess.

Slipping a bridle on in a practiced motion, but not bothering with a saddle, Gwain mounted his horse. Pulling Amelia up behind him, Gwain lightly touched Gabriel's neck before guiding him down the path, racing away from the battle.

"The men," Amelia protested.

"Are sworn to protect you first."

Responding to the danger, Gabriel moved swiftly without any encouragement, leaving Gwain grateful for the smooth path and nearly full moon lighting their way.

Gwain quickly realized they were not alone; one of Yarin's riders had managed to make it past his men to give chase.

Guiding Gabriel to the forest edge, Gwain lowered Amelia to the ground mid turn. "Go to the trees," he instructed, watching her run in the indicated direction without hesitation. Gwain managed to pull his sword in time to meet the oncoming man.

Without a saddle, Gwain struggled not to fall under the force of the weapons' collision. Gabriel instinctively shifted to better support him. When the swords drew back, the other man jumped from his own smaller horse, launching himself at Gwain, who dismounted as well.

"Never did like fighting on horseback," the stranger said. "Always preferred on foot myself."

Gwain did not respond, but lunged toward the man, bringing his sword to the attacker's right side. The man parried, blocking the intended strike. Gwain swung up, causing the man to step back to avoid losing control of his sword. At the retreat, Gwain followed, thrusting his blade toward his opponent's chest. The man jerked back, twisting out of the attack before bringing his own weapon to Gwain's right.

The captain sidestepped the stroke, turning to bring his elbow into the man's arm, pushing with all his strength. The man struggled for balance, his body turning farther than he'd intended as Gwain followed the motion with his sword, slicing the sharp edge into his attacker's shoulder and upper back.

The man screamed in pain, retreating again.

Gwain followed his attacker, delivering a second blow to the center of his back before the man managed to step far enough away to turn.

With a crooked posture, the man held his blade in a defensive stance. Gwain advanced, swinging toward the man's injured shoulder. To his credit, he managed to stop Gwain's sword, but a grimace betrayed his pain.

Gwain again swung to the man's right, down upon his injured arm. On the fourth stroke, the limb gave way, the attacker's blade falling to the ground. Gwain thrust up, the sword's deadly tip slicing into the man's now vulnerable throat, spilling blood and splattering both their shirts with the hot, sticky substance as the man fell to the ground with a gurgling sound, never to rise.

CHAPTER XIII

GWAIN SCANNED THE AREA. GABRIEL stood at the tree line where he'd left Amelia. He walked to the horse, holding out a hand, which Gabriel pressed his nose against as Gwain grasped the reins attached to the bridle.

"Good boy," he praised softly, stroking the stallion's mane.

Fearing the man he had killed might not be the last, he called the princess' name, half expecting her not to answer.

To his surprise, Amelia appeared at his call, emerging from a thicket, stray pieces of grass tangled in her long locks.

"Are you all right, my lady?"

"Yes," she answered, looking alarmed. "Are you?"

"I am," he assured, watching her reach toward the side of his face, though she paused before touching his skin. "The blood's not mine," he said, only now realizing how he must appear, face and neck covered by arterial spray. Tearing a piece of cloth from his cloak, Gwain swiped at the blood.

"Here." Amelia stepped closer. "Allow me."

After he handed her the cloth, she wiped at the thick liquid. "As good as I can do without water."

"Thank you. May I suggest we move from here, in case others head our way?"

Amelia nodded, allowing the knight to again lift her onto the horse before he climbed behind her, looping the attacker's horse's reins into his belt so the horse would follow them.

For a time they rode in silence until Amelia remarked, "I don't understand."

"My lady?"

"Why did they fight in human form? I mean, if they came to take me, and they had more men, would it not have been..."

"Dragon fire could burn the forest, especially this time of year. We're very close to the temples. If they had, even accidentally, burned down a temple, Yarin would have been held accountable for it. And, this close, the temples would have seen the battle and sent reinforcements. Far safer for Yarin to try and grab you in human form."

"Oh," was Amelia's only response as they continued down the moonlit path.

Gwain also grappled with what had transpired. Yarin's words rang disturbingly true.

By the time they'd reached the final turn toward the temples, Gwain was reasonably sure they were safe, and hoped his men had fared as well as he with their attackers.

As though reading his mind, Amelia broke their silence. "I'm sorry if any of the guardsmen were harmed. They were only doing their job. I would never wish any of them ill."

Surprised at her gentle sentiment, Gwain pulled on the reins and, after handing the smaller horse's tether to Amelia, directed Gabriel from the path into a thicket of trees. He dismounted, stepping cautiously to better lead the horses through the underbrush.

"What are you doing?" Amelia asked in alarm.

The captain did not answer, instead leading the two horses and remaining rider deeper into the woods.

They traveled for half an hour, until they reached a bubbling spring where he pulled her from the horse's back, lifting her effortlessly, and then tied the two horses' leads together, trusting Gabriel to stay put.

"What are we doing here?" Amelia asked, her voice holding fear.

"What I should have done from the beginning. Give you a choice."

"A choice?"

Gwain nodded. "My lady, what Yarin said about the temples…" His words, laced with sorrow, trailed.

"I heard him speak, but I don't understand what he meant."

"Gwen."

"Who's Gwen?"

The knight drew a deep breath. "She was my sister. I was seventeen, barely a man. She was only six, and terrified when they took her away. Everything happened so suddenly. Without any warning, they appeared, and within minutes, my only sister was gone."

"She was selected to become a priestess?"

He nodded. "My parents were largely absent in her upbringing. We were everything to each other. Best friends, if there can be such a thing between siblings. I was very protective. Her fear, that she put aside at my urging, still haunts me."

"I don't understand. It's an honor to be chosen to speak for the goddess, is it not?"

"That is what I was told, and how I encouraged her to go. But you see…the truth is a different story."

CHAPTER XIV

26 YEARS AGO

"HAPPY NAME DAY!" ROB GREETED, entering the room without bothering to knock. "Any special plans?"

"Not really," Gwain answered as his friend plopped down on a chair beside him. "Finishing a letter," he added, writing a final line before putting down his quill and glancing up.

"A letter?" Rob offered a teasing smile. "Did you finally get a girl?"

Gwain rolled his eyes. "You know who I'm writing."

Rob sighed. "Yeah, but come on, Gwain. Does it have to be every single day? What could you possibly have to tell her different from yesterday? And it's not like she writes you that frequently. What's it been? Three weeks since her last letter?"

"I made a promise," Gwain defended. "A fact you know well."

"Kind of weird. If you were writing a girlfriend, sure, but—"

"Leave it alone," Gwain warned.

Rob moved his arms palm-up in a gesture of surrender. "Why don't you finish and we'll go flying? Visit the field you like?"

"Sure," Gwain replied. "Sounds great."

After sealing the letter, and dropping it off to the carrier, Gwain enjoyed flying through the warm winds of a wonderfully sunny day. Time off with friends was a rare treat among upper academy students.

He had returned home only a handful of times over the years of training, having never forgiven his parents for the cruel way they surrendered his sister. When Gwain had confronted his father upon the lord's return, he had been met with more indifference than sympathy.

"An honor," his father had said, "to be chosen to join the temples. Not only for your sister, but for our house, and name as well. She will receive the finest education, and an esteemed position upon her completion."

"She was terrified!" Gwain had spoken with thick anger. "No one explained what was going on. She was…" He had drawn a breath, pain seeping through his voice. "I understand she had to go with them, but please, Father, allow me to visit her."

"Whatever for?"

Gwain had stared at his father, disbelieving. "To ensure she's all right. To let her know she has not been abandoned. To—"

"Your sister is in the temples. It is unbecoming of you to question their care of her."

"That's not what I—"

"You, Gwain, will leave your sister to the temple's care." His father's voice took on a commanding tone, which left no room for further arguments. "You going there would only confuse her."

"But—"

"You will report to the academy at once."

"Father, please."

"This is my final word on the matter."

And hence, it had been years without seeing the sister he had promised to watch over. The sister he loved. More recently, mature enough to be comfortable defying his father's edict, he had made multiple requests to visit, but the temple had refuted all of his attempts.

The communications he received from his sister were few, and far between, but those that arrived read cordial in nature. So casually worded the letters might have been written by a stranger.

He knew temple education had some similarity to a knight's training. Both involved a level of emotional distancing from one's family. Yet the cold, impersonal nature of Gwen's letters burned the edges of his heart. He wondered if his sister blamed him for allowing her to be taken in such a heartless manner. Did she hate him?

The questions were not frequently on his mind. But today, on the celebration he had spent years sharing with his sibling, the guilt weighed heavily.

Grateful to Rob for the day's distraction, Gwain was surprised to find a parcel awaiting his return. Assuming the package to be from his estranged mother, Gwain picked up the thick envelope, planning to discard it, when he spied the temple seal.

Heart leaping, Gwain closed the door to his chamber and opened the parcel. Within he found a leather-bound book, and a sealed letter, his name inscribed elegantly on the outer folds. With more care than he had used opening the package, Gwain unfolded the perfectly creased parchment.

My Dearest Brother,

Happy name day! I hope this finds you well, enjoying this day, and your continued academy training. Thank you for all your recent letters. Reading your kind words causes my heart to swell. I am delighted to know you are happy with your training. You will become among the most honorable and courageous knights the queen could ever hope to find.

Enclosed is a simple gift. A journal that, I hope, you will fill with your many adventures as your training ends and you fulfill the dreams you always hoped to live.

With Love and Affection,
Your Sister

p.s. I've included an additional gift in the center pages. I hope you enjoy, and had a wondrous name day.

Placing the letter on the bed with care, Gwain opened the journal, thumbing through the pages until he found the one to which the letter referred.

His breath caught.

Gingerly, Gwain walked to his wooden desk, and placed the open book upon it.

Between the pages: a pressed rose, petals flat between the bound pieces of parchment. Reaching out, Gwain touched the delicate remains.

I don't understand. Gwen would never pluck a flower, let alone a rose. He delicately lifted the blossom from the page.

Underneath, he read a final note.

Gwain,

This beautiful rose reminded me of the ones you picked and placed on the table the last day we were together. I hope it brings as many pleasant memories for you, my dear brother, as it has always done for me.

With Love,
Your sister

CHAPTER XV

"WHILE I HAD LONG SUSPECTED, I knew then that she needed me," Gwain informed the princess.

"The first time someone had given Gwen a cut flower, she fell to instant tears. She couldn't stand the thought of something so beautiful dying for her selfish pleasure. On her name day, I wouldn't have dreamed to cut the roses she loved. Instead, I took her up into the mountains to enjoy them. With the message, everything clarified.

"The cold, impersonal responses. The lack of communication. Someone was watching. Reading her letters. I could feel it in my bones. I knew..."

Gwain drew a deep breath, staring at the bubbling spring as he summoned the will to continue.

"I increased my requests to visit her, receiving a firm reprimand from my parents as the temple reported my pleas. I attempted to explain. Tried to convince them to visit instead, if they did not wish for me to do so." Gwain sighed. "They would not heed my worries.

"By the time I finished academy training, I was desperate. I considered going to my captain, but feared my request would negatively impact my pending assignment, making it even more difficult to help her. My sister was in the care of the temples, after all. Among the highest authorities in the land. I, on the other hand, was only in my mid-twenties, not even fully a knight yet. I..." His gaze remained intent on the water.

"What did you do?"

"I went myself."

CHAPTER XVI

26 YEARS AGO

CAREFUL PLANNING. FORBIDDEN SECRETS. HEARTBREAKING lies. Yet eventually, Gwain managed to find his way into the restricted sanctuary where his sister was being held.

Wearing loaned attire, Gwain entered the temple under the false guise of a visiting, high-ranking representative of the crown. One of the priestesses greeted him happily, and then escorted him to a surprisingly luxurious quarters with a bed draped in silken cloth, and chest inlaid with gold embellishments.

During the evening prayers, Gwain watched as those in training approached the altar to accept a sip of wine, which each worshiper was required to partake, in honor of Kamar. His heart raced as he watched the procession, each fire maiden lifting a red veil to sip from a golden goblet. When the fourth trainee reached the pyre, Gwain's breath caught.

Older, yet unmistakable. A rare beauty with golden hair, unblemished skin, and eyes like deep blue sapphires. It took all his strength to resist running toward her, lifting her into his arms, and begging her forgiveness. Breathing deep, Gwain resisted, watching his sister take the cup in her hands, and press the goblet to her lips, before replacing the veil, and returning to the pew from which she had risen.

Whatever you do, he had been cautioned by the organization who had helped procure his false documentation, *do not single her out in public, in any way. They are always watching, especially as the girls come of age.*

Forcing himself to remain on script, Gwain spoke with the head priestesses for several days, inspecting the grounds under the false pretense of having been sent by the crown. Visiting dignitaries, on behalf of the queen, were not unusual. For the most part, he simply nodded in silent acknowledgment as the priestesses proudly toured him around the grounds they were charged with overseeing. He saw lush gardens, towering buildings of worship, and church railings inlaid with strips of gold and silver supported on spiraling beams embellished with occasional jewels. Building interiors sparkled from the filtered light of stained glass windows, while depictions of ancient battles and famous dragons played out across delicate glass panels.

Each evening, he schooled his features as his sister approached the altar and accepted her sip of wine. Each night, his heart recoiled against the notion he was so close, and yet so far. He waited, dutifully fulfilling the mundane tasks required by one of his position, dining with the upper-level women, employing a limited answer policy, to decrease his chance of giving his identity away.

On the fifth evening, he was relieved to find the list of required visit elements completed. "Lady Penelope," Gwain addressed one of the high priestesses, "am I correct in my belief that an ascension ceremony is soon to be performed?"

"Yes, my lord. Four days from now, in fact."

"As is custom, the crown must be allowed to inspect the well-being and compliance of the girls, prior to the taking of their oaths."

The woman smiled. "Of course, my lord. Now I know why you're here. Would you like to meet with them as a group, or individually?"

"How many are there?"

"Three, my lord. Though I've a feeling, inspecting one of them might satisfy you. A true beauty, my lord, whom I'm sure would be happy to speak for her sister priestesses."

"What family was she selected from?"

"Noble enough for you, I promise. Daughter of a politician."

Gwain struggled to keep his expression indifferent. "Send her to my chambers, if you believe her to be the best representative. After I am done questioning her, we shall see if I need to speak with the others as well."

Penelope winked. "As you wish, my lord. I'm sure you'll give her a *thorough* examination."

The woman turned, laughing as she walked down the hall, leaving Gwain to return to his assigned chambers.

CHAPTER XVII

GWAIN PACED THE OPULENT CHAMBER, heart beating erratically. Penelope's implied assumption of his intentions made his blood run cold.

What would have happened if the real official had come?

He forced those foul thoughts from his mind, attempting to mentally prepare himself for the meeting to come.

At a knock on his door, Gwain moved to the center of the room, and drew a breath, praying for strength. "Come in."

The door opened at his invitation. Priestess Penelope led in a slender young woman covered in the red robes of her goddess, the mark of a golden flame etched into the material at her breast. A matching crimson veil shrouded her face, blocking him from view.

"On your knees," the elder woman instructed the younger. "A sign of proper respect."

The girl complied, kneeling before him, head down, gaze on the lush red rug covering the floor.

"Remove your maiden veil," the woman further ordered.

Again, the girl complied, never raising her eyes from the floor.

Gwain stared at the long golden hair, tumbling down her back in gentle waves. He wanted to speak, but feared his words would come unsteady.

"As promised," Penelope stated. "A rare beauty, and completely untarnished."

The woman reached out a hand and ran her fingers through the girl's golden locks. "Remember, Guinevere, you are to do all this man asks. Otherwise you will greatly displease both me and your goddess." As she stroked the girl's hair, Gwain witnessed a visible shiver his sister was unable to suppress. "Be a good girl now."

Penelope looked up at Gwain. "If she gives you any trouble, let me know. I hope you find your examination...satisfactory."

With those words, the woman left the room, closing the door with a profound *thud* that echoed through the room.

Alone at last with his lost sister, the air tightened in Gwain's chest, refusing to rise as he stared down at the girl who was a child no longer. Finally, he managed to squeeze out, "My lady."

"Please," her terrified plea broke his heart. "Don't make me do this."

Forcing air through his constricted throat, Gwain said, "I would have brought roses, my lady, but know that plucking them would upset you so."

Nearly a minute passed while his words were processed. Slowly, the girl raised her eyes, meeting her brother's pained gaze.

Her blue eyes widened, lips falling agape. She appeared to try and speak, but no sound came, Gwen as speechless as her brother.

Between ragged breaths, and with tears filling her eyes to slip down her cheeks, she asked, "Gwain?" The question came jagged and unsteady. "Gwain?"

"Little sister," he answered, kneeling before her.

"By the gods!" she exclaimed, throwing herself into his arms as her tears fell faster. "I can't believe...I—"

"I'm sorry. So sorry, Gwen, that it took me so long. I am so..." His own tears gathered.

"My letter..."

"I knew the moment I saw the rose that you needed me."

"Did mother and father send—"

"No." Gwain shook his head, though his cheek remained buried in his sister's long hair. "But I knew. I'm sorry, Gwen. You must hate me for letting them take you."

"You didn't do anything wrong. I knew you couldn't save...I knew."

"I should have," he replied, voice thick with regret. "I wanted to stop them. I tried to see you, I swear. I sent so many requests, pleaded with our parents." He pulled back to see his sister's eyes, but not enough to remove her from the circle of his arms. "I tried, Gwen. I'm..."

"Brother," she whispered, "I can't believe you're...here...I..."

"I had to see you."

Gwen's tears slowed as she attempted to explain, "I was scared. I didn't mean to drag you into...to get you in trouble. I never wanted to harm you."

"You haven't. Tell me, what's going on?"

"I..." She drew a breath. "I was selected to become a voice of Kamar."

"A voice?"

She nodded. "At the initiation ceremony, each priestess in training is assigned a future role. Some, like Penelope, are chosen to become high priestesses. Others are assigned different tasks to help serve the temples. But," she drew a wheezed breath, "I was chosen to become a voice."

"You mean the oracles who speak with the goddess?"

"Yes, but it's not true."

"Not true?"

Gwen's shoulders shook. "They give you something awful. If you refuse, they force it upon you. I've seen girls tied down, screaming, while this liquid was poured down their throats to ensure they ingest it. It takes away who you are." Tears slipped from the corners of her eyes, each glistening drop tearing at Gwain's heart. "Once the drug is taken, the girls speak in riddles and nonsense, which high priestesses interpret as the words of the goddess."

"Wait…" Gwain shook his head uncomprehendingly. "Are you saying the prophecies and proclamations from the goddess aren't true? That they drug the girls?"

"They drug and keep them…for the rest of their lives."

"I don't understand. What about their dragon halves? You can't have a half-competent dragon flying around without—"

"Someone chosen as a voice never transforms."

"What?"

"The drugs prevent them from doing so. That's why they do this as soon as we come of age. They never become dragons."

Gwain looked at his sister, this revelation difficult to digest. The temples were an elaborate lie. The words of the priestesses, false. A system to maintain their power in the kingdom.

"What were you told to expect by the woman who left you in this room?"

Gwen's voice grew faint. "I was to please you, in any desired way. They give girls my age to the officials sometimes. Safer, they say, to hand over a girl who has…"

"Yet to meet her dragon half," Gwain finished, before clenching his teeth. "Gods, Gwen. I—" Under the crushing weight of failure, he pulled his sister close, crying as he spilled his remorse onto the thick cloth of her robe.

She wrapped her arms around him, a sharing of mutual sorrow born of their cruel separation.

"I knew you would come," she whispered. "I always knew. I wanted to tell you so many times, but they read my letters. Forced me to destroy them if they found anything too personal. They wouldn't even allow me to express how much I missed you. Gods, I wanted to."

Gwain held his sister for a long time, releasing his fear and sorrow before finding the strength to stand. Lifting her as effortlessly as he had done during her childhood, Gwain moved Gwen to the spacious bed and laid her down, moving a chair beside the bed to face her more comfortably.

"I'm going to get you out of here. I promise, sister. But if this is going to work, we must do so carefully. Tonight, you are going to remain here.

Tomorrow, I will order you to accompany me on a ride, during which, the friends who assisted me in gaining access will cause a distraction. We'll only have that one chance to escape.

"You should be aware that our parents do not support anything I've done, nor do they know. If we run, we will live in exile. Away from all we've ever known."

"What about you?" Gwen asked. "You would have graduated from the academy by now, have you not?"

"A few months ago."

"Were you assigned to a guard?"

"It doesn't matter."

"Were you?"

"Yes," he answered reluctantly.

"Which one?"

"I said it doesn't—"

"Tell me."

"The royal guard."

"Royal? Gwain, that's your dream."

"It doesn't matter," he insisted. "All that matters is getting you out of here. I promised to take care of you, and I've failed. All these years, I have failed, and in such a spectacular fashion. I refuse to fail you anymore, sister. I can't live with myself if I do."

"Am I supposed to be able to sleep at night, knowing I took away all you have worked for? All the good you could have done?"

"Yes! I don't care about any of it."

Gwen took a deep breath and stared at her brother's intense gaze. "You're lying."

He sighed. "Allow me say what is beyond dispute. I love you, sister. Being your brother means more than any position or title. Can you believe that much?"

Tears reemerged, cascading down Gwen's cheeks as Gwain left the chair to again pull her close.

"Forgive me, Gwen."

"I do," she answered. "You came. You're here."

"I am." He kissed her brow, holding her until she gave in to exhaustion.

CHAPTER XVIII

DAWN CAME TOO SOON, BOTH siblings awakening in a disparity of mixed emotions. Luckily such a state was appropriate for convincing Penelope events had taken a far different turn in the chambers the night before. Having moved to the bed to create a false pretense, Penelope found Gwen covered by a thick blanket, lying on her side, while Gwain had removed his shirt, giving the illusion of nudity.

Taking the sharp tone of the pretended dignitary, Gwain glared at the intruding priestess. "Did I give you permission to interrupt?"

Smile faltering, the woman rushed to say, "Pardon me, my lord. I only came to see if you were finished examining—"

"Do I look finished?" he snapped.

"No, my lord." The woman lowered her gaze in a submissive gesture. "Forgive me."

"If no privacy can be found within these walls, I intend to take this examination elsewhere."

"Elsewhere?"

"Yes," Gwain answered, in a voice he hoped carried an air of authority. "In fact, tell me, how fairs the weather today?"

"The weather?"

"Are you going to repeat every question?"

"No, my lord. It's sunny today. Seems quite nice."

"Good. Saddle a horse." He reached toward his sister and, with an apologetic glance only she could see, placed a hand on her shoulder, slipping his fingers down her side over the blanket. "There's a clearing nearby. I intend to continue this line of questioning there."

"My lord, your request is highly unusual."

Lifting his gaze to stare at the woman, Gwain arched an eyebrow. "So is, I assume, the queen receiving an ill report from her chosen advisor. Would you prefer I inform her majesty that I found your institution less than accommodating? I'd be happy to recommend additional oversight."

"No, my lord." The woman shook her head. "Won't be necessary. I'll have a horse saddled immediately. Will you require two, or one?"

"One. The girl rides with me."

"Of course, my lord." Penelope lowered her head in submission.

She left without another word, leaving the two to properly dress.

"Sorry," Gwain apologized. "I didn't know how else to ensure she was convinced."

"It's all right," she answered, rising from the bed.

He did the same, grabbing his discarded shirt. "I'd let you change, but it might draw additional suspicion since…"

"It's fine," she assured. "Only…"

"What is it?"

"I can't believe you're here. I thought I would wake this morning to find this a dream."

"As did I," he answered softly, taking his sister's left hand and placing a kiss upon the back of her palm. "Are you ready to get out of here?"

Nervously, Gwen nodded, heart leaping at her brother's comforting smile.

Together, they walked down the halls, past occasional stares from the other women, until they emerged into sunlight. Awaiting them was a young woman holding the reins of a white stallion, equipped with a brown leather saddle.

"My lord," the woman offered a brief bow. "Is there anything else you require?"

He started to say no, then recalled his sickening façade. "A blanket."

"Of course, my lord."

"I'll take the horse," he stated, reaching for the reins, which the girl passed into his hand before she left to fetch the requested item.

He assisted Gwen onto the stallion while waiting, stuffing the blanket into a saddle bag the young woman had also thought to bring. Tethering the bag behind the saddle, Gwain mounted the horse, sliding behind his sister as he maneuvered the reins around her.

"Tell Lady Penelope we will return by nightfall. I shall be returning to the palace first thing tomorrow morning."

"Yes, my lord," the girl replied, again giving a slight bow.

Gwain guided the horse toward the wooded area around the back side of the temple grounds. The land was vast, the temples owning expansive sections of the surrounding area. After allowing several minutes for both of them to grow accustomed to the horse's cant, Gwain increased their pace to a gentle gallop, climbing over grassy hills, and gliding down gentle slopes to the scent of fresh grass and sparse wildflowers.

Heat from the rising sun poured down on the two riders. Gwain increased their mount's pace, inviting the breeze to cool their warm skin. His sister leaned trustingly against him, and both felt as though the past years had vanished. They were again two children racing along a well-loved path.

Gwen stared up, spying a bird flying overhead, brightly colored feathers dancing across the sky. "Pretty bird. It's been forever since I was allowed on a horse. Not since I was last with you."

The confession fractured his freshly glued heart, and he prompted the horse even faster. The beast eagerly responded, hooves pounding over the dry dirt.

At the increase, Gwen laughed, and the sound brought him a joy he had not known since their separation.

Eventually they slowed, moving to the temple's south side. The grounds were outlined with a massive fence of solid, thick wood, which functioned to both keep out intruders, and prevent those within from escape. Gwain slowed the horse to a walk, and directed it along the outer walls, praying the instructions he had received were accurate.

When they turned to follow the fence's southern panels, Gwain dismounted. Walking along the wood barrier, Gwain's fingers sought the hidden latch.

His finger touched a deep grove, and he pushed back a hidden panel, before releasing a breath he hadn't realized he had been holding. Moving back to the horse, he assisted Gwen from the saddle, placing her in the tall grass before gazing up at the sun, a hand moving to shield his eyes from the brightest rays.

"Should be any time now."

"What will happen?"

"They are going to—"

A roar arose, the bellow so loud it reverberated in the siblings' ears. A second roar drew a frightened squeal from Gwen's lips. She turned, staring toward the temples at two immense golden dragons circling the distant building.

Setting aside his blend of fear and awe, Gwain grabbed her arm, turning her back toward the fence. "The signal. We have to go now."

"Where?"

"This way." He guided her toward the fence, pushing on the hidden lever to open the panel.

A third roar filled the air, and she turned, gasping at the sight of yellow flames lighting the field in front of the temple.

"Go!" Gwain shoved her through the opening before ducking down to follow her.

"Wait, what about the horse?"

"He'll be fine. They are only burning the front field to distract them. They'll have the flames out in minutes, and the horse will be found when they search the grounds. As will we, if we don't hurry."

On the other side of the wooden barrier, Gwen was faced with a dirt path, shrouded in shadows from towering trees above.

With more hurry than care, Gwain guided her through the forgotten path, pushing aside branches and stepping over occasional rocks.

He had done it. His sister was free of her prison walls. However, they remained far from safety, and the next hour of their journey would be the most dangerous. If the dragons assisting him were caught, they might be interrogated and give away his plot. Regardless, it would only be a matter of minutes before someone realized they were missing, in spite of the disturbance.

Neither speaking, they followed the path to the spring, where it diverged, and he chose to continue in a thicker portion of the woods. With each crushed branch, Gwain cringed, fearing it might be the sound to give away their location. Around them, the forest remained eerily quiet.

By the time they emerged from the trees, the sun had begun to set. Leaving his sister a few paces back, Gwain entered the clearing and spied a man seated by the fire. He approached cautiously, crouched in the tall grass.

Once close enough to confirm the man's identity, relief poured through him. Gwain stood, waving at his long-time friend. "Rob," he called, alerting the other man to his presence. "We made it!"

In greeting, Rob raised his hand.

Gwain moved back to the tree line, and beckoned his sister forward, before escorting her across the field.

"You made it," Rob echoed, rising to his feet. "I have to be honest, I didn't think you would."

"Neither did I," Gwain answered, flashing a tired smile before turning back to Gwen. "Rob, this is my sister."

"Glad to finally meet you, my lady" he said, extending a hand before clasping his fingers around hers.

"Pleased to meet you too, my lord."

Rob smiled and moved to the log he had used as a make-shift bench. "You're welcome to have a seat. I have some water."

"That would be wonderful. Thank you."

"No need," he said with a dismissive wave before handing her a leather flask. "Drink your fill, there's plenty more."

Thirstily, Gwen took a deep drink of the quenching liquid before handing the flask to her brother, who partook as well, the liquid cool on his dry throat.

"Quite a ruckus you made today," Rob observed. "Your friends got away, so you know."

70

"Thank the gods," he answered, shoulders releasing further stress at this news.

"Your parents probably know by now she's missing, and given how much you've protested her placement, it won't take long before they suspect you helped her."

Gwain smiled at his sister. "I didn't expect it to. My only goal was to get her away."

"You can't take her back home."

"We're going to ride north, find refuge in the mountains."

Rob nodded. "You both must be exhausted, but I would suggest riding as far as we can under the cover of night. They're less likely to find us, and we are more likely to see them coming."

"I agree." Gwain glanced apologetically at his sister. "I know you're tired Gwen, but…"

"We can rest later," she concurred. "As long as I don't have to go back there."

"I brought a horse for each of you," Rob said.

"You should ride out of here," Gwain urged. "You've risked too much already."

"You're my friend."

"Thanks," Gwain replied, then assisted Rob in the retrieval of the mentioned mounts.

They rode through the night, each mile placed between themselves and the temple allowing Gwain to breathe easier. His elation at their escape finally tempered with contemplating the realities of providing food and shelter for them both.

They approached the forest's end at sunrise. All three riders were exhausted. They made a crude camp with pelts Rob had brought, and bedded the horses down. Gwen was already asleep as her brother lay down a few feet from her.

He slept for hours, despite the sunlight seeping through the thick branches overhead, but was awoken by a shrill scream. The sound lurching him to awareness, Gwain jerked up and called his sister's name.

Beside him, Gwen tossed and turned ferociously in the twisted pelts.

He rushed to her side, calling her name as he woke her. "Gwen, it's all right! You're safe. Gwen, wake up!"

His words pulled her from the nightmare, another shriek emanating as she scrambled up in a panic.

"Gwen!"

The sharp tone broke through her panic. She looked at him, recognition dawning. "Gwain?"

"I'm here."

She crawled toward him, pressing her cheek to his chest as he wrapped her in his arms.

Trembling, she clung to him. "I'm sorry," she spoke on a shaky breath. "I didn't mean to."

"It's all right. A bad dream."

"The same. Always the same."

"Same?" he questioned, thinking back to the many nights she had slipped into his room asking for sanctuary. "You mean…the dream of the dragon?"

"Yes. I was scared. There were flames everywhere. I called your name, but you didn't come. I…"

"I'm here now," he assured. "I promise, Gwen. I'll take care of you."

"I'm frightened," she whispered, her voice holding the same childhood fear he recalled in his memory.

"I am too. But whatever happens, Gwen, we'll face it together. I promise."

"Don't let them take me back there. I don't want to be locked in dreams. Please, Gwain."

"I won't," he answered with conviction, running his hand lightly through the golden locks of her hair. "I promise, Gwen. I'll protect you."

She curled into him, placing her head on his shoulder as he coaxed her to calm, and eventually back to slumber. Depositing her on her pelt, he sat beside her, rubbing her back.

Watching them from across the fire, Rob's voice came in soft tones. "Is she all right?"

"I don't think so. She's had nightmares since she was a small child. A field burning. A dragon with feathered wings, like those of a bird."

"What about you? How are you?"

Surprised by the question, Gwain turned to meet his friend's eyes. The word *fine* formed in his mind, but stopped short of being spoken. Inhaling, he paused before speaking a more truthful answer. "Terrified and relieved. They were going to drug her."

"What?"

"They don't hear the voices of the goddess at all. It's a sham, Robert."

"What do you mean?"

"They drug them—the girls too young to transform—and use the gibberish the drugs produce to proclaim hidden prophecies, which are then used to forge laws as they see fit. My sister's had nightmares all her life, and they wanted to condemn her to eternal dreams. To…" His hands formed fists, rage becoming a living, breathing voice that woke the beast within. His dragon rose to anger's call, forcing him to draw several deep breaths to calm his other half, his eyes transforming to a green glow.

Rob saw the dragon glinting through his friend's eyes, but said nothing, trusting Gwain to control his more lethal half.

"They were going to condemn her to a torment so profound...I can't even imagine what it would have been like for her. I can't..."

Silence fell. Gwain closed his eyes, corralling his beast with imaginary walls.

Rob's voice came soft and uncertain as he asked, "You're telling the truth, aren't you?"

"Why would I lie?"

Rob shifted, shoulders moving as he drew a deep breath.

"What is it?"

"I knew you loved her, but I had no idea she would be so," he seemed to search for the word, "fragile. Nor so lovely."

"And?"

"I didn't think you would escape the temple. Nor did I have any faith you would be there for as long as you were without getting caught. I..."

Tension renewed its path between Gwain's shoulders, his eyes trained on those of his closest friend, who refused to meet his gaze. "Rob?" he asked through a layer of fresh fear. "What did you do?"

Rob's eyes squeezed tight before he forced himself to look up and meet Gwain's worried expression. "I'm sorry," he confessed. "They expected you would try to free her at some point. You've made too many requests, and your behavior these past few months...they knew, Gwain."

"Knew?" The blood in Gwain's veins was replaced by icy fear.

"I'm sorry, Gwain. There was no choice."

With that contrite apology, hands laid siege to Gwain's arms.

He cried out, screaming for Gwen to run.

Too late. Far too late.

CHAPTER XIX

AMELIA STARED AT THE CAPTAIN as he wiped a tear from his pale cheek. "They caught you."

Gwain nodded, but did not speak.

"What happened?"

Words failed, requiring several additional breaths before Gwain was able to speak. "They told her she was wicked for attempting to run. Sinful for risking not only her own future, but mine as well. Selfish they…"

26 YEARS AGO

"LET HER GO!" GWAIN SCREAMED. "Please, for the love of all the gods, she doesn't want this! Please!"

"Silence!" a feminine voice interrupted his cries. The same woman he thought he had deceived the night prior stepped between the siblings.

Arms bound, Gwain was held on his knees by four men. "Please don't harm her," he pleaded. "She knew nothing."

"Highly doubtful," the woman replied. "Were the two of you anyone else, punishment would be harsh indeed."

Penelope extended her hand to trace a line along Gwen's high cheekbones, and down her chin. "A shame to mar such exquisite beauty."

"Don't touch her!" Gwain screamed, thrashing.

The man on his right punched his side, the blow landing painfully against Gwain's ribs.

"Do not fear," the priestess said, continuing to run her hands over his sister. "I will not harm her. Guinevere is, after all, destined to speak for our most revered goddess." She turned to him. "You, on the other hand..."

"I don't care how you harm me. Let my sister go."

"Such a noble spirit." Penelope gave a crude laugh. "No wonder you were chosen for the queen's personal guard."

"Please," he whispered. "Don't harm my sister."

"Harm her? I'm going to honor her."

"You're lying. She doesn't want this. She's never heard the goddess' voice."

"But I have," the woman cooed. "Kamar has told me your sister is to be her chosen vessel. Her words will be from the divine herself."

"If my sister speaks for the goddess, listen to her! She doesn't want this, so to force anything upon her, against her will, is to directly challenge the goddess' authority."

"Guinevere is too young to understand the goddess' desires," the priestess defended. "I am here to assist her in interpreting Kamar's will."

"Are you deliberately cruel, or completely delusional? She doesn't want this!"

The woman leaned forward and placed her hand on the side of Gwain's face.

He jerked from her touch, drawing a cruel laugh from the powerful woman.

Walking back to his sister, Penelope stepped behind Gwen. Gathering her golden hair, the priestess yanked Gwen's head back.

"Gwain!" the girl cried out, more from fear than pain.

His dragon roared at the sound, bursting forth, his eyes changing to vibrant, glowing green, while his pupils narrowed to thin slits, and scales rose from his skin. He was unprepared when one of the men moved forward, pushing something sharp deep into his skin.

The transformation stopped instantly, the dragon within screaming as a searing pain also caused the human to cry out. The men let him fall, pain spreading with a touch so cold, it burned. He tried to speak, but could only manage a second unbidden scream.

"Gwain!" his sister yelled. "What did you do to him? What did you—"

"Never fear, pet. His status is temporary, thanks to a concoction that controls unruly dragons." She clucked her tongue. "Did you not anticipate we'd plan for every contingency?"

"I'll go with you!" his sister promised. "Please, I beg of you, don't harm my brother. Please, don't!"

"Enough of this," a second, sharper voice called. "Get on with it, Penelope."

"Yes," the woman replied, turning back to Gwen. With the help of another woman, who tipped back Gwen's head, Penelope forced Gwen's jaws apart as she brought out a flask. Small enough to be concealed in one's palm, the vial was slender, and Gwen's eyes widened in recognition.

"For you, a taste of the dreams to come."

Gwen struggled against the women to no avail, her eyes flying to her brother as the vile, bitter liquid was forced between her lips.

"Swallow," Penelope instructed, "or your brother won't survive the night."

"No!" Gwain pleaded from where he writhed on the ground, agony wracking his body, every muscle tightening in painful spasms.

Tears streaming, Gwen allowed the poison to slide down her throat.

Once certain of her compliance, the women stepped back.

Surprised to be free, Gwen rushed to her brother's side, pulling him against her as she called his name. "Gwain! I'm sorry. I'm sorry."

"No." Gwain shook his head, an unsteady movement that involved his entire body. Another spasm caused him to cry out in spite of his best efforts not to.

The unseen priestess instructed, "I suggest you say goodbye. Soon, she'll know only the will of the gods."

"Let her go," Gwain bargained. "Take me. I'll be your voice. I'd do anything. Please, I…" His words failed, burning cold creeping further through his body, numbing his limbs while clamping down on his throat. Suffocating, words and breath becoming harsher, the cold surrounding his dragon in a sheet of ice even its fire could not melt. Blackness descended from a lack of oxygen, vision blurring as his hearing dimmed.

"I'm sorry, Gwen," he managed to whisper, her tears falling on his cheeks. "I wanted to save you. I'm sorry."

"I love you, brother. I love you."

GWAIN DID NOT BOTHER TO wipe away his tears as he finished the tale.

"I awoke in a cell, a failure. My sister had been taken back to the temples, destined to spend her life speaking incoherent rubbish, to be interpreted as the high priestess saw fit."

"I've never heard of a poison that prevented us from transforming before. What did they inject you with?"

"I don't know its name." He drew a slow breath. "It prevented my dragon from emerging. If I'd been given multiple doses, I think it might have done far greater, and permanent, damage."

He shook his head. "My best guess? It's one of the elements in the drug concoction given to my sister, based on how it paralyzed my dragon. As you know, when one transforms for the first time, the creature is young, and weak. It must be given time, and room, to grow, as our human halves had before the dragon emerged.

"And like a human child, young dragons are more vulnerable. What the drug did to me was terrible. If they administered a stronger dose to a dragon that hadn't hatched, it would prevent the creature from ever emerging. That's why, I suspect, it's so important for the girls to be given the drug at a young age. Far easier to destroy an unhatched dragon, than an adult."

Amelia stared, digesting both Gwain's story, and the horrifying information he'd conveyed. Finally she asked, "What happened next?"

CHAPTER XX

26 YEARS AGO

GWAIN SAT IN HIS CELL, a blanket wrapped around him as a shield against the dank, stale air. He was beginning to lose count of the days, the dungeon far enough underground sunlight could not penetrate its depths. Torches flickered from the room's corners, casting a constant mixture of light and shadow.

Broken hearted, the young knight did not bother protesting his imprisonment. His failure to protect his sister had left him defeated. The knowledge of her fate, because of his failure, a crushing weight. He had spent numerous nights screaming against the temple's actions before those cries devolved to pathetic pleas and, finally, silence.

I deserve to be imprisoned.

A few weeks into his captivity, a temple official had come to speak with him. Without entering the cell, the man had trained his golden eyes on the younger man through the rusting iron bars. "Have you come to see the error in your ways?"

"I was a fool," Gwain answered.

The corners of the official's lips curved upward.

"To ever think the temples were anything but a horrifically corrupt institution. For failing to save her years ago!"

The official's smile never faltered; a perfect reflection of the brainwashed status the temples had instilled. "I see you have not learned your lesson."

Gwain moved closer to the other man, wrapping his hands around the cold cell bars. "Let my sister go," he begged. "Please, she's done nothing to deserve what is being done to her."

"I assure you, young man," the visitor's voice remained sickeningly cheerful, "she's in the best of hands."

"Bullshit! What you have done to her is worse than a death sentence. Do with me what you will, punish me, but release my sister! If you require a voice, let it be me. I'll take your drugs. I'll do anything you want. Please, I beg of you, let my sister go."

The official shook his head. "It's admirable, how you fight for her. To do so showcases all the qualities of the profession for which you have been trained; the promise of a remarkable future knight. But now you must call upon the discipline instilled in your training, and trust in the goddess, who has chosen your sister for personal service. I'm certain, in time, you will see the truth in my words. May the goddess bless you with peace and understanding."

The official offered a brief bow before turning to leave Gwain to his solitude.

Once a month, the official returned, each time leaving the younger man with the same words. Gwain refused to yield, welcoming the punishment. If his sister was to be confined, surely he should face the same fate for his failure.

He was frequently dosed with a milder form of the strange concoction he had been injected with when they'd taken Gwen from him. Not enough to cause the searing pain of the first instance, but sufficiently potent to suppress his dragon form. He had recently been medicated when footsteps alerted him to a disruption in his preferred solitude.

"Go away," he preemptively rejected the expected official. "My answer remains the same."

"I can't do that, Gwain."

At the familiar voice, Gwain turned, jaw tightening. "What the hell are you doing here?"

"Gwain," Rob replied, "I must speak with you."

"I don't converse with traitors."

"Gwain—"

Seized with overwhelming rage, his dragon attempted to push past the sedative, screeching through his mind as the beast thundered against his narrow confines. Gwain walked to the bars and wrapped his hands around them, glaring at his former friend through eyes flecked with green. "What could you possibly say that would help?"

"I came to explain."

"Explain what? How you betrayed me, condemned my sister to…"

"You made too many requests, Gwain. They knew you'd try to rescue her."

"And your best solution was allowing us to walk into a trap?"

"I didn't know."

"Know what? That you're a backstabbing conspirator?"

Rob drew a sharp breath. "Against everything we'd been taught, everything we'd been trained to defend, you claimed the temples were corrupt. Decided your sister was in trouble…because of a flower." Rob shook his head. "Do you know how ludicrous you sounded? Because of a dried flower—a name day gift—you had to break into the temples and steal her away.

"I was raised under the same values as you, Gwain. The temples are a source of all good. They speak for the goddess. Your ravings went against everything we've been taught to believe."

"You should have stayed out of it! Not pretended to be my friend, and—"

"I am your friend."

"Bullshit!"

"When the temple representatives came to me they expressed compassion, explaining you were delusional. They were concerned you were throwing away what you had worked your entire life to achieve."

"I don't care what they said!"

"The representative advised me that if I helped, you could be safely captured, spend a few months here, get treatment, then be released back to your life. If I had refused, and you made it to the mountains, you might be killed, and if captured alive, held indefinitely. Because you're my friend, I agreed to assist to ensure your safety, your future."

Gwain stared, attempting to process Rob's justification. "You should have warned me. We'd have taken a different route. Escaped another way."

"She's a voice of the goddess. They would have pursued you to the world's end."

"You condemned her to a fate worse than death. You betrayed me!"

Rob lowered his gaze to the grimy stone floor. "I didn't believe you, when you said she needed you, nor did I anticipate she would be so fragile. I didn't..." He shook his head. "I'm sorry, Gwain."

"Sorry?" The word came out as a deep growl. "You're sorry? Well, I suppose that fixes everything."

"No, it doesn't."

"You gave her to monsters! Condemned her!" The words were venomous. "My little sister. I promised to protect her. I swore she would never be forced to return."

"I'm sorry."

"I hope your actions haunt you, Robert. Every night for the rest of *her* life."

"Please—"

"What you did is beyond any realm of forgiveness. You condemned her to never-ending dreams." Anger transformed to anguish as Gwain fought to breathe. "You trapped her in nightmares, Robert. The very thing I promised would never happen."

Overcome with grief, Gwain hung his head, leaning against the gate, hands digging into rusted metal.

Reaching between the bars, Rob placed a hand on Gwain's shoulder in an attempt to offer comfort. For a time, Gwain allowed the contact, the pain too deep to even react to the touch, his failure as fresh now as it had been months before.

"Gwain," Robert said, "I thought I was doing the right thing."

Jerking back from the gate, he spat, "I don't give a damn. I want you to leave."

"Gwain, please—"

"There's no forgiveness." He met the other man's gaze head on. "There never will be as long as she remains captive."

Robert's lips parted as though to speak, then closed. He offered a single bow, and turned from the cell. As he reached the end of the corridor, he paused. "For what it's worth, I am sorry, Gwain. What I did, was out of friendship. Yours was the best I've ever had."

With that, Rob departed, leaving Gwain to anguished solitude.

CHAPTER XXI

GWAIN TURNED FROM THE PRINCESS, fixing his gaze back on the running spring. "Six months after I was taken into captivity, my father used his influence to retrieve me. However, before being returned to my family, the priestess escorted me back to the temple, to see my sister.

"She was…comatose, eyes vacant. She…wasn't there anymore. My bright, beautiful sister, who would not so much as pull a rose from the vine, was no more. I walked to her, but she shied away from my touch, unable to recognize…" He drew a deep breath. "I kissed her cheek, even though she flinched at the contact, and asked her to be strong. But…my sister was gone.

"I left brokenhearted and, once home, endured additional months of punishment, at the hand of my father. For trying to save my sister, he said I was a disgrace to the family. Had brought shame.

"But it didn't matter. His words couldn't touch me. I'd failed Gwen, and no amount of additional punishment could compare to that horror.

"Eventually, I returned to the guard. I had expected they would reduce me to a menial position, but given my father's influence, and connections, the entire incident was virtually erased."

"And your sister?"

Gwain shook his head. "I went back, but they had moved her to a new location, and I lacked the heart to learn where. A coward, I was unable to face my failure, and thus allowed them to condemn her to eternal nightmares."

"You were too young to protect her the first time, and your trusted friend betrayed you the second. You can't blame yourself."

"But I do. I failed my sister. I had promised to protect her, and I did not. The very definition of failure, Your Highness."

Gwain turned to face Amelia, whose golden hair and blue eyes were strikingly like those of another. "Your sister claimed you would join the temple to become a high priestess. If you were to succeed in this endeavor, by the ancient traditions of this land, your position would one day be as powerful as her own. Tell me, Princess Amelia—and I pray you answer truthfully—do you believe your sister will share her power so easily?"

Amelia stared, wanting to defend Kaliyah, even now. The silence lingered. She knew the truth, but to speak the heresy became another matter entirely. "No." The word tore at the fabric of her soul. "I don't believe she would."

"Nor do I."

"So you believe she sent me to the temple to…meet the same fate as your sister?"

"I do not wish to believe it," Gwain answered. "She is my queen."

"But you do."

"Yes."

Fear gripped her. "What would you have me do, Captain?"

He withdrew a key from his belt, released the single lock in her remaining chains, and threw them into the water. "Run north to the mountains. To the ice and cold. The one place in this realm where anyone, even a princess, can disappear. For I fear, my lady, should you enter the temple's sacred walls…you shall never leave."

Her eyes widened as she rubbed her wrists and shoulders. "What about you, my lord?"

Moving to the tethered mounts, he explained, "I shall ride back on the dead man's horse. I will tell the guard you took Gabriel during the battle, and I chased after you." He patted the ebony stallion affectionately. "The smaller horse is no match for him. I'll send them in the wrong direction. They will search for a long time. With no sightings of your dragon, they'll presume you are bound by horse travel, and can't break your chains to fly." He held her gaze. "I have one request, Princess. A promise, if you will, to be made upon your royal bloodline."

The words seemed important, and Amelia paused before nodding. Her words came soft, yet certain, knowing the vow he demanded was not one she would be able to refuse. "What would you have of me, Captain?"

"Do not go back to the palace. You will find no help there. Not from those you knew. Not from your sister. Not from the man you loved."

Reality crashed around her at his words; the truth found within undeniable. "I understand."

"Your promise, Princess. What I intended to allow to happen is unforgivable. But I'm asking, Your Highness, promise you'll not to return to the palace for help. There is none to be found."

"I promise," the words ripped through her, re-opening the wound created by her sister's cold pronouncement of her fate. "As a princess of Kalleen, you have my word."

CHAPTER XXII

AMELIA RODE NORTH, TRAVELING MOSTLY during the cover of night, and resisting the urge to take her dragon form, lest she be recognized before reaching the mountain sanctuary. She used fire sparingly, opting instead to bury herself between the warm layers of pelts and cloaks Gwain had added, including his own, after transferring the dead man's saddle to Gabriel, and carefully packing as much as he could into the attached bags.

"The fewer risks you take, the better," he had said. "Once you reach the north mountains, you will be outside your sister's reach. Those lands are not technically under her rule, but instead, a region with no ownership between our kingdom and the next."

She had been riding for the better part of two weeks, hunting as she could for small game, and gathering berries. Thankfully water was plentiful along her path.

Amelia did not fear traveling in the dark; her eyesight had adjusted to darkness since her first moonlight transformation. Each morning after bedding down, she offered a silent prayer for the man who had helped her escape, and for the sister he had lost long ago. Once those prayers were spent, she would close her eyes against the sunlight, hoping when she woke, it would be in the safety of Stephen's arms.

Her heart ached for him to tell her this was naught but a dream. She was still in the palace, her newly crowned sister waiting with a smile Amelia had not seen since their mother had died. When had her sister become so cold? So heartless? Had it been at the death of their last parent? Or before? She tried to remember, but never seemed to grasp an exact timeframe before her consciousness gave way to slumber.

Temperatures steadily declined the closer she came to the mountains. She switched from her own cloak to the one Gwain had sent with her, grateful for the added warmth of the thicker material, then added a blanket over Gabriel, stroking his mane. "Sorry for getting you into this, boy. If it gets any colder, I'll start a fire, I promise."

The air was crisp, but the wind was worse, blowing on an icy breath, which penetrated the skin to chill bone. Arriving at the mountains' base under dense gray skies, Amelia considered the towering peaks rising to touch the clouds, tops shrouded in mist. The austere sight was enough to place a fresh layer of despair over her heart, having exchanged one form of exile for another. A strong gust sent a shiver down her spine as she led Gabriel upward, occasional patches of snow dotting the ground as dead grass crunched underfoot.

After traveling a ways up the mountain, she encountered a cave. Cautiously, she entered, finding it deep and barren. Large enough, Amelia brought the horse inside and lit a fire, using the surrounding rocks to cover the flames' light. Ensuring Gabriel was close enough to benefit from the warmth, she settled herself against a rock wall.

Relatively safe, she reached for her leather satchel and dumped the contents. The journey had resulted in a cluttered disarray, which she intended to remedy. Sorting through the blankets, and what little remained of her emergency rations, she found a scroll she had not noticed prior. Lifting the dry parchment, she glanced at the wax seal and recognized the mark of her sister's signet ring.

She considered tossing the scroll into the fire, but resisted the urge, instead breaking the wax to flatten the carefully rolled letter. In her sister's unique handwriting, she read the note within.

High Priestess,

I write to inform you of two equally important events.

First, as discussed, I deliver unto you my sister, Princess Amelia. I appreciate you taking her off my hands, and shall rest at night knowing she is safely out of the line of succession; neither she, nor any child, will be able to challenge my rule. Your idea of transforming her into a voice of Kamar is one I agree with wholeheartedly. You have my permission to grant my sister this position, and administer any force deemed necessary to ensure her compliance in her new role at the temple.

Second, I wish to inform you I have decided to name my chosen consort, Lord Stephen, son of Lord Terrance. He shall stand by my side throughout my reign, and together, we shall provide children to the realm. Stephen has consented to this position, and our union shall be announced shortly. I would advise not informing my sister, as such news might cause her to act even more unruly than I already expect. Stephen and I are eager to begin our venture together and, soon, to provide this kingdom with a future king or queen.

Again, thank you for your assistance in confining my sister, and ensuring the stability of my reign.

Faithfully,

Queen Kaliyah of Kalleen

Stunned, Amelia stared at the imprints on the parchment, and traced her finger over the signature she knew well, desperately wanting to believe the words were false. Yet there they were, in her sister's own hand. Unchangeable. Unquestionable. Undeniable.

A numbness spread, tears coming to her blue eyes for the first time since her last nightmare, from which Gwain had awoken her. Had the captain known? His repetitious admonishment that Stephen would not help her echoed with newfound meaning.

If Gwain knew the truth, why didn't he tell me? Followed immediately by the answer. *I never would have believed.* But this letter, meant for the high priestess, crushed her in a manner so profound it overwhelmed. The loss of all she knew. Her position, her friends, her sister, and now, irrefutable proof of her lover's betrayal.

Did he trade me in so quickly? A princess for a queen?

Amelia gave herself to grief. Sobs spilled from an emotional wound as blood would slide from a physical one. Her shoulders shook as she wrapped her arms around herself, the salty taste of tears reaching her lips as she cried. Even as Gabriel moved closer to nudge her affectionately with his head, she did not attempt to stifle her emotions, allowing them to flood her system. She welcomed her grief as numbness spread, seeping through her veins.

As she surrendered to her pain, her dragon stirred. At first the warmth was comforting, a soothing heat that pushed back the deathly chill. It spread, accelerating from comforting warmth to burning heat.

Amelia waited for the expected sense of well-being as the beast awoke within her. However, instead of a gentle rumble, the dragon roared. A sound that shook her, though heard by her alone. Belatedly, she attempted to calm the beast, but it burst forth with a boundless rage.

Wrath overwhelmed, the hurting girl surrendering to mythical power, blue scales emerging from pale skin with ferocious speed, the suddenness of the shift stealing her breath in a gasp of unexpected pain. First pulling off her mother's ring, and then throwing her clothes aside before they were completely shredded, the sharp sensation of splitting flesh was swallowed by the emergence of her dragon half, to whom such pain was but a trifle. Wings emerged from her back, melting into shoulders as cracking bones rearranged within her to accommodate the creature's immense form.

Beside her, Gabriel squealed, rising to paw the air at her changing scent. Amelia raced from the cave, exiting before her size threatened the shelter's structure. Her wings expanded, soft, itchy scales covering tender flesh, transforming it to a nearly impenetrable hide. Her vision sharpened, neck and face stretching. When the transformation was complete, a sky-blue dragon stood before the cave's entrance.

Snarling, her forked tongue licked the air, tasting the scents of barren bark, and creatures hiding from the bitter cold of ice-tipped mountains.

As Amelia gave herself to the dragon within, her pain dimmed. All thoughts faded behind the desire to survey this new land. Surrendering, she allowed the dragon to spread its massive wings and took to the air, the ground fading as each powerful beat carried her closer to the mountains' ridge.

Nothing painful could harm her here, among the clouds. Pain, anger, even the rage which had drawn the creature forth, vanished under the dragon's power. Refusing to struggle for control, she took comfort in the solitude and forgetfulness she found within her beast. Slipping into the wet clouds, the dragon drew a breath, roaring its dominance to the mountains below, before releasing a stream of hot, blue fire. Intense heat clashed with icy wind as Amelia gave herself fully to the dragon's embrace.

CHAPTER XXIII

NAKED IN THE CAVE WHERE she had taken shelter, Amelia awoke with no memory of how she had returned. Groggily, she sat up, grateful the cold air had less effect on her kind than it did mortals, but she nevertheless pulled Gwain's cloak over her, cinching it around her waist as best she could, snuggling into the extra warmth.

Checking on Gabriel, she was relieved to find the horse unharmed. After stroking his neck for a time, she walked back to where she'd dumped out her saddlebag and, retrieving a leather pouch, extracted a handful of oats.

Offering them in her cupped hands, she apologized, "Sorry I scared you, boy. Not sure what came over me last night."

With a soft huff, the horse ate.

After giving one more affectionate pat, Amelia walked back toward the center of the cave where her bag's contents waited, strewn over the dirt. With a heavy heart, she picked up the discarded letter and again read the heartbreaking words she desperately wished to deny. Tracing her fingers over the familiar signature, she could not summon the required doubt.

"Stephen," she whispered, clutching the paper to her chest, eyes closing as she resisted the urge to renew her tears. "Why?"

Questions ran through her mind. *Did Stephen love my sister? Had he loved me? What was—*

Amelia drew a harsh breath and forced herself to pause her contemplation. "It doesn't matter," she spoke to the empty cave. "Results will be the same."

No amount of tears would change the fact that Stephen must have agreed to the arrangement. Nor that he was now by her sister's side. The thought of his lips, which had coaxed her to sweet release, now moving over Kaliyah's pale flesh caused her to shudder, but she forced the emotions back. Obsessing would not help her current situation.

After a deep breath, she lit a new fire to warm Gabriel. She then removed her outer cloak, and pulled back on the shirt and trousers she'd discarded the night before, along with her mother's ring.

Replacing the outer cloak, she carefully repacked her saddle bags as she'd intended to do the night before. She then turned to the fire and, not wanting the letter to reveal her identity to strangers, tossed the parchment into the flames. Eating a simple meal of rations, she watched the scroll turn to ash before extinguishing the blaze.

Thus prepared for an uncertain future, the exiled princess saddled Gabriel and journeyed deeper into the mountains, seeking one of the scattered villages she had been told of during her childhood studies.

From what she could recall, those who lived in the Kalleen Mountains were a secluded people, whose villages dotting the valleys were generally populated with non-shifters. Recalling this limited detail, she found a dirt trail, praying she was far enough from her sister's land she could travel in relative safety. The path seemed rarely used, covered in thick layers of leaves.

Three days passed before she came upon the first outcropping of civilization: a row of quaint huts snuggled against the mountain backdrop. Amelia approached warily. Locating what appeared to be an inn, Amelia rode to the rails and dismounted, considering if she wanted to enter, when a boy of perhaps twelve years of age approached.

"Hello," the young man addressed her. "Would you like me to take your horse?"

"My horse?"

"We have a stable." He nodded in the direction of a wooden structure in the distance. "Can get him warmed up, and fed for the night, if you'd like?"

Amelia nodded, reaching into her saddle bag and withdrawing one of the few coins that had been within. "Would this cover it?"

The boy eyed the piece of silver. "Of course, my lady. If you go inside, and give it to my Aunt Chris, should be enough for some soup and a cup o' wine as well."

"Thank you," she said, unlatching the saddle bag and handing the boy Gabriel's reins. "Take good care of him."

"I will, my lady. Promise."

Grasping her meager belongings, Amelia turned and entered through a pair of squeaky wooden doors into the main room. Sparse, the tavern was scattered with wooden tables, splinters protruding from abused legs. Only three people were inside: two men sitting together in the back corner, half-empty goblets the likely reason for their boisterous voices, and a woman behind the counter, whom Amelia presumed to be the stable boy's aunt.

Amelia approached, noting gray strands disrupting the continuity of her plain brown locks, which lay straight down her back.

Glancing up, the woman smiled in greeting. "Good day. May I help you?"

Amelia nodded. "A stable boy was kind enough to bed down my horse. Said you were the one to speak to."

"Ah, yes, my nephew, Jimmy. A good lad, he'll take care of the animal for you."

"Thank you," Amelia replied, holding out the piece of silver and placing it in the woman's hand.

Her eyes widened at the shimmering metal. "I'm afraid this is far too much for simply feeding your horse."

"I was hoping to get a meal for myself, and glass of wine as well."

The woman studied the circles under Amelia's bloodshot eyes, and the excessive dirt on her cloak. She looked as one on the verge of collapse. "I'll fetch a bowl of soup, and some bread. 'Tis not the fanciest of meals, but it should help warm you up, at the very least."

"Thank you, ma'am."

"Please, call me Chris."

Amelia did not answer, but gave a single nod, and moved to a seat at one of the tables near the fireplace. The heat warmed her skin, but not the chill lacing her soul. Even the comforting scent of freshly baked bread did little to draw her out of her own head, and so she jumped when the tavern keeper appeared, her soup in hand.

"Didn't mean to frighten you," Chris apologized.

"No," she mumbled. "It's fine. Sorry."

"Quite all right." Chris placed the soup and bread, then returned shortly, adding the requested glass of wine. "I'd imagine you've had quite the journey. If you'd like, I have some spare rooms upstairs. You're more than welcome to stay here tonight. It's not much, but there's at least a place to rest."

"Thank you, but I couldn't possibly—"

"Nonsense," Chris interrupted. "You look tired as death. Some quality sleep would do you good. And if he's as tired as you are, I suspect your horse will benefit from a night in."

Amelia considered arguing, but exhaustion prevailed, and the idea of sleeping in a bed instead of on the cold ground won out. "That would be very nice."

Chris nodded. "I'll have some extra linens taken up for you, and a bath drawn. I'm happy to wash your clothing as well, and hang it by the fire to dry."

"Thank you."

"It's no problem."

She turned to attend to her other guests, leaving Amelia alone to finish her meal. The food was simple, but welcome. The hot broth soothed her throat, and the fire warmed her chilled flesh. Once finished, bag in tow, she climbed the rickety inn steps, and was taken to the prepared room.

Stripping her soiled garments, Amelia handed them to the innkeeper before sinking into a narrow tub of warm water. Using the provided bar of unscented soap, she scrubbed her skin and hair to remove as much dirt as she could, then remained in the water until it had completely cooled before rising. Wrapping a towel around her thin form, the princess lay down on the bed, slipping between the layers of provided pelts.

A knock on the door caused her alarm, but she managed to steady her thumping heart. "Yes?"

The door opened and Chris entered. "Forgive the intrusion. I wanted to ensure you didn't require anything further."

"No." Amelia shook her head. "Thank you for asking, and for your hospitality."

The older woman smiled. "Happy to help." Chris moved to the door, but paused and turned back around. "I want you to know, there's nothing to fear here. This place was made for people like us."

"Like us?"

Chris nodded. "I know what it's like, to be rejected by your family."

Amelia's heart resumed a faster pace as she stared at the other woman. "I assure you, I don't—"

"Forgive the presumption, my lady, but a lot of our kind come through here."

"Our kind? Sorry, I don't..." Words faltered as Amelia watched her, fearful of her meaning. She had come here to hide. Did this woman know her identity?

Chris stepped closer, eyes offering a kindness Amelia did not comprehend. "People who didn't shift, from families who did. I was one too."

Not the expected answer, Amelia gaped at the woman, who smiled with misplaced understanding. She wanted to say she didn't understand. *There were villages near the castle for people who failed to shift. Why would they come here?*

"Lots of people run for the safety of these mountains," Chris explained, not completely answering the unspoken question. "You're among friends here, if friends are what you seek. I'll not ask you any questions. Respecting privacy is another part of the rules here, unspoken as they may be."

Silence followed before Amelia shook her head. "You're being awfully kind, with me being a stranger."

"Kindness should be granted to all, but strangers especially, because you never know what they have been through." She put up her hands. "Again, not prying. I only want you to know you're safe here. But now, you must be exhausted. Get some sleep. We can speak more in the morning, if you wish."

With a never-faltering smile, the older woman turned and left the room, leaving Amelia alone, a hint of moonlight filtering through the room's single window as she burrowed under the soft pelts.

CHAPTER XXIV

AMELIA ENJOYED A RARE, BLESSEDLY dreamless sleep. Waking refreshed, she found a set of clothes draped neatly over a wooden chair beside a matching desk, the only furnishings in the room other than the bed on which she lay.

Stretching, Amelia rose and walked to the window. Though the sun was high in the mid-morning sky, the light imparted little warmth to the frigid air. Surrounded by mountains on every side, the snowy valley was dotted with rows of wooden homes and shops. She observed for a while, watching the occasional passerby below before turning to the desk. Atop the clothes pile, a note:

Your clothes were still damp this morning, and your shirt needed mending. These are my daughter's. Hopefully they will fit close enough. Come down for breakfast when you're ready.

~ Chris

Amelia picked up the dress, a simple garment but not without a certain charm, the crushed green velvet pretty against her pale skin as she slipped the gown over her head. The sleeves ran down her arms, ending in sharp angles at her wrist. The gown was large for her thin frame, but not so much it looked out of place. Running her fingers through her hair, she arranged it as best she could, and pulled on her boots, before walking down the creaking stairs.

"You're awake," Chris greeted as she emerged, straightening from over the table she had been wiping down. "Hungry?"

She nodded.

"Take a seat." Chris motioned to the now clean table. "I'll bring food."

"Thank you."

Amelia took the indicated seat, and moments later a bowl of porridge, swirled with honey, was placed on the table with a wooden spoon. Eating,

Amelia listened to the mixed banter of additional guests, who had increased in number since the previous night. Chris flitted between the tables, greeting the newcomers as old friends, filling bowls, and wiping down tables as people came and went through the tavern.

Across the room, Chris paused to converse with a man who appeared in his late forties. "So, picked up another stray, have ye?" He nodded in Amelia's general direction.

"Poor thing came in last night. Looked like she's been on quite the journey to get here."

"You know you don't have to take in every refugee that passes by, right?"

"And you know that if I can help someone, I'm going to do so. The girl was near frozen and utterly exhausted."

"Chris—"

"No different than what your uncle once did for me, George."

"Yes, but you were a special—"

"I was no different than her. Nor is any other who comes here seeking aid."

The man eyed his long-time friend critically, then relented, settling his gaze back on the newcomer.

Amelia busily ate her breakfast, eyes downcast.

"Wonder what happened to her?"

"Probably the same as what happened to us all, once cast from the dragon realms."

"She's older than the typical refugee."

Chris shrugged. "Perhaps the family hid her for a while, or she survived in the local villages. But you know what happens to the young women sent to those villages who failed to transform. Especially the pretty ones."

"I do." George nodded solemnly. "Hope she escaped before it came to that."

Bitterness laced Chris' words as she agreed, "Yes, let's hope she did."

Chris continued about the business of running her tavern before working her way back to the young woman. "Get enough to eat?"

"Yes, thank you."

"Would you care to take a look around the village?"

Amelia shook her head. "I must be on my way."

"Nonsense. A storm's coming tonight, and there is no way anyone should be out in it, let alone a young woman such as yourself. You'll stay another night."

"I really should be—"

"I'm refusing to take 'no' for an answer. You'll stay until the storm passes. From the looks of you, I doubt you've ever been in an ice storm such as the ones we have here. Monstrous. No reason for you to be out in it, especially when you don't have to."

"I'm afraid I don't have much more silver with me."

"Never you mind. I wouldn't accept it from you in any case."

Dropping her head, Amelia's silence conveyed consent, causing Chris to nod.

"Feel free to explore the village, but be sure to grab a cloak. We have some extra ones in the back." She motioned to the left side of the room. "Your cloak is hanging behind the kitchen fire, and will hopefully be dry in a few hours. Until then, make yourself at home, and borrow anything you'd like from the closet."

"Thank you. You're being far too kind."

"My pleasure," she said. "By the way, I failed to ask your name last night."

"It's...Elizabeth," she gave her middle name in lieu of her more well-known first.

"Well, Elizabeth, please consider my tavern home for the time being."

Before Amelia could answer, the elder woman turned and walked away.

Following instructions, Amelia walked over to the indicated closet and withdrew a woolen gray cloak. Securing it across her shoulders, she tied the belt around her, enfolding herself into the warm garment. She stepped outside, walking carefully to avoid slipping on the ice lining the wooden porch.

Snow crunching under her steps, Amelia walked through the village, inhaling the aromas of freshly cooking bread, and sausage, as she passed by a bread maker and butcher. Residents she encountered offered her warm smiles and a few nods. Laughter echoed through the settlement as well, from children playing in the snow, chasing each other merrily.

When Amelia turned back toward the inn, she paused by the stables to check on Gabriel, grateful she found him munching on a generous portion of oats, and covered by a warm blanket. After stroking the horse's neck, she turned and re-entered the tavern to find Chris preparing the evening meal.

"I hadn't realized I was out so long," Amelia apologized.

"More than fine. I'm glad you went exploring."

"May I help you prepare supper?"

"You don't have to."

"I'd like to. You've been so kind. I would love to help."

"Sure." Chris smiled, handing over a wooden spoon nearly as long as her arm. "Would you mind stirring the soup while I set out some bowls? Be careful not to touch the cauldron. Wouldn't want you to burn yourself."

"No problem." Amelia flashed her own smile, taking the spoon, stained by countless meals, to stir the kettle.

When Chris would call for one, she'd fill the bowls as guests arrived for dinner. While she worked, Amelia listened to the friendly banter exchanged by those in the village, where everyone seemed to know each other, making her the only stranger in sight.

Later, she assisted Chris in cleaning the kitchen before sitting down to her own supper, sharing a table with her benevolent hostess.

"So," Chris began after devouring several bites of the warm broth, "what did you think of our humble village?"

"It's lovely. Everyone seems nice."

Chris nodded. "More or less."

"May I ask, what is this place?"

"A refuge of sorts. For those who brought *dishonor* to their families for failing to shift."

"Failing to shift isn't a choice though. There's no dishonor in something you have no control over."

Chris looked at her critically, studying Amelia's sapphire eyes. "Was I incorrect in my assumptions of you?"

Amelia hesitated, deciding upon a half-truth. "I too have brought dishonor to my family. I could not fulfill my expected fate, and came to these mountains hoping to find refuge."

Chris nodded. "I was born to two dragon shifters of a prominent family. I had two siblings, who both made their first transformation when they were fifteen. When I reached my name day, I was filled with excitement. At last, I too would be able to fly with my elder sisters, and join the family in the sky."

She paused her story, reaching for a pitcher of wine on the table, and pouring the red liquid into a pair of goblets. Handing one to Amelia, Chris placed the other to her lips and drank deeply before resuming.

"However, much to everyone's surprise, the year came and went, without my dragon awakening. Same for my sixteenth and seventeenth year. By the time I had reached my eighteenth name day, my parents had determined I would never transform, and sent me to live in one of the villages set aside for others such as myself. Children of powerful families who never became dragons."

Amelia recognized the pain in Chris' voice. The same sadness that had plagued her dear friend, Kelsie. For years, the two girls had planned all the flights they would have together. But Kelsie had never transformed.

Amelia spoke softly, "You were sent to a local village, near the castle?"

Chris nodded.

"Why are you…"

"Difficult, to make a new life. Even more so to be abandoned by my family. Despite the challenges, I managed to make the best of my situation. Bonded with new friends, others who had also failed to transform. Found new ways to live. Even found a man I came to love deeply."

Chris paused to again take a sip from her wine goblet.

"When I turned twenty-three, an unexpected message arrived. My mother wished to speak with me on a matter of great urgency, and would be arriving at the village. I hadn't seen her since I was sent away, so I was both excited and worried. However, once she arrived..."

CHAPTER XXV

25 YEARS AGO

CHRIS RUMMAGED IN THE BOTTOM of her dusty chest, withdrawing a dress she had not worn since she was sent away. Wrapped lovingly in a piece of protective muslin, Chris untied the ribbons holding the bundle together and unfolded the garment.

Full length, the crimson satin gown looked as beautiful as the day she had left the dragon courts, being forced to not only give up her hopes of transforming with the rest of her family, but also the life of luxury into which she had been born. Upon arrival, her wardrobe had been replaced with plain garments of dull colors, better suited to those required to live outside of shifter status.

After airing out the gown as long as time allowed, Chris stepped into the dress, pulling the material up over her torso. Relief flooded her as she confirmed the fit, though looser than she had recalled. Her life of labor kept her thinner than she had been as a noble lady.

Once dressed, Chris ran a brush through her hair, taming the thick mop as best she could before checking her appearance in a hand-held mirror her friend, Rachel, had given her on her twenty-first name day. After confirming she looked as tidy as she could hope to, Chris carefully tucked away the mirror, covering it with a soft cloth on the dresser before walking downstairs in preparation for her mother's impending visit.

Regal as ever, Lady Selena arrived with several ladies in waiting, and a large honor guard consisting of no fewer than fifteen of the kingdom's finest knights, each garbed in matching emerald cloaks. All but two of these men were left outside as Selena entered the dwelling, careful to avoid touching anything she did not have to.

Chris dropped into a low bow at her entrance. "Mother."

"Daughter," Selena replied, lifting her hand in an upward motion. "Rise, child. I wish to see you."

Expectations uncertain, Chris rose to meet her mother's scrutinizing gaze, which slid the length of her body.

"Come closer," Selena instructed.

Taking several steps, Chris stopped a single pace from the older woman, who stared at her daughter without speaking. Reaching out a hand, Selena grasped Chris' chin, coldly forcing her head back, eyes studying the long line of her neck as she moved her daughter's head left, then right. She released her, only to move her hands toward Chris' waist. Selena gathered the sides of her crimson gown, pulling the material so it clung tightly to Chris' waist and chest.

"Hmm…" her mother mused. "Skinny, but not so much as to be unsuitable."

"Unsuitable?" Chris asked in confusion. "I don't understand."

Her mother sighed, stepping back from her daughter, and again running down her body with a piercing gaze. "It will have to do."

"What will? Why have you come to see me? I didn't think you ever would." Chris smiled, a hopeful expression. "I've missed you, Mother."

"Yes, I would imagine you have," Selena answered. "After all, look at the diminished state of your life."

"It's been difficult, especially at the beginning. But with time, life has become better. I've learned lots of new skills, including becoming a good cook. And I have been teaching local children to read." She searched for words, uncertain how to explain her new life to a woman she no longer knew.

"I'm engaged," she sputtered.

"Engaged?"

"To Brian. He's a non-shifter like me. We've been courting for a few years."

Her mother stared intently, but Chris resisted the urge to squirm under her scrutiny. "Tell me, daughter, how long has this engagement been in place?"

"A month. I'm really happy. He's so kind, and he helps me with so much. You'll like him." She smiled again.

Her mother did not return the gesture.

"What's wrong?"

"Did you ask permission, before agreeing to marry this…man?"

"Permission?"

"Yes. Shifter or no, you remain the daughter of a noble family. Did you ask your father's permission to marry? Or inform anyone, for that matter?"

"I…"

"I'll take your silence as a no."

"I haven't seen you in five years! You abandoned me."

"Don't be dramatic, Christina. You know how I detest tantrums."

"Tantrums? I haven't seen you since the day you sent me here! Nor received any help."

"Did you wish for my assistance?" Selena challenged. "You did not ask."

"Because I knew what your answer would be."

Her mother scoffed, "You knew no such thing. You were sent here because tradition, and the laws of the land, dictated we do so. You were never disowned, girl." Selena shook her head. "You are not yet married, correct?"

Chris shook her head.

"Good, then it's not too late to save you from such an error."

"Error?"

"Of course. Just because you did not transform, does not mean you have no further value."

"What are you talking about?"

Her mother smiled, perfectly lined ruby lips lifting to a gesture without the faintest hint of warmth. "Christina, you are the daughter of a noble lord. A child of a shifter line. Though you personally were not blessed by the goddess, you may bear children who are. Therefore the passing of our lineage is very much a matter of concern."

"I don't understand."

"You will provide children, and hopefully those children shall be blessed by the goddess, even if you, personally, were not."

Chris stared blankly. "What are you saying?"

"The son of Lord Randall, Marcus, has agreed to father your children."

"Father my…"

"Yes. In fact, he has agreed to begin immediately, provided you had not become too ghastly during your unfortunate stay here. Thinness aside, you shall do nicely."

The world shifted as Chris' heart rate increased, blood pounding against her left temple as she attempted to process her mother's words. When she had finally gathered her thoughts enough to speak, her voice came soft and childlike. "But I love Brian. We're going to be married. I can't simply leave and marry someone else."

"Of course not," Selena snapped. "The esteemed son of a noble family marrying a non-shifter? Would never do."

Chris shook her head, not understanding. "I don't—"

With an exasperated sigh, her mother clarified, "I don't recall you being this dense, but I suppose intelligence isn't required for this duty. I said he offered to father your children, not marry you. You will be his concubine, Christina. He also intends to take a wife, and impregnate you both. Should any of your children be born shifters, they will be legitimized upon their first transformation. Otherwise, they will be sent here, to whatever fate this miserable place may have in store."

Panic set in at the full explanation. Her eyes widened. "No."

"Come now, Christina, this is no time to be foolish. You will be well cared for. How hard can it be to lay on your back? In return, you'll be provided with the life of comfort to which you were once accustomed. Surely better than this ghastly excuse of an existence."

"No!" Chris exclaimed, rushing toward the exit. She threw open the door, only to find herself faced with her mother's guards, who stood clustered around porch. As she rushed down the stairs, one of the men grabbed her, the thin girl no match for a trained knight. She struggled as a second man stepped forward, the two gaining complete control over her writhing form even as she yelled, "Let me go!"

The men forced her to turn, her mother emerging from the house as she was compelled forward. Walking gracefully down the stairs, Selena reached out and pressed her palm against Chris' right cheek, maintaining the same cruel smile she had displayed during their exchange. "Come now, daughter. For one of your unfortunate disposition, this is a great honor."

"I don't want this!" Chris protested. "Please, Mother!"

In response, her mother gave her a sharp slap to the face, carefully applied to sting, but not leave a mark. "Come now, Christina. No more tantrums."

"I'm not—"

"Chris?" a new voice entered the conversation.

She jerked her head in the direction of the voice, managing to glimpse Brian's approach from the right.

"Chris, what's going on?"

"Brian!"

"Ah," her mother said, "so this is the man I can thank for tarnishing my daughter."

"Who are you?"

"Mother," Chris pleaded, "let's discuss—"

"There is nothing to discuss. You are a daughter of a noble house. You are to be used as the heads of the family see fit."

"Please." Tears burned her eyes as she realized her pleas were in vain.

Brian rushed forward, slipping past the outer guard to reach the ones holding her. Throwing his weight against the guard on her left, the one on her right let go of her arm in alarm.

Chris ran to her right, managing to slip past the first guard, but was quickly recaptured, her arms grabbed roughly as she was turned in time to see Brian rushing toward her.

"No!" Chris screamed at her love's valiant attempt to set her free. "Stop! Please!"

Brian pulled back a fist, landing a punch against the knight's left cheek, hard enough the guard fell to the ground, dazed.

Another of her mother's guards stepped forward, drawing a large, heavy blade.

"Brian, no!"

Faced with men on multiple sides, and vastly outnumbered, the men forced Brian back, away from Chris.

"Mother, please stop this!"

As though in slow motion, Chris watched as more blades were pulled, until her fiancé was encircled by a wall of lethal swords.

"I'll do what you want!" she bargained in desperation.

The words came too late.

Surrounded, Brian attempted to dash between two of the men, but was pushed back, right into a waiting blade.

Chris screamed as she watched the weapon pierce the chest of the man she loved. A sound between a shriek and wail. She screamed again, calling his name as he fell, the act skewering her heart as sharply as the blade had sliced into his.

Managing to wrest herself free, Chris raced toward Brian, and this time, the guards allowed it, watching as she fell to her knees.

She attempted to press her hands against the wound, but there was so much blood, she only succeeded in drenching herself with the hot, sticky substance. Gathering him against her chest, she sobbed his name.

"Brian, no. No. Please, no."

"Chris," he managed to say. "Beautiful Chris."

She leaned her head down, not caring as blood soaked her hair, pressing her cheek to his gasping chest. "Don't leave me," she begged, but she shook so badly the words came broken and incoherent. "I love you. I love you."

"Fight them," he managed to whisper, words a wheezing gasp only she could hear. "Promise me."

"No," she shook her head. "Please, no."

"Promise...love...promise me." He coughed, and blood splattered her face.

"Brian, I..."

"Promise, Chris. Promise...Prom..."

Against her cheek, she heard his heart beat once more, and then never again.

Unable to believe this was real, the pounding of her heart so fierce she lay frozen in fear, pain, and rage. She let out an ear-splitting scream as she tucked herself tightly against his body, her beautiful red dress darker now, saturated with his blood.

Chris screamed for a long time before, in a hoarse whisper she managed to say, "I promise."

With that, the guards pulled her away from her dead love and shoved her into the waiting carriage, destroying all semblance of the life she had known.

Chapter XXVI

A<small>MELIA STARED AT THE OLDER</small> woman, who reached up to wipe a tear from her eyes.

"Oh my gods," Amelia sympathized, attempting to find the right words. "They...I mean..."

"Forgive me. These events happened so long ago. Yet thinking of Brian...well, you'll have to forgive me."

"No, please, don't apologize. I only...I'm so sorry."

"Thank you," Chris' words were soft.

"What happened next? How did you end up here?"

Chris closed her eyes and drew a breath, before centering her gaze on the far wall. "I wish I could tell you that Brian's sacrifice saved me from my mother's plans. But..."

"They forced you to the lord's..."

Chris nodded. "I resisted, at first, but...when I did, they simply tied me in whatever manner Marcus wished, and he had his way. I spent two years as his slave; he would violate me each night in hopes of getting me pregnant.

"No children were conceived though, and I managed to make a few contacts, who eventually helped me to escape. They brought me to the base of these mountains, where I ran, until I stumbled upon this village. My friend, George—his parents were very kind. They took me in; treated me like a daughter. It had happened to George's mother also, you see. Her story is very similar to my own."

"You said Marcus was the son of Lord Randall."

"Yes."

"The brother of Lord Terrance?" she named Stephen's father.

"The same. Did you know him?"

Amelia drew a sharp breath. "In a manner of speaking."

"The entire family has been corrupt for generations. Each member struggling to move a step closer to the throne."

"The throne?"

"Of course. They marry a step higher with each generation. Bedding me was a favor to my family, which outranked theirs. Had I borne him a child, who could have been legitimized, it would have added prestige to both lines."

Amelia stood from the chair, feet itching with the need to flee as a horrible realization descended. "I'm sorry, would you excuse me?"

"Certainly," she said. "Though please, I did not mean to upset—"

Amelia did not hear her remaining words, turning to the wooden door to race down the steps. Inside her, the dragon stirred as she raced forward, desperate to escape the valley. Her steps were slow, the beast within roaring against her resistance to taking the form it desired.

The storm Chris had warned her about had arrived, in full, horrific glory, slush soaking through her borrowed gown. As her skin heated, creating steam, she ran faster, splashing through mud and muck as ice pelted her.

Inside her, the dragon reared up with a ferocity she had rarely known from the normally gentle beast.

At last, she reached the forest's edge, slipping between the first row of trees to fall on her knees in the wet dirt. Curling on her side, she struggled against the dragon, fighting to maintain control while her mind replayed Chris' words, along with the crushing confirmation of what she had most feared.

"He never loved me," she spoke to the chilled wind.

Curled into a ball, she let out a scream, swallowed by the dragon's eager call, which only she could hear. "Why, Stephen? Why?"

World crushed, she lay in the ice and mud for a long time until someone shook her.

"Are you all right?"

Amelia lacked the will to glance up, strength sapped by the internal exertion required to keep the dragon at bay.

When she didn't respond, her rescuer reached down and gathered her in his arms.

She silently struggled for control, the dragon switching from rage to sweet promises in a voice only she would ever hear.

The pain will vanish, the dragon promised. *No pain.*

The offered hope verged on more than she could bear as she was carried back to the inn. She had no idea how long they traveled, until light intruded, causing her to close her eyes tightly.

Chris' voice instructed, "Take her upstairs."

No pain. The silent promise rose again, heat searing her flesh.

Amelia shrieked at the sensation, like a thousand embers burning her internally.

K.L. BONE

A cool hand touched her forehead. "She's burning up," Chris said, but her words came from a distance. "I'll fetch a cool cloth and extra pelts."

The man who had carried her pushed her hair back. Leaning down, he whispered, "Speak to your dragon, my lady. The creature is a part of you. It will listen, if you ask."

Losing the battle, and too panicked to care how the man knew, she heeded the stranger's advice, calling to the dragon coiling within.

Hear my plea. Please, I beg of you, be calm.

At her request, the dragon quieted, her skin cooling instantly as she was laid onto the room's bed. She opened her eyes enough to briefly take in the image of a young man, about her age with light brown hair.

His lilac eyes studied hers intently as Amelia's gaze moved to his smooth, strong jawline and expanded to his broad shoulders.

"Thank you, Conner," Chris spoke to Amelia's rescuer, returning with the cloths and pelts that would no longer be needed.

"No problem," the man answered, his deep voice settling against her skin. "I hope she's all right. Is there anything else I can do?"

"I'll take it from here," Chris replied before Amelia slipped to unconsciousness.

Chapter XXVII

THE BANISHED PRINCESS WOKE TO Chris' tender care.

"I'm sorry," she apologized. "I—"

"No need, Elizabeth," Chris assured. "Each of us must deal with life's twists in our own way. No one here will judge, nor pry. We all have our stories to tell. If you find one day you wish to share yours, I am happy to listen. Until then, please know you are welcome to make this your new home, if you wish, or continue on your journey."

"Thank you," Amelia whispered, shame lacing her words at her uncontrollable behavior the night before, and regret over using a secretive name. "I'm sorry if I damaged your daughter's dress."

"The gown doesn't matter. I am only glad you were returned safe, and don't appear to have caught cold from the storm. You had quite the fever when Conner brought you back last night."

"I'm fine," she answered. "Tired, but well."

"To be expected." Chris motioned to the wooden desk, where a fresh gown, in lilac this time, had been laid out. "Your own clothes are underneath, if you prefer. Otherwise, feel free to borrow the dress. Come down for breakfast when you're ready."

And so time passed. Six months later, Amelia had cautiously accepted the full breadth of the older woman's hospitality. Now, as she wiped down tables, Amelia attempted to focus on her blessings, instead of the lost life she mourned.

But each night, alone in her room, her mind inevitably turned to thoughts of her sister, and the lover that had betrayed her. The heartbreaking realization she would be forever banned from the land, and people, she loved. She no longer cried at these thoughts, but instead stared longingly at the waning moon, while the dragon inside silently promised to take away the pain, if she would but allow it.

Amelia resisted, restraining the dragon deep within, refusing to allow the beast to take wing, even as her heart longed to do so. The most difficult nights were those when the moon was at its brightest, her soul crying out to fly among the crisp clouds. She feared the reaction of her new friends, were they to learn she was among the blessed and had invaded the sanctuary created to escape her kind.

Many times, Amelia had asked of her rescuer, the mysterious Conner. She had never seen him again, after the night he had returned her from the woods.

"He lives on the outskirts with his brothers," Chris had informed her. "They prefer it that way, though I've tried several times to get them to reconsider." She shrugged. "They seem content by themselves."

"I wanted to thank him."

"He knows you're grateful, child. Trust me."

Her mind played over the events of that night. The intense pain in her head. The exhaustive struggle to contain the dragon. The stranger's voice. *Speak to your dragon, my lady. The creature is a part of you. It will listen, if you ask.*

Who was her savior? Had he actually known what she was, or had she imagined the words? If he knew, why hadn't he exposed her secret?

Forcing these troubling thoughts from her mind, she lay down on the bed, tension ebbing with each deep breath, until she reached the rhythm of sleep.

CHAPTER XXVIII

THE DRAGON PRINCESS STOOD IN a burning field, throat dry from thick smoke, each breath forced into her protesting lungs. Her heart lurched as she spied the skeletal crumblings of the once lush land, birds fluttering helpless, unable to fly through the falling ash.

She walked over the charred ground, hot air stinging her dry eyes. A thick fog blanketed the land, partially shrouding the devastating aftermath. Attempting to keep her coughs to a minimum, Amelia sought the source of the flames, but as she searched, she was overpowered by a familiar sense of dismay. She herself was a creature of flame. A raw force, which consumed and destroyed; never soothed.

When she came upon a struggling squirrel, she spoke softly to the creature, which calmed at her gentle assurance. In desperation, she called on the little power she held, and light emanated from her fingers as she willed the creature to live. But as the healing radiance burst from her palms, a chilling, familiar shadow fell over her kneeling form.

Fear crawled over her skin as she forced herself to glance toward the sky.

The strange feathered dragon glared down. Fangs protruded from its open mouth, its forked tongue flicking the air, tasting her terror. Intense silver eyes stared down, causing Amelia's heart to pound painfully against her ribs. She swallowed, dread mixing with smoke, forcing her to suppress a coughing fit.

"What do you want?" Her voice a soft whisper, but she knew the dragon would hear. "Tell me what you want."

To her surprise, a deep, masculine voice slid silkily through her mind as the creature hovered. "The flames of Kalleen…must die."

With those words, the creature opened his mouth, sealing her fate in a spew of golden flame.

"Elizabeth!" Chris' voice drew her from the all-too familiar nightmare.

Eyes open, Amelia clawed her way from the bed, twisting in panic as she crossed the room before full awareness dawned.

"Forgive me, Elizabeth," Chris addressed her again by the middle name she had given. "You were having a nightmare."

Amelia faced the wall, drawing labored breaths, hesitant to turn lest her eyes appeared other than human. Her dragon rumbled beneath her skin, heating her flesh to a rosy flush as she struggled to contain the protective nature of the beast within.

Please, she begged silently, pleading for calm over the racing of her heart, and sweat breaking on her brow.

The dragon quieted, retiring to patience, though not to slumber.

Thank you, she said without words, before turning toward Chris. "I'm sorry."

"Another dream? Would you like to talk about it?"

Amelia shook her head.

Chris persisted, "You get nightmares a lot. Sometimes it helps to share."

Amelia shifted uncomfortably, wanting to trust the woman who had shown her nothing but kindness, yet cautious. If she confessed her dreams, she might be unable to prevent herself from revealing all.

"It's all right. If you ever do wish to talk, you know where I am." Offering an understanding smile, she moved toward the door.

Against her better judgement, Amelia decided to take a chance. "May I ask you something?"

"Of course."

Amelia took a breath, steeling herself for unknown outcomes. "Have you ever seen a dragon who looked...different than others?"

"Different? How so?"

"Like a dragon, but with wings of a bird."

"A bird?"

Amelia nodded. "Wings that look more like feathers, but you can see the fire inside of them, glowing embers lighting the wings from within. The front legs are also more bird-like, with claws, but the back legs have hooves, like those of a horse."

Chris walked to the desk, moving its wooden chair to beside the bed. Once seated, the older woman met the gaze of the younger. Chris appeared pale, eyes wide as she reviewed the princess' words. "A dragon, with the wings of a bird, you say?"

"And the hooves of a horse."

"A dragon with..."

"Have you seen such a creature?"

"No," she answered. "No one has. Not since..."

"Since when? Do they exist? Where are they?"

"Only in stories, songs, and glimpses of dreams."

"Glimpses of dreams? I met a man who said his sister had seen the same creature in her nightmares."

Chris nodded. "Those who do are sent to the temples, never to be seen again."

"What?"

"Individuals who have dreams of the feathery dragons are always sent to the temples."

Understanding dawned. "Where they are given potions," Amelia finished, "to ensure they never transform."

"Yes."

"But why? Are the people who dream of this meant to become a different dragon?"

"Some claim that is the fear. Yet the songs, the myths, they are as old as the temples themselves."

"What do the myths say?"

"That there was once an abundance of such dragons. Long ago, they were cast from the Kalleen kingdoms by a high priestess and queen, who stood united. They have many different names, however they are most commonly referred to as Amethystine Dragons, due to their purple coloring. Whereas the Kalleen Dragons are generally pastel-toned, Amethystine Dragons were meant to blend with darker skies. And just as it is rare for a Kalleen Dragon to be borne by moonlight, stories say it is equally rare for an Amethystine Dragon to be borne by day."

"What happened to them, according to the stories?"

"Supposedly they attempted to wrestle control of the kingdom for themselves. When they failed, the dragons left, vowing to one day return, and vanished into the mist, never again to be seen."

"Yes." Amelia's voice sounded haunted. "Something must have happened. The dragon in the dream, he has such…rage." A chill raced down her skin, causing Amelia to rub at her arm. "I've never known such anger."

"Yes, the Amethystine Dragon, raging against banishment of his people. Forced into eternal exile." Chris leaned forward. "Is there anything else you wish to tell me, my lady?"

Amelia desired nothing more than to relieve her lonely burden by telling the truth. All of it. To explain who she was, and what her sister had done, but fear stayed her tongue. Instead, she shook her head.

"You ask if these stories are true. I do not have answers, only a caution. The temples are a powerful and ancient force in these lands. They have ruled for centuries as keepers of the realm's most damning secrets. There is a reason they gather all those who carry such dreams. A reason they hide them from the world."

Amelia drew a sharp breath and struggled to speak, her next word a strained whisper. "Why?"

"The temples once honorably assisted the crown in governing the land. They spoke for the goddesses, guiding those blessed by her power through the entangled path of living in two worlds, but belonging fully to neither. A spiritual bridge, if you will, between dragon and human.

"Over time, their power became corrupt. People saw the temples as a path to conquest. Those with a true calling were reduced to lesser roles, and eventually…"

"Prevented from ever transforming."

Chris nodded. "It happened to my cousin. She had such terrible nightmares of disasters similar to those you describe."

"I don't understand."

"Some say having these dreams are a sign of being divine. Others, a warning of what is yet to come. I can tell you though, the land my cousin saw was far away. A place she had never seen, yet could describe in exquisite detail. A few months after she was taken away, that land experienced a terrible fire. Hundreds perished. Yet the temples never spoke of the priestess who had predicted the tragedy."

Amelia shook her head. The field she had seen was not a foreign land, but the forest outside her home. *No*, she reasoned. Surely if these visions were predictions, not even the temples would attempt to hide them. What possible benefit could there be to hiding a warning that would protect the people the temples were sworn to serve? And besides, Gwain had said nothing of his sister's predictions coming true. This must have been a mere coincidence.

Even as she formed this protective line of reasoning, Amelia began to doubt. "I've had these nightmares for years. The forest in the dreams, it stands still."

"For now," Chris noted, furthering disturbing Amelia's mind as she rose to leave. "I only ask you to act with caution, my lady. Those chosen by the goddesses, in any capacity, often experience hardship few shall ever know. Try to get some rest. You know where I am, should you need anything further."

Chris did not wait for Amelia's reply, but turned and left the room, leaving her to contemplation.

CHAPTER XXIX

FIELDS BURNED. GROUND CHARRED. TREES *shriveled. Ash clung to her throat, clawing its way painfully to wheezing lungs. A plain brown bird fluttered in her hand as she desperately attempted to heal the gasping creature, toxins stealing its life faster than her magic could repair the damage.*

The shadow fell, familiar dread spilling over her skin with an icy touch so unlike the flames of her suppressed beast.

The Amethystine Dragon bellowed its challenge. Silver eyes as enthralling as they were lethal in their deadly gaze.

"What do you want?" she again asked the question. "I don't understand. Why must the flames die?"

The dragon reared back, opening his mouth with a fresh snarl as flames burst forth.

Waking from the dream with a shriek, Amelia tumbled painfully to the wooden floor, knee stinging as she fell upon it.

Angry, Amelia pulled her legs against her chest, wrapping trembling arms around her knees to bury her face against them. Mouth pressed to the cloth of her shift, Amelia groaned in frustration, both at her continued failure to resist the lethal intent of her nightmare's monster, and her inability to rid herself of the plaguing dream.

"Why do I always cower?" she asked the empty room. "I'm a dragon princess. I shouldn't stand there and wait for my inevitable death. Why? Why can't I run, or fight, or…" She shook her head in frustration before reaching to grasp her mother's ring from a hidden drawer, the cold metal a familiar comfort against her skin.

When she finally managed to climb back into bed, the low murmur of voices gave her pause. Never having heard anyone awake at this hour, Amelia grabbed a thick robe and pulled it around her waist, cinching the material with a wool belt.

After opening the door and proceeding down the hall, she realized the voices were coming from the tavern's lower level. Quietly, she made her way down the wooden steps, grateful the creaking wood remained abnormally quiet.

Halfway down, previously mingled voices transformed to distinguishable words.

"You know what I desire," a man stated.

"I've told you before, my lord," Chris' words were soft, but firm, "you've already taken them all."

"You lie," the masculine voice replied. "You will hand them over, and shall do so now."

"I promise, there are no more."

"Hand them over, or I shall take you to your brother. There's a reward for your return, you know? You embarrassed the family a great deal when you left the lord you had been assigned to. Brought great shame. I'm sure your brother would honor your father's promises to pay handsomely."

"I have a few pieces of silver, but I swear, there's nothing else left. Now please, leave me in peace."

At the bottom of the stairs, Amelia peaked around the corner, grateful for the wall between herself and the men surrounding Chris. There were five men total, four standing in a circle, and the speaker in front of Chris, his bronzed hand holding tight to her right arm.

After a pause, the crude man said, "I'll consider the silver. But you'll have to throw something else in as well." He turned to the men standing around him. "What do you say, boys? I've never been with the daughter of a noble house before. Have you?"

"Seth, please. Don't do this."

"Oh I am going to do it. Only question is if you're going to be a good girl and let me, or force me to mark your pretty face while I do so. You're a fine looking woman, in spite of your years. I'm sure your experience will make up for the lack of youth."

Chris attempted to pull away, but found herself grabbed roughly by the man she had referred to as Seth. "No!" she protested as her back was forced against his front.

"Oh quiet down now, Chris," he instructed, pulling up her skirts. "Not like you haven't done this often enough."

Uncertain, but knowing she could not stand by and allow these barbarians to have their way, Amelia stepped around the corner. "Wait!" she called, her appearance startling the men. "Leave her alone."

"What's this?" a blond to Chris' right spoke for the first time.

"Don't hurt her," Amelia said. "If it is jewels you seek, I can oblige."

All eyes trained on Amelia as she reached toward her right hand and removed her gold ring. Topped with a deep pear-shaped ruby, surrounded by diamond baguettes, her mother's ring was of vast value, and all she now possessed of the late queen. She resisted the sentimental urge to pause, and handed it over without preamble to the man who had spoken at her appearance. "Here, this should be worth enough to clear up any misunderstanding."

Stepping toward the firelight, the man held up the ring, the baguettes causing light to dance in multiple colors, speckled across the room.

He turned back, eyeing Amelia with a critical eye. "How did a tavern wench come into a treasure such as this?"

"What's it matter? Take it, and be on your way."

"Be on our way?" Seth's voice re-entered the conversation from where he held Chris firmly against his chest. "Do you hear the wench giving us orders, Mitch?"

"I do. Some spunk in this one, and she's much prettier than the old woman."

"You asked for jewels, and you've been given them. Now I am asking you to leave us in peace."

"Oh, we will," Mitch replied, grinning to show several teeth missing from his upper gums. "Soon as we get to know you better."

Amelia stepped back, causing the other men to grin in anticipation.

From her captive place, Chris offered, "I'll be good for all of you. Like you said, Seth, experience makes up for youth."

"Youth, yes. But a beauty like this? I think not. Bring her closer, Mitch. Let's get a better look at her."

"Run!" Chris screamed.

But Mitch managed to grab the princess before she could so much as turn. A second man stepped forward to seize her other arm, forcing her toward Seth.

"Let me go!" Amelia demanded, struggling against the stronger men.

She was held tight, captive hands bruising her upper arms as she struggled. Handing Chris over to another companion, Seth approached the outraged girl, and reached for her chin, forcing her to meet his gaze, brown eyes connecting with sapphire.

"Pretty," he said. "Didn't know beauties such as you existed in these mountains. Thought only the shifters held such fire." He laughed, a crude sound. "What do you say you show me how pretty?"

Without waiting for a reply, Seth pushed aside her robe, moving his dirt-caked hands to the top of her simple gown, where he ripped through her coverings. The thin material easily gave way to brute strength, and the gown opened nearly to the floor. Her rose-tipped breasts hardened as they were exposed to the frigid air.

Seth stepped back, allowing his gaze to feast on her flawless skin. "And to think I was going to settle for the old tavern maid." He shook his head.

"You're exquisite." His eyes swept from the bottom up, starting with her long, lithe legs, flat stomach, succulent breasts, and finally, her flushed cheeks and wide blue eyes.

Her face gave him pause; her angry expression notably lacked the fear he expected. He stepped closer, leaning enough to let his putrid breath warm her cheek. "Are you afraid, girl?"

"No," she gave the startling answer. "Let me go, and leave in peace. I won't ask again."

Throwing his head back, Seth laughed. "Bravo for effort!" He clapped his hands as he turned back to the men behind him, who shared in the mockery. "Can you believe this girl is threatening me? Oh, this is going to be good."

"Hope she keeps some of that sprit for when I'm between—" The man's expression instantly sobered.

"What is it?" Seth demanded.

A sound drew his attention back toward Amelia. The two men holding her had stepped back in alarm.

"What are you doing?"

Returning his gaze to the nude girl, his breath caught, body stiffening as he met not the blue eyes of a human, but a sinister reptilian green. Glowing through the dark, Amelia's dragon growled, a sound that rose unnaturally from her human throat. Blue scales burned along her skin, piercing through her more fragile form.

"She's a dragon!" Mitch screamed, scrambling around the shifting girl to rush toward the exit.

At their fright, Amelia attempted to rein the beast back inside. But this time, the creature was not to be denied. A twisted shriek escaped her lips, rising from her lengthening neck, arms transforming to wings. Rushing forward, she followed the men, managing to escape the doorway a mere moment before she would have been too large to do so.

"Enough," she pleaded to the beast, but the running figures proved her undoing, the dragon demanding she give chase to its fleeing prey.

Scales hardened as her wings expanded, the girl replaced by the creature, awoken at last. Another roar rose, and this time, the sound filled the air, echoing through the valley as her wings expanded, causing the village to stir.

The last of her resistance was stripped away when additional bandits emerged from nearby houses, several clutching villager's valuables between grubby fingers.

With a flap of her fully formed wings, Amelia took to the sky, each beat carrying her higher. From the air, she surveyed the confusion below, her enhanced vision zeroing in on the men she sought who ran down the valley toward the safety of the trees.

The dragon had other plans.

Plunging through frigid air, the dragon raced them, a blue streak above.

Amelia appealed to the beast, but the dragon refused to be restrained. Wings expanded, bringing the dragon to an abrupt halt as it reached the men it sought, lips parting to a snarl as menacing as the one from Amelia's dreams.

Drawing a breath, the last of Amelia's human consciousness gave way.

The dragon issued another dreadful roar before channeling air through a second chamber, inhaling the oxygen required to fan the fires within.

Without further warning, the dragon exhaled, blue flames streaming from between its lethal fangs.

The blaze engulfed the men, burning through clothes and haphazard armor to melt the materials along with layers of skin. Aflame, the men screamed, flailing on the charring ground, nerves unaware of the body's inability to further sustain life. Its primary prey executed, the dragon did not watch the dying men, nor take satisfaction in their agony. Instead it turned, spying more thieves attempting to flee the inferno. With another breath, they too were set ablaze, and more screams filled the once tranquil valley as the dragon princess incinerated those who had dared to cause harm.

Vengeance exacted, the dragon paid no mind to the burning fields, nor to the villagers who rushed to ensure the fire would not spread to the village. She did not notice the farmhouse, which burned in spite of their efforts.

Swooping through the air, the dragon roared its victory, soaring high to illuminate the night with streaks of blue light as it danced through icy skies.

CHAPTER XXX

AMELIA AWOKE AT THE FOREST'S edge. Nude, but covered in patches of dirt, leaves and twigs knotted in her hair. Every muscle hurt, and her skin itched terribly as she struggled to adjust to the costs of transformation after having denied the dragon for so long. After lying still for a few minutes, Amelia rose.

Wiping her eyes, she walked the path she had learned well over the previous few months, until she found a particular spot. Lifting several rocks, she pulled out a hidden satchel, retrieving a spare pair of pants and shirt she'd stashed for such an occurance. Amelia dressed as she recalled the previous night's events.

As usual, with an undesired transformation, memory returned slowly. She had experienced the familiar dream, and went downstairs for... She jerked to a standing position as she remembered. Men had attempted to rape Chris. Their refusal to heed her warnings. The wrath of the dragon as they burned.

"Oh my gods!" Her hand flew to her mouth as she rushed forward, running in the direction of the village.

Reaching the clearing, Amelia spied the charred fields, smoke assaulting her nostrils. As her eyes trailed down the valley, relief flooded her at the unscathed houses. Yet her heart crumbled when she saw the distant farmhouse, utterly destroyed by her dragon's unquenchable wrath.

"No!" Amelia shook her head, guilt overcoming her.

Did I hurt someone?

The horrific thought plagued as she ran past the fields, toward the skeletal remains of the home. Several people stood around the blackened timbers.

When she reached them, one of the men ordered, "Stay back!"

Amelia froze, cheeks flushing as her eyes searched the faces in earnest, attempting to determine if lives had been lost. "Please," she asked, "was anyone hurt?"

"We don't want *your* kind here," the man replied.

"I didn't mean for this to happen. They were going to harm Chris. I was only—"

"Your kind causes more destruction than any of these thugs have ever done."

"They were hurting her. I tried to help."

"You *helped* all right. They would have taken a few pieces of silver. You helped us right into destitution."

"I didn't—"

"My brother was burned in your flames."

Her blood ran cold. "Is he okay?"

"No thanks to you," the man said sharply. "Now leave! You're not welcome here."

Close to tears, Amelia hung her head. "I'm sorry," she mumbled, before turning away from those gathered.

Amelia walked back toward the woods, but paused as the ground transformed from wild grass to charred stubs. Moving along the edge of the soot, she hissed as something sharp pierced the sole of her left foot. Hopping on one leg, she raised the stinging foot, and withdrew the jagged shard. Holding up piece marked with her blood, Amelia was horrified to realize the splinter was not of wood, but bone.

Pressing the fragment between her fingers, the brittle remains crumbled, blowing away in the breath of a gentle wind, which carried the sickening scents of smoke and burnt flesh.

Her eyes focused through her tears to take in the ghastly scene. She realized she stood beside not bodies, but instead piles of ash in the shape of men. Where once souls had been housed, not even the bones remained.

Running from field of death, she raced toward the shadowed forest.

"Elizabeth! Wait!"

At the sound of Chris' voice, Amelia paused, but could not bring herself to face the woman who had been so kind.

"Please look at me?"

Miserably, Amelia turned.

To her surprise, Chris stepped forward and pulled her into a tight embrace. "Thank you."

"Thank me?" Amelia extricated herself from Chris' arms as she glanced up to meet her gaze. "How can you thank me? Look at what I did!"

"You saved me, along with dozens of other women in the village. These fools are not intelligent enough to realize it."

"I killed those men."

"They were evil."

"So am I. I only wished to frighten them. To make them stop. But…the dragon. I couldn't control her. She killed them, and I couldn't stop her. The village, I…"

"You have been suppressing the dragon for a long time, I suspect. Far too long to control, once unleashed."

"I don't understand; it's never been this way before. The dragon, she's always been a natural part of me. But this…I…"

"There exists a balance, to being a shifter, my princess."

Startled by the formal address, Amelia jerked back, eyes wide with fear.

"The ring." Chris reached into a pocket to withdraw the gold band topped with the deep red stone. "Before I failed to transform, I served as lady-in-waiting to the dragon queen, whom I now suspect to be your mother. I may not have recognized you, Your Highness. But the ring, I put it away every night, and retrieved it each morning when your mother dressed. The men dropped it in their rush to escape. When I saw it, I realized who you were, my lady—"

"Amelia," she whispered her name. "I'm sorry I lied. You were so kind. I…"

"Quite all right, Your Highness. I understand why you did." Chris drew a breath, handing the ring back to its rightful owner, watching as Amelia slipped it back onto the third finger of her right hand. "Please, my lady, come back to the tavern. The villagers, they were taken by surprise. I promise, they will realize what you did for them soon."

"No," Amelia answered. "They won't, and as long as my dragon half is so enraged, no one is safe. Every time I have that dream—nightmare—I can't count the number of times I've awoken and could barely contain the flames. I must go where I can't harm anyone."

"Please, my lady. Give last night's events time to settle."

Amelia considered Chris' invitation, wanting nothing more than to grant her request. Closing her eyes, Amelia again saw the fleeing men, her blue flames rushing forth to turn living flesh to ash.

"No." Her eyes flew open as inside, the dragon stirred, brought forth by the memory of its triumph. "I'm sorry. I can't." She pulled her mother's ring off, handing it back to Chris. "Sell this, and use the money to repair the farm, and anything else I damaged. And please take care of Gabriel," she spoke of Gwain's horse, who had carried her on her journey. "He's been a faithful companion."

"My lady, please."

"No," she said again, eyes bleeding from sapphire to emerald, pupils narrowing as the dragon took control of her vision. Stepping back, she quickly shed the shirt and pants, scales already lining her body, transforming her skin from silk to leather as her wings emerged.

Chris gave her distance as the dragon burst through.

Guilt, embarrassment, and remorse vanished, replaced by the elation of having conquered its enemies. Pain forgotten, the dragon's strength enfolded Amelia, eradicating all traces of humanity.

The dragon knew nothing of shame. It did not care about the villagers' harsh words, nor the cold stares that followed her steps toward the woods. A creature of legend; a powerful, fire-breathing entity of strength and divinity. Lord of the sky, the dragon soared high, taking the human girl securely in its protective embrace, guarding her from those who would cause her harm.

No pain, the voice only she could hear issued the comforting promise. *In safely, shall I keep you. In my protection, shall you be. Until the end of time.*

With those final thoughts, Amelia lost herself to the enthralling creature within.

Below, Chris watched her leave, familiar ring clutched tightly in her palm. Her heart was heavy remembering the late queen's kindness as she watched her daughter vanish from sight. She remained there for a long time, part of her hoping the princess would change her mind and return.

She did not.

With a sigh, Chris turned back toward the village, when Conner emerged from between the trees, covering the distance between them in a few quick strides.

"Conner," she called in greeting, covertly tucking the precious ring in a hidden pocket.

"What, by the gods, happened here?"

"Well—"

"The girl? I told you keeping her here was dangerous. I knew this would eventually happen."

"You knew no such thing."

"Mother, you could have been killed! The entire village could have... Was anyone harmed?"

"One farmer got a few burns on his arm—"

"Gods!"

"Not what you think," she defended her young charge.

"What I think is that girl transformed, and burnt most of the fields to a crisp on some uncontrolled joyride."

"Seth came back!" Chris snapped.

Conner stared at her, lilac eyes meeting her angry gaze. "Seth?"

"Only this time, he brought an entire group of thugs with him."

"Oh...did he?"

"He tried to..." Chris said quietly, "with the girl, while his men entered other houses, likely seeking similar entertainment."

Conner's eyes shut, teeth digging into his bottom lip.

"She saved us, Conner. Probably saved the majority of the village. Yes, there was some damage, and an injury, but nothing to compare with what might have happened, had Seth's men finished having their way."

"I'm sorry. I should have been here."

"No." Chris shook her head, offering a tight smile. "You made the right decision, when you chose to leave. You know you did."

"And what about the girl?"

"The girl is more than she seems."

"What do you mean?"

"She's…" Chris considered telling her son the truth, but hesitated. She had known the girl was a shifter from when Conner had carried her in from the storm. The kind of fever she had displayed, followed by the absolute cold, was a classic symptom of repressed transformation. Her nightmares marked her as well, for only those blessed by the power of Kamar were granted the gift of foresight.

"Are you telling the truth?" Conner's question brought her out of her thoughts. "Did Seth, or his men…"

"No," she assured him. "And they won't be bothering us again, thanks to her."

"I'm sorry, Mother. I wish…"

"You had to choose your own path, even if that path rarely leads you to my door."

"I wish there were more I could do for you."

"There is, Conner. Watch out for the girl."

"The girl? I meant for you."

"As did I," Chris replied. "The girl is special. I worry she may need assistance, and I'm not able to be there for her."

"How so?"

"She's like I once was, abandoned by those who should have cared for her most. Hesitant to trust."

"Why would a dragon shifter, at her level of power, have been cast out?"

"I can't imagine. I only know she's very special, and may require our help to find her place in the world."

"Should I go after her?"

"No." Chris shook her head. "To do so now would only cause harm, to you or her. Give her time to cope with—to process—whatever trials she has faced. Watch her from afar, and wait until the time is right."

"When will the time be right?"

His mother issued a soft smile. "I believe, my son, when the time is right, you'll know."

With those cryptic words, Chris kissed her son's cheek, before leaving him at the forest's edge.

CHAPTER XXXI

7 YEARS LATER

WINGS SILHOUETTED AGAINST MIDNIGHT SKIES, the dragon soared through moonlight, thriving on the crisp, frigid air that soothed the creature's heated flesh.

Consumed by grief, the human girl had given herself over to the beast within, allowing the dragon to reign. Knowing nothing of fear, of anguish, nor the heartache and loneliness that plagued the fading girl, the dragon moved with confidence, each muscle adjusting seamlessly in flight, its power protecting Amelia from all who would seek to harm her...including herself.

She thrived in this solitary existence. After leaving the village, Amelia had found a secluded cave miles away. Thankfully, the dragon's hunting and eating sated the hunger of both halves. And on the rare occasion she took human form, she would gather berries from a nearby thicket, or fish from the stream. She had managed to fashion basic clothes using the hide of one of the dragon's kills, putting her limited sewing knowledge to use. Every six months or so, she would venture into a different nearby village and trade for a few supplies, including the finely cured two-layer sleeping sack, made from pieced-together rabbit fur on the inside, with a durable leather exterior, which she used for sleeping on the infrequent nights she remained in human form.

Amelia preferred the dragon's care-free mind. Over the years, she had come to detest her weaker half; the girl who longed for the arms of a man who had never loved her, and the sister who had seen her only as a threat to her crown. Over and over, she attempted to force her mind and heart past those events, yet continually failed to do so.

She hardly spoke, even to herself, instead going through the motions of life in silence, grateful she was now far enough away from others to avoid harming anyone else.

In spite of the bandits' ill-intentions, she had never meant to kill them. The slaughter haunted her, a daily reminder her choice to leave was the right one for all concerned. Here, at least, she could harm none but herself.

These thoughts carried her through many twilight hours as she curled by the fire, exhausted from the dragon's exertions, enduring until her next shift into blessed oblivion. She managed to sleep for a short while, before rising and venturing out into the area she had come to know well.

Pausing by a thicket, she gathered a handful of blueberries, savoring the slight sour taste on the back of her tongue. She took her time, eating her fill.

The forest around her was filled with the sounds of chirping birds, and the sweet aroma of fresh grass. A tranquil scene, all was well in the forest she had come to view as home.

Leaving the thicket, she walked along a grassy path until she eventually came to the river. Moving along its length, she reached a bend where the water calmed. Shedding her simple hide garment, Amelia stepped into the current, grateful the early summer sun had warmed the water enough not to steal her breath. Dipping her head beneath the surface, she allowed the fresh running water to rinse clumps of dirt from her blonde tresses, running her fingers through the strands, assisting in the removal of grime.

Finally, Amelia leaned back, floating on the surface, staring into the blue sky above. Cloudless, it would be a beautiful night for a flight. Closing her eyes, she floated for another minute before turning to swim back toward the riverbank.

Perched on a log, Amelia ran her fingers through her hair, attempting to detangle it while she air dried.

To her left, a crow squawked and flapped as it furiously moved past.

Her gaze followed the bird, and she silently apologized for having spooked the creature, who let out another terrified sound, which was swallowed by a deep-throated growl.

Amelia turned toward the sound as something solid collided with her left side. Falling face down, she attempted to climb to her feet, but the weight landed on her back, sharp claws ripping her lower abdomen, tearing through skin and slicing into muscle.

The exiled princess screamed, clawing at the dirt in front of her. Struggling, she attempted to rise again, this time angling herself enough to identify the attacking creature as a large cat. A mountain lion, she guessed, who must have jumped from one of the overreaching trees. She tried to scramble back, but the lion was again on her, teeth sinking into her left arm. Her dragon surged forth as she screamed again, but the transformation would come too late as claws dug into her hips, drawing arterial blood.

Unable, or unwilling, to struggle through this new kind of pain, Amelia collapsed. In terror, she watched as the lethal cat stalked closer, baring its teeth, this time focused on her exposed neck. A kill strike.

Inside her, the dragon roared, scales emerging with their familiar burning itch.

The cat did not pause to wonder at this strange transformation, instead focused on lowering its head for a better angle on her throat.

In contrast to her dragon's defiance, for Amelia, an understanding of death dawned. She closed her eyes, hoping the bite would be less painful if she simply accepted her fate.

Another roar filled the air, reverberating in her ears. A deep-throated bellow louder than any cat could ever make.

At the sound, the mountain lion turned.

With a second roar, the creature appeared, a shadow swallowing the ground.

The cat backed away from Amelia, before turning to run toward the woods.

Blood pouring from multiple injuries, the princess tried to rise, to meet this new threat, but groaned in pain as she attempted to use damaged muscles. The gash on her arm was deep, and the pain in her lower back made her wonder if the claws had reached through to her spine.

The second dragon circled, but Amelia closed her eyes. As in her recurring dream, she lay perfectly still, unable to do more than breathe as the creature circled above.

When the dragon landed nearby, the ground shook.

Gritting her teeth, Amelia managed to turn enough to witness the form of a man appearing from beneath the dragon's bulk.

Tall, and well built, the man finished his transformation before approaching, unbothered by his own nudity, or hers.

Amelia's heart pounded, both from pain and fear. "Please," she whispered, as he reached her side. Her first spoken words in months, since her last village visit. "Don't hurt me."

"I'm here to help," he promised, kneeling in the dirt to examine her injuries.

Long gouges marred her back, flesh skewered on either side of the deep cuts by the cat's curved claws. The wound was ugly, but the deep puncture on her hip, and the ragged gash in her arm, concerned him more.

Scanning the riverbank, he spied Amelia's sparse clothing, and walked over to grab her tunic. "I have to bind your arm."

He took the garment and, with brute force, tore the soft hide into long, uneven strips before proceeding to tie pieces around her arm.

She screamed as he tightened the crude bandage, torn flesh protesting at being forced back together.

"Sorry," he offered with real regret. "You're going to be in pain for a while."

"Will I..."

"You're lucky to be a shifter. We're harder to kill than most, though I must say the cat made a good effort."

"I don't…"

"You'll recover," he assured. "But it will be a painful few days."

"Who are you?"

"A passerby."

"There are no other dragons in these mountains."

Without answering, he pressed a second piece of hide against Amelia's hip.

She yelped at the unexpected pressure, head pounding from the pain.

Noting the tremors, the man offered, "I have a cabin not far from here."

Amelia shook her head, protesting even as the man gathered her in his arms. "You can't carry me."

"Why not?"

"You're naked."

The man shrugged. "So are you."

Realizing he was right, a blush rose to Amelia's cheeks, which only deepened as he lifted her higher.

With his first step, she cried out in pain at the jarring motion.

"I'm sorry. Your injuries are quite severe. Though they will fully heal, they must be treated in order to so. Please, allow me to take you to my cabin where I have supplies, including food, and clothes as well."

Questions filled Amelia's mind. *Who was this man? How did he find me?*

As more blood oozed from her injuries, the task of focusing on even these simple thoughts grew exhausting.

Closing her eyes against the throbbing pain, Amelia attempted to relax against his chest, wincing as each step brought a fresh spasm of pain.

Seeming to understand, the man walked at a slow, even pace. At that rate, it took over an hour to reach the cabin, but when he eventually did, he took her directly to a side bedroom.

Though quaint, the room was warm, and the bed on which she had been deposited was the softest surface she had lain on in over five years.

Lying on her stomach, Amelia remained still under the blanket he'd draped over her.

When her rescuer returned, wearing a pair of black trousers but no shirt, he placed a leather flask to her lips. "Here. Drink."

"What is it?"

"To help with the pain."

Complying, Amelia took a deep gulp of the foul liquid, which burned going down her parched throat. Gagging, she attempted to hand the flask back.

"Drink more," he advised. "All of it, if you can. It tastes like paint thinner, but trust me, it will help with the next part."

Holding her breath, Amelia forced herself to do as he'd asked, draining the bitter liquid before handing the empty container back.

With efficient motions, tempered by a degree of care, he meticulously cleaned each wound, and applied medicine to her injuries, the stinging ointment causing her to writhe. Finally, fresh bandages were applied, complete with globs of more salve.

He moved to her arm, maneuvering her shoulder to check the severity of the injury. "I think it's fractured. I ought to splint it, just in case, to be sure it heals cleanly."

The man left the room again and came back with a narrow wooden plank. When he moved her arm into proper position, tears filled her eyes. With sympathy, he explained, "I'll need both of my hands to tie this, but you can grab my upper arm if it would help."

Amelia shook her head, instead lacing the fingers of her opposite arm into the bedding.

"Sorry," he apologized again, when he'd finished. "I don't want to risk anything healing incorrectly. Fixing it would require re-breaking the arm, and that would be even more painful."

Amelia nodded, confused by the day's strange turn of events, and exhausted from the prolonged ordeal.

Her trembling grew worse as he lifted her higher into the pillows, helping her find a semi-comfortable position, before placing several layers of pelts around her for warmth, careful to avoid pressing on her bandages.

As he moved her, Amelia caught the man's gaze. Lilac eyes, as pale as her blue were deep, stared back. She studied him: the familiar high, pale cheekbones, short brown hair. She searched her memory, her mind focusing on his eyes.

"You carried me from the storm."

At her words, he turned, ripping his eyes from her inspection.

"You brought me in from the cold. Told me to ask the dragon for calm."

With a deep breath, the man turned back and nodded. "At your service, my lady."

"Who are you? Chris said you lived outside the village."

"I have lived all over these mountains. They, more than any particular place within them, are my home."

"You're a child blessed by Kamar, like me."

"Yes, though I'm uncertain if I would call this particular gift a blessing."

"Of course it's a blessing. We are children of Kamar. Chosen to carry on our ancient lines."

"Sounds like temple garbage."

"I am not from the temples," she snapped, voice cross even laced with exhaustion. "Don't compare me to those monsters."

Amelia's words brought both to silence.

"Fair enough," the man nodded, truce restored. "My name is Conner, by the way."

"Elizabeth," she gave her middle name out of habit.

"Well, Elizabeth, I suggest you get some rest."

"Wait. I don't understand what you're doing here. How you found me."

"I'll answer what questions I can in the morning. For now, rest. I'll be in the alcove across the way."

CHAPTER XXXII

CONNER LAY UPON THE NARROW bed that was more of a shelf, really, but sleep remained elusive. The girl was sure to have questions, and as he stared blankly at the ceiling above, he realized he could no more answer her inquiries than he could his own.

Though his mother had asked him to watch the girl, he had done so sporadically, and from afar, primarily observing she spent an abundance of time in dragon form. He had considered warning her of the dangers in allowing the dragon such a great amount of control, but decided against doing so. Better if she came to the realization on her own.

Now, having seen her wildness, he realized his error and experienced a deep-seated regret for not attempting to give her warning. Though why he carried so much responsibility for the girl, he knew naught.

Awoken the previous morning by an intense drive, his normally dormant dragon stirred with an urgent aggression that Conner had rarely experienced. He had attempted to sate the beast with practiced calming techniques, but even in his most relaxed state, the dragon had roared, demanding freedom.

Eventually giving in, Conner had transformed, his dragon taking control of their flight, heading toward the east mountains. They had flown with a fierce determination, in a line straight for the young woman, as though the dragon had been aware of her plight. But how his dragon would have known this, Conner could not begin to explain.

Coincidence? he wondered, then dismissed the thought.

Somehow his dragon had known the girl was in trouble and had, in desperation, come to her aide. There was no doubt about this. But how? And who was she?

He had been told by the villagers that her dragon was an unusual blue. A color generally reserved for those kissed by moonlight. A rarity among the Kalleen dragons.

Turning to find a more comfortable position, Conner closed his eyes, struggling to calm himself enough for sleep to come. Normally shifting left him exhausted, but tonight his blood hummed with vigorous energy, senses attuned to every sound of the old cabin, which had once belonged to his paternal grandmother.

After a while, he gave up. Walking to the kitchen, he added wood to the stove and began to assemble breakfast, grilling thick pieces of meat, and frying some eggs he had found in a nearby nest. Ensuring everything was cooked as well as could be without being burnt, Conner shuffled the meal onto two plates, left them on the table, and went to check on his charge.

Initially, he thought the girl still asleep, but her eyes opened at his footsteps across the wooden floor. She blinked, revealing her green, elongated pupils, the glance shooting another pang of guilt through him, though again, he did not understand why.

Pushing back his thoughts, he forced a slight smile. "Would you like breakfast?"

Amelia stared, wondering if she should refuse further aid, yet the rumble of her stomach announced otherwise. Slightly embarrassed by the sound, Amelia nodded. "Breakfast would be much appreciated."

Conner watched as Amelia struggled to her feet. "Why don't you let me bring the food in here? The less you move, the lower the chance of reopening your injuries."

"Okay," she agreed, the sharp pain in her hip, from the simple movement of her leg, enough to make her fall back in the bed.

"I have some clothes for you as well. They'll probably be too large, but not so big you can't wear them." He walked to the closet and pulled out a simple, faded blue cotton dress. "Belonged to my grandmother, so not quite in style, but…"

"Thank you," she replied as he placed the garment on the bed beside her.

"Think you can get into it by yourself? We could just tuck the covers around you for now."

"I'll manage," she answered, watching as he left the room to retrieve the promised breakfast, closing the door behind him.

Throwing back the pelts, Amelia grasped the thin material and pulled it over her head, biting back a groan as she had to lift her leg to slide the material under it. Because of its large size, as Conner had predicted, she didn't have to fiddle with any of the buttons.

A knock at the door alerted her to the return of her mysterious rescuer.

After arranging herself as best she could, thanks to the sore hip, she beckoned, "Come in."

The door opened at her invitation, Conner reappearing with the eggs and meat, whose smell had lured her from slumber.

Pulling herself higher, Amelia pushed her back to the wall behind the bed, grateful for the support as Conner handed her the plate.

"Not the fanciest," he said, "but it should be filling at least."

"Looks wonderful. Thank you. It's been a long time since someone cooked for me."

"You're welcome."

Starving, Amelia devoured her first bites, the red meat juicy, seasoned with a generous portion of salt and pepper.

Conner moved to leave when Amelia said, "Thank you, as well."

"You've already said—"

"For saving my life."

Meeting her reptilian gaze, Conner nodded, a solemn movement, his lilac eyes studying her.

The plain garment served to underscore her extraordinary beauty, from lush gold locks, to her nearly flawless skin; only the unusual dark imprint along her left shoulder disrupted her smooth complexion. But even this flaw failed to mar her beauty, instead adding to it, the patterned markings appearing in the likeness of an exotic tattoo. Starting at her shoulder, the textured lines ran up the side of her neck, creating a cluster of diamond shaped rows. With a start, Conner realized that not only had her eyes been affected by her extended use of dragon form, but her skin also bore permanent evidence of her inner beast.

"Are you all right?" Amelia asked. Self-consciously, her hand moved to her neck where the pattern lay. "The skin grew rough a few months ago. Doesn't hurt but...I imagine it doesn't look pretty." Amelia shook her head. "Who are you? How did you find me?"

Conner stepped closer, keeping his eyes on hers, his dragon pacing beneath the surface of his skin in response to her challenge. "I didn't find you, my lady."

"What?"

"I didn't. My dragon did."

"Your dragon?"

Conner nodded. "He knew you were in trouble, and where to find you. I wish I could tell you how, but I can't."

Her eyes went wide, pupils becoming more circular, specks of blue showing, but they did not transform back to the blue of the first time he had seen her.

"Please don't be afraid, my lady. I mean you no harm, nor does my dragon."

Protect, the dragon's vow reached Conner alone. *Save girl.*

Jarred by the normally dormant voice, Conner attempted to step away from the girl, but found himself unable to do so. By compulsion, he knelt to the floor. "I promise," he spoke unplanned words, "I will never harm you, my lady."

"Bold assurances from a stranger."

"Perhaps." Conner shook himself, spell broken by sheer will. Standing, he said, "I only wish for you to know you have nothing to fear from me, my lady. I'll return after you've eaten to redress your injuries."

He hurried from the small room, as confused by his words as the girl whom, he was certain, they had failed to assure.

CHAPTER XXXIII

AFTER DOZING SPORADICALLY OVER THE following days, Amelia felt more like herself. The cuts on her back were nearly healed, and the one on her hip had reduced to a dull throb. Only her arm remained painful, the fracture proving more difficult to mend than expected.

Conner would apologize frequently as he was forced to check the injury, shaking his head as it had not reknit the way he had hoped. "You shouldn't shift until it's better," he had informed her. "Doing so might cause further damage."

With her physical progress, she had moved from the bed to a nearby chair, and was staring out the window when Conner entered through her open doorway.

"I was wondering if you'd like dinner?"

She nodded, with an appreciative smile.

"Shall I bring it to you?"

"Would it be possible to eat outside?"

"Of course! It'd be nice to get some fresh air, and I'm sure you could stand for some as well after these past few days."

"Yes, thank you."

Amelia stood, but too fast, her tender leg failing to support her weight.

Conner caught her as she collapsed, sliding an arm around her back, before pulling her against his chest in an attempt to steady her, and take the weight off the sore joint.

Her hand reflexively grabbed his upper arm, her slender fingers unable to fully wrap around the well-developed muscles underneath.

Heat rushing to her cheeks, Amelia met his eyes. "Perhaps I'll have supper in the room after all."

"Nonsense," he replied, bending to wrap his arms under her legs. Effortlessly, Conner gathered her into his embrace, cradling her to his chest as he carried her from the room.

"This isn't necessary."

"I don't mind."

"I can—"

"Put your arms around my neck so I don't drop you."

Her cheeks grew warmer as she complied, and he shifted his load, allowing him to better hold her as they transitioned from the bedroom to the cabin's back deck. Held close, she breathed him in, liking his fresh cedar scent, with a hint of citrus from the soap he used, blended with the smoky aroma of his dragon. A comforting mixture, she was surprised to find she liked the sense of safety that came with being enveloped in his strong arms.

When they emerged onto the deck, Conner placed his charge on an oak bench before a matching table. The deck was vast, a high wooden rail lining the edge. Surrounded by lush forest on all sides, the cabin centered the tranquil setting, further lowering Amelia's defenses as she enjoyed the spring sun's warmth.

"A lovely view."

"It is. I don't make it here very often, but enjoy spending time when I can."

"Where do you usually live?"

"The opposite side of the mountains. Farther north."

"Is it cold there?"

"Freezing, most of the time. Probably wouldn't survive for long, if we were mortal."

"Hmm...guess it's a good thing we're not." She smiled, but his expression did not soften to match hers.

"Let me fetch the food."

"Sure. I'm starving."

He left Amelia to enjoy the peaceful backdrop. She struggled to her feet, careful to keep as much weight on her good leg as she could, and hobbled over to the deck's rail.

The tall trees sported fresh leaves, and a gushing stream babbled in the distance. Birds busily flitted from the bank into the trees, twittering in their playful courting. The sun rode high in an azure sky, only a few sparse clouds disrupting its brilliance. Turning her body slightly, she welcomed a cool breeze to tug at the tresses of her blonde hair.

One of the birds flew near, coming to rest on the rail with a curiously cocked head.

"Hello there," she greeted the inquisitive creature.

The bird chirped, hopping closer at the sound of her voice.

"I'm sorry, little one. I don't have any food."

The bird chipped again, insistent.

Enamored, Amelia held out her hand, slowly extending a finger in the bird's direction.

In response, her new friend opened its wings, hopping from the wood to land on her hand.

Amelia remained as still as possible, so as not to spook the tiny creature.

Ruffling bright blue feathers, its tiny feet bit lightly into Amelia's flesh.

"Aren't you pretty?"

The bird considered her again, tilting its head as gold flames erupted, incinerating the small creature with a single blaze from above.

CHAPTER XXXIV

HER BODY COLLIDED WITH THE deck as she fell back from the menacing figure of the Amethystine Dragon hovering above. She screamed, ignoring the sting of the hard wood against her hands and the renewed pain in her leg as she struggled to evade the inevitable attack. Issuing a second shriek, she scrambled farther away, struggling to maintain control as the flames within burst forth, her dragon reacting protectively to her overwhelming fear.

"Elizabeth!" Conner appeared beside her, moving to his knees to grab her in hopes of preventing her from causing further damage to her wounds. "Elizabeth, what is it?"

Her gaze moved past his worried expression, to the horizon. Where there had been an inferno, the sky was now clear. The bird she had been holding peered at her from the rail in concern.

"What happened?"

"I'm sorry." She shook her head. "I don't…"

"It's all right. There's nothing there."

He stood and carefully scanned the area to confirm his words, seeing nothing but tranquil land, amorous birds, and a few skittering squirrels. "There's nothing out there, my lady."

Heart rate slowing, Amelia attempted to raise herself from the ground.

Conner came closer and assisted her to the bench before taking a knee, so as to not tower over her. "Are you all right?"

Drawing a shaky breath, she nodded. "I'm really sorry. I don't know what happened. I…got spooked."

"As long as you're okay."

"I am," she assured. Turning back toward the rail, she smiled. "Sorry, little one," she apologized to the bird. "Didn't mean to frighten you."

Chirping in acknowledgment, the bird flew toward her, landing on the table to peep softly. "Really." Amelia smiled. "Everything is all right."

With a brief happy dance, the bird flapped its blue wings and flittered away, returning to the trees.

"I've never seen anything like that," Conner remarked, drawing her attention back to his kneeling form.

Amelia shrugged. "They like me," she spoke softly. "Birds, bunnies, squirrels. Always have."

"Normally they run the other way from me."

"I have dreams sometimes, where I can help the injured ones. But…" She shook her head. "Never actually happens."

"Help them how?"

"With my touch. I take them in my hand, there's a glow, and they get better. I don't know why, but I've dreamed of being able to do so all my life."

"It's good the animals like you. Shows you have a kind heart."

"I didn't have a great number of friends growing up. Birds, and other small creatures, kept me company."

Conner smiled before standing and moving a platter of cheese and cooked fish in front of her. "I went to the spring this morning and got lucky. Thought fish would be a nice change from the steak."

"It looks wonderful."

Smiling, Conner served her a generous fillet, block of cheese, and a goblet of wine.

Grasping the glass stem, she put the ruby liquid to her lips, savoring the rich taste of cherries and blackberries in the full-bodied blend. "This is wonderful."

"Thank you. I make the wine myself."

"You make this?"

"I spent a few months learning from a local vintner, though it's taken years to create a palatable blend."

"It's really good."

"Glad you like it."

The two sat comfortably speaking of the mundane and enjoying their dinner, after which, Conner cleared the table. Amelia moved from the bench to one of the comfortable, reclined chairs, while Conner retrieved another pitcher to refill their goblets.

"So," Conner prompted gently, "are you ready to tell me how a young woman, blessed by Kamar, ends up spending years alone in the Kalleen Mountains?"

Amelia cast her gaze to the horizon, focusing on the sky as the clear cerulean canvas was splashed with rays of orange and pinks, the sun itself becoming more orange than yellow as it surrendered to the night's sweet embrace. "Does it matter?"

"To me."

"Why?"

"You've been out here for what, almost seven years? Alone in the woods." Conner turned in his chair to better face her, though Amelia kept her gazed fixed on the horizon. "What happened, my lady? If this is about what occurred in the village, I can assure, you've punished yourself enough."

"I hurt someone, because I couldn't control what I am. I killed those men."

"They were thugs, attempting to rob families and rape women."

"They were living beings. I didn't simply punish them—I killed them. Burned them alive like they were nothing. I can still see their bodies flailing in the flames." She shook her head. "What I did was awful, and not only that, but I harmed an innocent—"

"A flesh wound only. The farmer barely had a scar once the burn healed."

"What I did was reckless. It's a miracle more were not injured."

"I understand how you might feel this way, my lady, but you must know what happened was an accident. You shouldn't punish yourself for it."

"What do you know?" Her words should have held anger; instead they were spoken with a soft resignation. "You know nothing about me."

"I would like to."

She finally turned toward him. "Why?"

"Because I'd like to help you find balance. To show you how your dragon and human halves can work in harmony."

She turned back to the sunset. "I'm fine with my dragon. She keeps me safe. What happened in the forest would never have taken place, if I had allowed her control instead of myself."

Prolonged silence followed as Conner considered her words, eyes sliding to the side of her neck, where the distinct shadow, and texture, of scales lined her skin. He knew from dressing her injuries, the mar had not spread beyond this particular patch of flesh, but it would, should she continue to allow the dragon free rein.

"May I show you something, my lady?"

She looked hesitant.

"Please."

Amelia nodded, allowing him to escort her back into the cabin.

"Nothing untoward," he promised, leading her back to the bedroom.

He pulled a circular, hand-held looking glass from a dresser drawer. Wrapped in a soft cloth, his grandmother had treasured the silver piece, which he now gingerly handed to the girl beside him.

"What is this?"

"Look."

Confused, Amelia raised the looking glass. Glowing green eyes gazed back from the reflective surface, elongated pupils in sharp contrast to her otherwise human face.

Her lips parted, shock emanating through her. Mirrors were a rare commodity, outside of wealthy lands, and the streams where she'd bathed were not calm enough to offer a solid reflection. In fact, it had never occurred to her to attempt to see herself. What's to appreciate in wind-blown hair, and a layer of grime, her constant companions since she had taken refuge in the Kalleen Mountains.

Now she stared in a mixture of awe and horror, her dragon's green eyes glowing like colored embers, no trace of her sapphire irises found within them. The marks on her shoulder, which she had blamed on an illness, under closer examination proved to be neither scarring nor disease, but instead the unmistakable pattern of dragon scales, which had left a permanent imprint on her skin.

"What is this?" she demanded. "What is happening to me?"

"This is what occurs, my lady, when a shifter spends too much time in dragon form. The imprint of scales, and persistent dragon eyes, are the first signs."

"Of what?"

"Spending excessive time in your other form. More than you should."

"I don't understand. My eyes...they're supposed to be blue."

"Not anymore," he answered, gently prying the mirror from Amelia's fingers.

"Will they change back?"

"I don't know for certain..." He re-wrapped the soft cloth around the family treasure before placing it back in the drawer.

"But?"

Conner turned to her, keeping his face as neutral as possible. "It's unlikely."

Amelia's hand moved to press against her lips, her voice dimming as she asked, "What is happening to me?"

Moved by her fear, Conner guided her to a chair in the corner of the room before taking a knee. "With your permission, my lady, I have a story I would like to tell you."

Amelia nodded.

"I had a friend once, a long time ago. He had a difficult childhood, leading to an even harder life. He had a group of friends, you see, and one day those friends betrayed him in a way so fundamental he could not move past the hurt." Conner drew a deep breath. "My friend, he, well...he wanted to—"

"Escape the pain," Amelia offered.

"Yes."

"My dragon doesn't comprehend betrayal. The threat of physical harm, yes. But not the emotional anguish of a bitter word."

Lies cannot harm a dragon. The memory caught Conner by surprise; the similarity of the young woman's words to the sentiments expressed by his friend long ago.

"My friend, like you, hid in these mountains. Many times I attempted to coax him back to his humanity. To remind him of a better world, beyond his anger. But he would not hear my pleas."

"What happened?"

Conner's lips formed a thin line, his eyes closing in an expression of deep regret. "In the beginning, he refused to hear my words. As time passed though, what was once a conscious refusal, became an inability to do so, until finally, he could no longer understand my words even if he wished to."

"You mean…"

"The man he was has vanished. The dragon is all that remains. He's naught but a beast now, a creature roaming the eastern skies, forever doomed to his chosen solitude."

"He refused to change back?"

"He can't change. Even if he wished it."

Silence fell for a time, the consequences rolling through Amelia's mind as she considered his story in the context of her transformed eyes and skin.

"Your friend, I'm sorry."

"So was I."

"May I ask…"

"Go ahead."

"Is he free, as a dragon? Free from the hurt of betrayal? From the heartache of knowing those who supposedly loved him most were also the ones to cause him pain?"

"Free?" Conner drew a deep breath, not wanting to give anything less than an honest answer to her heartfelt question. "I would like to think, my lady, a part of him is happy with the choice. Yet, sometimes, from afar, I see him, flying through the clouds. Smoke rises from his lips, fire painting the air as he breathes. Some part of him, buried deep, rages still. I don't think it's possible to be happy—to be free—filled with such rage."

Amelia reached out, tentatively placing her hand on Conner's. "I'm sorry about your friend. Truly."

Conner nodded, a gesture of thanks for her gentle understanding. "No question, the dragon is a magnificent creature. The power it grants our kind is to be both protected and feared.

"But spending too much time in dragon form is dangerous. I've seen the dragon's nature take too many of those I care for, reducing them to a base, animalistic nature.

"And this is why I beg you to consider this warning, my lady. Your eyes, the imprint of scales, these are the first signs of losing oneself to the creature within."

"I didn't know," she admitted fearfully. "I didn't…"

"It's all right. The dragon is a powerful force, and while it works cooperatively with us in many ways, it remains a creature of dominance. The dragon wants to live, to thrive, to be in control. You must learn to be stronger, or the creature will consume you."

Struggling to maintain her composure, Amelia nodded. "Thank you for the warning, and for letting me see. I didn't…"

"Quite all right, my lady." He squeezed the hand she had placed upon his, offering gentle reassurance as they sat together in silence, until she eventually pulled her hand away.

"After a lovely dinner outside, and these revelations, I'm tired," she explained. "Would you mind excusing me?"

"Of course not," he answered, standing to assist her from the chair.

"I'll manage." She motioned for him to step back as she limped to the bed.

When she had settled, he left the room, softly closing her door.

In contrast with her posture, her heart raced as she sat, body trembling from the realization her sanctuary could easily become her prison. Her dragon had protected her, washing away the loneliness that only her human half suffered from. But it had also betrayed her, diminishing what made her human through seductive promises of freedom and power.

Alone, her tremors transformed to sobs, tears slipping from unnatural reptilian eyes to splash onto her lap.

A knock at the door alerted her that her sobs had carried beyond the room. "Elizabeth?"

"I'm sorry," she apologized, attempting to stifle her tears.

Conner opened the door and moved to sit beside her on the bed. "I didn't mean to frighten you. I only wished for you to understand the risks."

"I've lost everything I held dear. The dragon's all I have left."

"And you will never lose her, my lady."

"I don't understand. I had transformed most nights before I came here. Nothing like this ever happened."

"It's not a matter as simple as how long you've transform for," he explained. "It's about being in control while you do so. You've allowed the dragon to utterly control your mind. It's the control, my lady, for which there must exist a balance."

"I was balanced before. I don't—"

"And I do not know what evils befell to bring you into this isolation, but I can see its toll."

Amelia shook her head. "Why do you care?"

Conner met her glowing eyes, his dragon stirring to pace the narrow confines of Conner's smaller form. A low grumble echoed, though only Conner could hear the protest.

Protect, the voice he rarely heard rose from his confined beast. *Protect the girl.*

"I wish to help you."

"But why?"

His dragon roared at the question, forcing Conner to close his eyes, draw a breath, and calm the frustrated creature.

"Christina is my mother," he offered, a more platonic explanation than the one the dragon would have preferred.

Amelia blinked. "Your...mother?"

"You saved her from rape, for which I am grateful."

"Why didn't she tell me?"

"Not something we advertise. You saw the village where she lives. If they knew her son to be a shifter, they would be less likely to treat her as she deserves. She has many friends in the village; not a life I wish to disrupt."

"I don't understand why you're out here."

"What do you mean?"

"Those blessed by Kamar, even if their parents were not, are welcome in Kalleen lands. Why did you not return to court, and to your mother's family?"

Conner gave a hard chuckle. "Go back to the people who treated my mother with such disdain? To the family who disowned her for being born without the ability to shift? Why would I want to go to them?"

"Because they're your family?"

"Only by blood. My mother is family by choice, and love. I would never go back to the people who treated her so poorly."

"I'm sorry they did that to her. Your mother was kind to me." Amelia lowered her gaze to the floor. "I had a friend, Kelsie. They sent her to the village as well, for the same reason."

"It's not right, though I doubt there's anything to be done. I had heard good things about the future queen. Whispers that perhaps she would be the one who took the initiative to make some changes. Unfortunately, her rule seems to be the same as all those who have come before."

"What do you mean?"

"She clings to the same archaic laws as all the rest. Chose a consort from the same family who made my mother's life hell when she was young. They say she even sent her own sister off to the corrupt temples to be a *voice*, likely never to be seen again."

"What do you know of the temples?"

"Same as you, I'd assume. A corrupt organization where those in power use their influence to prevent those who are truly blessed from gaining authority, lest such oracles prove their self-created prophecies false."

"Do you know where they keep the voices of Kamar?" she asked, thinking of Gwain's tragic tale.

"Only rumors. The most likely candidate would be the eastern temples. They're isolated, easy to defend, and should anyone attempt to escape, they would likely perish."

"Have you heard what they do to the voices?"

Conner nodded. "My mother had friends who were among the chosen. She told me stories of what was done to them." He shuddered. "I can't imagine how horrible it must be, even for child. But to force an adult woman, and princess…"

"Why would being sent to the temples be worse for her than a child?"

"The children know no other world. They've been raised to serve goddesses, shielded from the outside world, and are never taught anything else. But someone who has lived a life outside? I imagine the princess would have a more difficult time watching all she had ever known being stripped away."

Amelia found herself completely drawn to the man before her. His compassionate sentiments, toward a woman he was unaware he had ever known, pulled at the strings of her heart. "You are very kind. I'm certain, if the princess heard your empathy, she'd be grateful, as would all those forced into worlds and lives they would rather escape."

Conner shifted closer to where she sat. Moving a hand to her cheek, he slid a finger down the right side of her face before pressing up on her chin, guiding her gaze to his own. Staring down, his dragon growled possessively, delighted by the intimate proximity. "Do not mistake me for a nice man, my lady. You may find yourself disappointed."

Confused at this change in tone, she challenged, "Why did you save me?"

"I…" Conner's dragon reared forth, his eyes narrowing to slits, soft lilac transforming to deep amethyst. His dragon fought for control with the same intensity he had on the day he had rushed to save her life.

He could fall into her eyes for days. Blonde locks tumbling loosely down her back appeared soft as silk; his fingers ached to run along the tresses. Her lips were ruby red, full, irresistible, teasing him.

Taste, the dragon urged.

The compulsion jarred Conner from his trance. He stood from the bed, but could not prevent his eyes from trailing down her form, appreciating how the straight cut of her gown showed the top of her breasts, trapped beneath the tied material.

Realizing the danger, to them both, Conner forced himself to step back. Drawing a breath, he turned and said, "Goodnight, my lady."

She did not challenge him leaving, instead watching in confused silence, lost between the desire to retire to the solitude she had come to find comfort in, and the inexplicable urge to call his name.

CHAPTER XXXV

CORDIAL WOULD BE THE ONLY word to describe the following days. Conner was a perfect gentleman; no more, no less.

The switch to this new, cold, and formal behavior was confusing, yet not completely unwelcome. After Stephen had shattered her heart, Amelia was not eager to fall for anyone, let alone this stranger in the woods, who seemed as cryptic in his personal stories as she herself was forced to be.

He had done a wonderful job helping with her physical healing process. Her leg no longer ached, and the mark on her hip, once an open, ugly gash, was barely visible. Even her arm was coming back into use.

She had not transformed since her injuries, respecting Conner's caution that to do so might slow, or even reverse, her recovery process. Now well enough to embark on a winged journey, she was reluctant. Fear stemming from a combination of Conner's story and her own seemingly irreversible transformations, caused her to resist the increasingly restless beast within.

A few nights after Conner had removed the final bandage from her arm, he asked if she would like to fly. When she shook her head, he attempted to assure her the type of flight he proposed was not one she should avoid. "I don't care to fly often; I've never allowed mine to have control. However, your dragon is accustomed to longer journeys. You must appease her, at least for now."

"Why?"

"Because if you do not choose when you transform, the dragon will do so instead, and generally, as you have learned, not in a healthy manner."

She considered relenting, but found she could not. "I'm sorry."

Returning to her room, Amelia lay on the bed, attempting to sleep. She tossed in the warm pelts for many hours before surrendering not to a sweet embrace of rest, but one of sheer exhaustion.

Her dreams were restless. Walking through the familiar valley. The looming dragon. The inevitable breath.

"Elizabeth!" Conner's firm voice drew her from the dream. "Wake up!"

She did, scrambling toward the head of the bed, her back touching the wall. Pulling up her knees, Amelia dug her teeth into her lower lip to prevent the pathetic sounds building in her throat from escaping, but a deep sob rose in spite of her efforts. "I'm sorry."

"It's all right," he assured.

Trembling, she fought for a semblance of control. Fear, which always arose from the horrific dream, mixed with anger at her inability to escape the repetitious nightmare. Normally she regained her senses, but tonight the dreams seemed to overwhelm every defense.

Conner sat down on the side of the bed and reached toward her. "A dream, my lady."

"It's so real," she confessed. "Always so real."

Touching her shoulder, Conner coaxed her gaze up from its steadfast stare at the rumpled bedding. "My lady?"

The soft spoken plea was too much. Amelia jerked forward, wrapping her arms around his back as she trembled.

Returning the embrace, Conner wrapped his arms around her, allowing her to lean into him as she pressed her cheek to the side of his neck.

Her tension ebbed as he ran his hand down her hair in a soothing caress. She had forgotten how comforting the simple act of touch could be. How being held close could ease the worst of her fears.

It had been nearly seven years since her self-imposed exile. Seven years since she had been held or comforted from the pains of her world. She had put the basic need from her mind long ago. Now it returned with intense desire.

She knew she should pull away, but found herself unwilling to do so, instead loving the weight of his arms around her. The strong assurance she was safe for the first time since leaving Stephen's embrace. "Thank you. I..."

"Here." Guiding her back toward the opposite side of the bed, Conner backed against the wall where she had been, and pulled her to his chest.

"You don't have to..."

"I know what it's like to go without touch. For our kind, it's a torture in itself. I won't make you stay, by any means. If you wish for me to leave—"

"No!" the word came more forceful than intended. More tears slid down her cheeks.

He reached up and touched them, catching the droplets on his fingertips. "Please, my lady, don't cry."

Conner held her until her tears ceased, and her breathing slowed.

"Thank you," she whispered as sleep reached her.

"No need," he answered.

143

"Conner?"

"Hmm?"

"Amelia."

"What?"

"My name, it's Amelia. Elizabeth's my middle."

"Amelia," he tried the name. "Sweet dreams, Amelia."

CHAPTER XXXVI

AMELIA AWOKE WRAPPED IN CONNER'S warm embrace. For a moment, she tensed, then gradually relaxed as she recalled the comfort he had given so freely. Another drastic change in behavior from the man who had claimed to be unkind.

She eased back down to again settle herself across his chest. Amelia pressed into his warmth, refreshed from the simple act of being held after so many nights of self-imposed isolation. She had slept deeply and, more importantly, dreamless, in his arms, for which she was grateful.

Now awake, she attempted to remain still, enjoying the even cadence of Conner's breathing.

Hand on his chest, she explored the corded muscles, moving up to his shoulder, caressing the arms that had carried her so effortlessly across grassy fields and around the house during her recovery.

He was handsome, his face free of stubble, and his chest smooth as well. A light tan had darkened his skin to a golden tone. He appeared peaceful in his sleep, a fact which comforted her further as she resumed her position beside him.

She stayed for another hour before attempting to slip from the bed, but his eyes opened as she swung her legs over the edge.

A slender smile lifted the corners of her lips. "Good morning. I—"

Her words were cut off as Conner pulled her down unexpectedly, and one of his hands wound its way into her hair, guiding her to a searing kiss.

Amelia tensed, eyes wide as the demanding sensation stole her breath.

When she pulled back, his eyes transformed to glinting amethyst, his reptilian gaze a match for her unnatural emerald.

She moved from the bed to her feet, and he followed, forcing her to tilt her head to gaze up at his taller form.

"I've been resisting you since the day of the mountain lion attack," he said, his dragon deepening his voice with a gruff tone. "I have a limit though, Amelia. I'm afraid I've reached it." He forced a breath. "If you wish me to leave, I'll return after I've granted my dragon a time to cool down. Or..."

The second option lingered.

Amelia stared at him, emotions pulling her in various directions. A third option materialized. "Fly with me."

Drawing a frustrated breath, Conner nodded, leading Amelia out the front door. Less than a minute later, above a pile of clothes where they had stripped, two dragons flew through a morning sky.

CHAPTER XXXVII

DRAGONS SOARED, THEIR MASSIVE WINGS carrying them high above the land. One a brilliant blue; the other, a deep purple, but together, the winged beasts ruled the skies. Fearless, the dragons rose and fell, diving with abandonment toward grassy fields, only to pull up at the last moment. They twirled and twisted through the air, circling each other, teasing playfully as they took turns giving chase.

Amelia had missed this silent companionship, and the ease of sharing the sky with another in a manner only those blessed by Kamar were able to understand. She'd attempted to explain it to a non-shifter once, but words had not done the experience justice; the absolute freedom such flights offered from all worldly concerns.

Playing in the air was easy with Conner, and for the first time since she had killed the bandits, Amelia felt at ease with her dragon. Conner had been correct in his assessment that her flights over the past few years had been drastically different from those of the time prior to her sister's betrayal. Her dragon was gentle now, enjoying the freedom as much as she.

Conner sped up, glancing back in unspoken challenge. Amelia merrily gave chase, the cool wind soothing the flames within. Pulling to the left of her, Conner drew a breath before letting out a hot stream of golden flames, which Amelia matched, her blue fire clashing with the gold to create a unique swirl of light.

Elated, Amelia rose higher, turning on her back to create a large loop, fully circling Conner as he paused to hover in the air, allowing her to complete the aerobatic oval.

Then Conner took his turn. Amelia allowed him to twist around her in an ancient dance of wind and flame.

They flew for hours, the tireless dragons delighting in their momentary abandon.

When they finally did land, transforming back to their human selves, Amelia burst into laughter, a joyous sound so different from the sorrow that had clung to her for longer than she cared to recall.

Once fully transformed back to human, Conner reached for his discarded clothes, but Amelia touched his shoulder. Turning to meet her green eyes, he was unprepared for her to pull him down into a heated kiss.

As his lips molded to hers, his dragon gave a growl of approval, while his hands grasped her bare hips. Using all the willpower he could muster, Conner drew back enough to caution, "Are you sure? If we start, I don't know if I'll be able to stop."

"I want this," she answered.

All the invitation he needed, Conner laced his fingers through her golden strands, jerking her head back before bringing his lips down on hers with bruising force. Her dragon rose meet his, though both remained locked behind human forms.

The kiss continued as Conner slid his hands down Amelia's back before moving one hand up between them, cupping her breast to flick his thumb over her tightening nipple.

A gasp escaped her at his touch, which he swallowed with another kiss, slipping his tongue between her teeth to dance with hers.

She tasted sweet, like the lilacs she gathered from a nearby shrub and added to her bath. Her hair smelled of them too, and he basked in her heady aroma as he kissed her. His fingers explored along her left side to her outer, then inner thigh.

When she shivered at his touch, he moved both hands to lift her off the ground. "Wrap your legs around me."

She complied, pressing against his lower stomach as he held her to him, his lips trailing down her throat to end above her flushed breasts.

As though she weighed nothing, Conner carried the young woman into the cabin, depositing Amelia onto her bed. He followed her into the soft pelts as he wedged himself between her spread thighs.

His body covering hers, he again moved to her neck, planting soft kisses along her throat before reaching the center of her chest, where he moved a hand to circle her right nipple while trailing his lips to her left.

She moaned, thrusting her hips as his lips enveloped her now hardened tips. He lapped at the delicate flesh, drawing tiny sounds from pouting ruby lips.

He continued his way down, softly kissing her stomach, and outer thighs, before moving inward.

When he reached her core, she moaned again, an impatient sound. "Conner," she pleaded, the sound of his name falling from her lips delicious to his ears. "Please, Conner."

148

At her heated request, he moved a finger, parting her petals, running the digit up and down her inner lips before pressing inside.

She was tight around his single finger, but also deliciously wet. Adding a second digit, he moved his hand back and forth inside of her, delighting in how she writhed under him, her breasts rising with each sharp intake of breath.

Removing his hand, he positioned himself above her, but paused, to his dragon's snarling displeasure. "You're sure?"

"Yes," she said on a breathy utterance, pushing all fears aside as she gave herself over to the touch and sensations long denied. "Please, Conner."

Stealing further words with another kiss, Conner thrust his hips as she gasped against his lips. Tight, but hungry, her body closed around him snuggly. With a hiss, he withdrew and pushed forward again slowly, attempting to cause her as little discomfort as possible.

Breathing deeply for control, he slid a hand down to where they were joined, moving his finger up against her until he found the spot he sought. Her eyes wide, she moaned his name, her channel moistening in sweet response to his attentions.

Pushing deeper, Conner buried himself fully into her, pausing to enjoy the exquisite warmth of her yielding body. Radiant beneath him, her long blonde hair cascaded down her flushed chest, framing her rose-tipped breasts. She wrapped her legs partially around him, encouraging him even deeper inside her, back arching as she acclimated to his girth.

"You're beautiful," he breathed. "In every way."

In response, she beamed a smile, a soft light emanating from her emerald eyes.

His dragon snarled within, expressing his displeasure at Conner's delay in completely claiming the young beauty.

To the complaint, Conner pushed the dragon back. *No,* Conner spoke silently. *You had your flight. Tonight, she's mine.*

Reluctantly, the dragon withdrew, coiling back inside of him as he began a steady thrust of his hips.

Beneath him, Amelia moved her hips up to meet his. Together, the new lovers fell into a gentle rhythm, delighting in the joining of their bodies.

"Conner, please."

At her breathy request, he thrust harder, lifting her torso toward him to again claim her mouth, rubbing his chest against her sensitive breasts. She cried out at the adjusted position, reaching her peak, clenching tight around him, which caused him to give his own cry before spilling himself inside her.

He lay panting for a few breaths before finding the strength to roll to his side. "Are you all right?"

She nodded, and seeing the relief cross his features, she smiled. "Better. Oh gods, so much better than all right."

Her happiness brought a reflective smile to his lips. He reclined, opening his arms. "May I hold you, Amelia?"

"I'd like that," she answered, her mirth turning to softer tones, a fresh blush coloring her cheeks.

Conner drew her to him, slipping an arm around her as she snuggled against his chest, her blonde hair covering them both. He held her close as she closed her eyes in contentment. It felt right to have her in his arms. Like she had been missing all his life.

He didn't fully comprehend what fears plagued her, but whatever they were, he would do all in his power to eradicate them from her mind, life, and heart.

Running his hands lightly through her blonde tresses, the dragon's voice returned with a single utterance.

Mine.

For the first time in his life, Conner and his dragon were in perfect agreement.

CHAPTER XXXVIII

AMELIA AWOKE SPRAWLED ACROSS HER lover's chest, one long leg intertwined with his. She found Conner had been watching her sleep.

"You looked peaceful," he explained. "Didn't have the heart to wake you."

Amelia flashed a radiant smile and offered a chaste kiss, different from the passionate ones of the day before.

She snuggled down and pressed against his warmth as he maneuvered the bedding more securely around them.

After a brief pause, Amelia inquired, "Conner, may I ask a question?"

"Sure."

"How did you learn to appease your dragon? I mean, did someone teach you? Your mother isn't a shifter so, I was curious…"

"Trial, error, and a lot of practice. I'd be happy to teach you a few techniques that work for me, if you'd like."

"That would be helpful, considering…" She waved a hand toward her face, indicating her eyes.

Conner nodded. "I'd be happy to."

"Thanks."

"I was trying to figure out—"

"Conner!" a feminine voice called.

Jumping from the bed, Conner scrambled to the closet. "Crap!" He pulled a shirt, inside-out, over his head.

"Who is it?" Amelia asked, heart pounding.

"She can't find us like this."

Conner's panic caused her heart to plummet. Did he have a girlfriend all this time?

"Conner!" the voice came again, this time from inside the cabin.

"Hold on!" he shouted, pulling up pants as the door flew open.

"Conner, is everything all right? I heard them say…"

The words died as Chris spied Amelia lying on the bed.

"Well, now I know who the other dragon was that the travelers reported seeing."

"Chris!" Amelia exclaimed, in a mixture of relief at recognizing her friend, and horror at being found naked in her son's bed.

"I see you two have found your way to each other. Was starting to have my doubts."

"What?"

"Mother!" Conner said crossly. "I'll be out in a minute!"

Chris nodded, flashing Amelia a smile before turning from the room.

Conner closed the door, pressing his forehead to the wood with a groan, then he chuckled as he turned back to Amelia, whose entire body had turned red with flushed embarrassment. "Sorry. I'd make an excuse, but…"

"It's all right," she answered, mortification giving way to laughter as the two exchanged an awkward glance.

Five minutes later, both were dressed. When Conner opened the door, Amelia paused, prompting him to reach for her hand. "Not like she doesn't already know."

She gave a bashful smile. "True."

Fingers interlaced, they entered the room together when Amelia stopped dead in her tracks. Chris was not alone.

Beside her sat a woman. She had wrinkles around her eyes and sparse gray strands disrupted her once lush auburn hair. But her eyes held the same childhood spark.

"Kelsie?"

The woman stood and walked toward her.

Amelia dropped Conner's hand at her approach.

"Amelia, it's been a long time."

Swallowing hard, Amelia gazed into her friend's pale green eyes and nodded, unable to find words.

The woman stepped forward, embracing her lost friend. "When I first heard they'd sent you to the temples, I thought you must have chosen to go." Kelsie shook her head. "But when Kaliyah announced Stephen would be her new consort, I knew something was wrong. I tried to find out where you'd been sent, but everyone was so secretive about the location. No one knew anything, other than you had been chosen to become a voice of the goddess."

"What are you doing here, Kelsie? How did you find me?"

"I have a cousin who works a trade route covering all of the non-shifter allocated lands. On a recent visit, he told me a story about a band of thugs, and the blue dragon who saved a village. Your coloring is so rare, I knew it had to be you."

Amelia pulled back, shaking her head in wonder. "Wait." She moved her gaze to Chris, who stared blankly before turning back to Kelsie. "Why did you want to find me?"

Kelsie drew a breath. "I need your help, Amelia."

"With what?"

"I have a daughter. They took her."

"Took her to the temples?"

Kelsie shook her head, miserably.

Glancing back at Chris, understanding dawned. "Not to the temples?"

"No."

"If your daughter has shifted, she's been restored to full status. Heir to your parents' rank and wealth. No doubt it's difficult to be separated from her, but you have to admit her prospects are far better than life in the villages."

"Only she wasn't."

Amelia attempted to better read her friend's expression. "Wasn't what?"

"Restored to full status."

"I don't understand."

"Shifters born of those who are not are no longer being granted full status. You have to prove a pure bloodline, at least three generations back."

"Since when?"

"The day your sister took the throne."

"Wait…" Conner's voice interrupted the conversation. "Sister?"

Eyes squeezing tight, Amelia struggled to draw a breath, and with it, addressed Kelsie, "I'll ask again, what are you doing here? My sister sent me to the temples, to be turned into a mindless drone for the remainder of my life. Do you expect the queen will listen to me? Have your parents speak to her."

"They tried, but the queen refused their pleas. Chris brought me here because she agreed, you're my daughter's last hope."

Amelia shook her head. "I'm sorry, but I can't—"

"When she comes of age, they're going to force her to serve as a concubine to Stephen's brother."

Amelia's mind struggled to comprehend. "That makes no sense."

"He had wanted me, but I didn't transform. My daughter, though…"

"Why wasn't she taken back to your parents? Why would someone of your bloodline not be granted—"

"They're rounding up the non-shifters, distributing most into forced servitude. Young and pretty ones, who once belonged to noble houses, are being gifted."

"Gifted?"

Kelsie nodded.

Amelia drew a breath. "No. She wouldn't."

"She has. Stephen he—"

"Don't."

"Amelia, please…"

"I don't know who you think I am, or what you believe I might possibly be able to do."

"You're of the royal bloodline."

"I'm an outcast—in exile!"

"Amelia, please, if you would but listen…"

"I hear you." Anger flared, coming clearly through Amelia's tone.

"You don't know what I'm asking."

"Oh, I'm fairly certain I do."

"Amelia—"

"You show up years into my sister's reign, just as her rule becomes challengeable? Should I take a wild guess at what you're asking, or should we cut the pretense?"

"Amelia, she's my child. They're going to do horrible things to—"

"There are worse fates than being a pampered concubine to a powerful lord. And now that you've proven you can bear shifter children, I'm certain you will be taken back into the palace yourself, where you can be closer to her."

"Please—"

"I am not challenging my sister."

Chris now stood, walking toward her with a gentle expression. "My lady," she said softly, "what your friend has told you is difficult to hear, and likely more difficult to process. We'll give you time to think."

Overwhelmed by the multiple eyes, Amelia stepped back, her dragon rising in response to her agitation.

"Everyone step back," Conner advised. "Don't crowd her."

A tremor raced down her back as she turned and met her lover's gaze. "I'm sorry," she finally addressed his earlier question. "I should have told you."

"You're a princess."

"I was, once." Tears burned her eyes. "I have to go."

"Wait!" Chris called as she fled the room. "You have to—"

"Let her go," Conner advised. "She'll return when she's ready."

The three watched her vanish from the room, their uneasy silence broken by a dragon's roar.

"Should you go with her?" Kelsie asked.

"Amelia can take care of herself in that form." Conner turned to face his mother. "Why didn't you tell me who she was?"

"Wasn't my place, or the right time, to do so."

"But now?"

"Now the situation has become dire. Non-shifters born into high families have always been treated as less than those who shift, but what happened to me was a rarity, not the common practice. Most non-shifters live their entire lives in happiness, in villages protected by the crown, as opposed to persecuted. The stories this woman has told," she nodded to Kelsie, "are horrific. The queen seems intent on protecting pure bloodlines at all costs, and her new consort is no better."

"The consort..." His eyes moved to Kelsie. "Why did you know something was amiss when you heard who the consort was?"

"Stephen was Amelia's lover. The day after Kaliyah became queen, Amelia was sent to the temples, and Stephen took his place at the queen's side. Rumors of the betrayal reached even our village."

"Wait, he left Amelia...for her sister?"

Kelsie nodded, causing Conner's heart to constrict.

Betrayed by her family, and lover. Condemned to the life of a mindless drone at the pleasure of corrupt temples. No wonder she had chosen absolute solitude.

Conner looked at his mom, putting the pieces together. "You knew who she was when you sent me to watch over her."

"After all she'd been through, she could use a friend." When Conner raised a dubious eyebrow she added, "And yes, I like Amelia, and hoped that more would bloom. Seems it did."

"She's a princess of Kalleen. Don't you think I should have known before we..."

"If I had told you, would you have helped her?" Chris shook her head. "You're a child of Kalleen as well, whether you choose to acknowledge such lineage or not. Your great-grandfather was a prince of the dragon realm. You have grown up despising that world, in part because of what they did to me, but Conner, Kalleen is your heritage and birthright, as much as hers."

"You should have told me."

"You would never have given her a chance if I had. And you needed to, Conner, for both your sakes."

"My dragon knew she was in danger. Do you know how the dragon knew? Because I don't."

Chris met her son's gaze. "I will answer your question, however I must ask you something very personal first. It's important for you to answer honestly."

"Fine."

"I mean it, Conner. It's important."

"Okay."

"When you took the princess to your bed, was it you, or your dragon?"

"Mother!"

"Answer the question."

Conner drew a breath, heat crawling up the side of his neck. "The dragon wanted her, but so did I."

His mother nodded, a slight smile on her lips. "I didn't tell you, Conner, because I wanted it to be your choice. A choice not generally afforded to one of your bloodlines. For it is *both* of your bloodlines, Conner."

"I don't understand."

"You've never been interested in your Kalleen line. If you had been, you would have learned you're from a line as ancient as the royal one. Dragons often have fated mates. The line from which you are descended, and Amelia's line, have long been intertwined. When you appeared the first time, during the ice storm, and found Amelia in the woods, I realized your appearance was likely no accident. Your dragon knew she was in trouble, and compelled you to help her. You say your dragon knew she was in trouble later as well? This doesn't surprise me in the least.

"Were you a weaker man, I might have warned you. But you have always been skilled in controlling the dragon within, better than most shall ever be. Had I told you the truth, you either would have run away from her, or toward her. My remaining silent allowed you to make a choice, as a man."

"And if it had been the dragon who bedded her?" Conner asked, anger and embarrassment lacing his words.

"Were that the case, I would recommend caution."

"And because it wasn't, I should…what, exactly?"

"Follow your heart, as you have always done." Chris smiled. "And remember, Conner, the animosity you hold toward those of Kalleen is for wrongs done to others, shadows of a past you never knew. The crimes committed against the princess are raw and bleeding. Had she been delivered to the temples, horrific abuses would have been performed upon her. It is difficult enough to bind the dragon of a lower-born child. For a woman of royal blood, it's nearly impossible. Her sister knew this when she sent Amelia into their hands. As did the man to whom Amelia had given her heart."

"I wasn't there personally," Kelsie added, "but my sister was. The princess was escorted from the palace in chains, her own sister watching from above in apparent delight." Kelsie shuddered. "I never cared for Kaliyah, but even I would never have dreamt…Amelia's her little sister."

At this, Conner left the room. The women let him go.

"They both need time to process what they've learned," Chris informed Kelsie.

"I understand," she replied, "but time is something my daughter does not have."

Chapter XXXIX

Wanting to avoid the two women she suspected were still inside, after retrieving her discarded clothes, Amelia returned to the cabin's back porch.

The flight had cooled her temper, for now. Apprehensions swirled through her human mind; things her dragon did not concern herself with.

Top of the list? That her sister would force the people she was sworn to protect into horrific servitude. In spite of what Kaliyah had done to her personally, she had wanted to believe her older sister would lead the kingdom with the same grace of their mother's reign. A kind, yet powerful woman, Eliana had ruled with wisdom, maintaining a fair balance between the strong and weak.

Or had she? Chris' personal tale jarred her long-held beliefs, causing her to wonder how the woman who had soothed her childhood fears could allow such an atrocity to take place. Forcing a non-shifter into the bed of a high ranking lord? Surely, her mother couldn't have known.

She shook her head, wishing for her mother's gentle guidance. "I have so many questions," she spoke to no one. "I don't know what to do, nor whom to believe."

Amelia did not doubt Kelsie's story, though a part of her longed to. However, neither did she desire to believe its truth. A contradiction within her, compounded by the simple fact she did not wish to be queen. She never had. A fact none seemed to believe.

Hearing the door open behind her, Amelia tensed, not ready to face the women again.

Her dread grew worse at the sound of Conner's voice. "May I join you?"

Muscles locking painfully, she remained staring at the horizon.

When he touched her shoulder, she jumped. "My lady?" The words were gentle.

"I'm sorry. I should have told you."

Various responses came to Conner's mind, but what he said was, "I hold bitterness over what has happened to others. My family. Friends. But…" His mother's words came to him. "None of my anger is based on personal grievances. What you've been through…it's more."

"I shouldn't have kept such a secret."

"I don't begrudge you secrets, my lady, if you will forgive me my own."

Drawing a deep breath, she turned to face him, and offered her hand. "My name is Amelia Elizabeth Castel, Princess of Kalleen."

Accepting the offered handshake, he replied formally, "Conner Brion Ardarg, grandson of Lord Tryon of Kalleen."

Amelia tried to smile, but faltered as deep exhaustion set in. "I'm sorry I didn't tell you. Especially considering how well you cared for me, I should have, long before we…"

"It's all right," he assured. "I understand."

"My sister, Kaliyah, ordered me to the temples. She—"

Conner's heart ached at the pain in her voice. "Come here." Pulling her into his arms, Conner held her gently.

"I hear what they're saying, but she's my sister."

"I understand," Conner answered, a coldness she could not place seeping into his voice. "It's difficult to be faced with the worst in one's family."

Amelia did not answer, allowing him to hold her, drawing on his strength.

He ran his fingers through her blonde tresses for a long time.

The door creaked open behind them. "I'm sorry to disturb…" Kelsie's words ceased when she saw Amelia in Conner's embrace.

It took several breaths before Amelia found the strength to face her childhood friend. "Kelsie, I'm sorry. I understand it's your daughter, but…there must be someone else who can help you. I can't return to the palace, and have no desire to challenge my sister. She is the queen. I swore an oath to follow her. And while what she did to me was unimaginable, she remains the rightful ruler."

"Your sister is a monster, Amelia."

"No, she's not."

"What she's done to the kingdom…" Kelsie shook her head. "It's appalling."

"You can't speak that way about your queen."

"Our queen is enslaving non-shifters. Reducing some to manual labor, while the others go to fates far worse. Fates my daughter and I will soon be faced with, unless someone challenges her rule.

"She's also cut off trade and negotiations with neighboring kingdoms, and is taxing the people to starvation in preparation for the conquest she's planning." Kelsie shook her head. "You have no idea what is going on in the kingdom, or how its people—your people—have suffered since the day she took the throne."

"I don't believe you. She would never."

"Never what, Amelia? Condemn her own sister to a fate worse than death?"

Amelia met Kelsie's gaze and found her denial faltered. Instead of offering protests, she shook her head. "I don't know what you came here seeking, but I am not the answer."

"I came seeking help from the only person who can."

"I can't help you."

"Can't or won't?"

Amelia's focus moved from Kelsie to Chris, attempting reason. "She's my sister, and my queen. No matter what she's done, nothing can change those two facts."

"No, it won't," Chris agreed. "However, sometimes the worst trespasses are committed by those we love the most. It makes the betrayal far worse than any a stranger could hope to commit."

"And what would I be, if I betray her?"

"After what she's done to you?" Kelsie spat. "How can you even ask such a thing?"

"My sister cast me out, but her actions do not dictate I must do the same. Can't you understand?" Internally, Amelia's dragon rose, the shadow of her scales transforming to a vivid blue, skin itching where they appeared. Struggling for control, she stepped back, moving toward the rail until she touched the wooden barrier. "I am not going to do this! Don't ask it of me!"

Conner grabbed her, pulling her close. "Breathe, Amelia."

She did as he instructed, not realizing her breaths came in wheezing gasps.

"I've got you." Lifting her into his arms, Conner walked past the other two women, who had fallen to silence as they witnessed panic overwhelm the broken princess.

Cradling her, Conner laid her down upon the bed, covering her with multiple layers of pelts before tucking himself in beside her.

Sheltered by the safety of his embrace, Amelia gave herself to grief.

CHAPTER XL

THE FIRST AWAKE, AMELIA UNTANGLED herself from the warm pelts, and slipped from Conner's embrace. After pulling on a chemise worn to perfect softness, she wrapped a shawl around her shoulders then walked back to the porch. Tranquil, the sounds of birds in the thicket and the rushing stream soothed her troubled heart. Familiar and comforting, the scene reminded her why she didn't want to return.

She had never desired to be queen, not even as a child. She had always preferred flight, nature, and adventure to the mundane requirements of running a kingdom. Challenging her sister, even if such a task were not surely a lethal venture, held no appeal.

Conflict filled her when the door opened. "Go away."

The footsteps paused, but did not recede.

"Please understand, I can't help you. I don't want the throne, and no matter what she's done, to me or others, I love my sister. There's only one way to dethrone a dragon queen."

The intruder remained silent as Amelia stared into the horizon.

"You're not asking me to dethrone her. You're asking me to kill her." She shook her head. "Ask another."

Chris' voice broke through her sorrow, "There are no others."

"Dozens of nobles can challenge her."

"At the initial coronation, yes. But not after she claimed the throne. Now, only those of royal blood may do so."

"Nothing she has done can be enough to justify taking her life."

"Amelia…"

"I am *not* killing my sister. Even if I had reason, and the heart to do it, which I don't, who's to say I would win? Have you seen her in dragon form? I have. She gained the throne uncontested for a reason, and it had nothing to do with her charming personality."

"My lady…"

"No." She finally turned to face the older woman. "I won't do it. Find another."

"Go see for yourself."

"See what?"

"The consequences of your sister's rule. If you fly, you'll get there quickly. No need to go near the castle; any of the outskirt villages will do. See with your own eyes what your sister has done to the land you love. To the people you were born to protect."

"Kaliyah was born to protect them. Not me."

Chris eyed her critically. "We both know that's a lie, my lady. You are also of the ancient, royal line. It is the sacred duty of *each* family member to protect those in their care. This, your sister has forgotten, or perhaps, never knew."

"I'll fly with her," Conner's voice entered the conversation as he moved onto the deck, the wooden planks creaking at his steps.

Chris offered a weary smile to her son. "Thank you for—"

"Don't thank me. I'm not agreeing with you, Mother. What you're asking her to do is horrendous." He moved his gaze to the dragon princess. "I will fly with you, Amelia, but only if your desire is to go. No one is going to force you, and I'll support any decision you make."

Amelia wanted nothing more than to deny their claims with all the vigor she possessed. To return to the solitary life she had come to appreciate, with all the simplistic pleasures and protection it brought. But her inquisitive mind had already decided otherwise, even as her heart rebelled against her next words. "Fine, we'll go. But we'll fly at night, and only just past the border."

She noted Chris' hopeful expression. "Don't expect me to change my mind. No matter what she's done, Kaliyah is my sister…and queen."

CHAPTER XLI

TOGETHER, THE TWO DRAGONS FLEW through night skies, expansive wings carrying them with ease toward their destination. With the lightening sky, the dragons landed, transforming back to their human forms. They'd each packed one set of clothes in a small leather duffle, which Conner had carried in his rear claws.

Comfortably dressed in a pair of black slacks with an emerald shirt, Amelia added a gray woolen cloak, which featured a hood to hide her golden tresses and most of her face, though nothing could be done to disguise her reptilian eyes.

"Probably for the best," Kelsie had said. "They won't be able to mistake you for a non-shifter."

The pair walked an additional two hours, finally reaching a village on the outskirts of the Kalleen Mountains. A simple town, rows of plain wooden huts lined a clearing with sparse marketing stands offering food and clothing for sale or trade.

Entering the village center, she found the town eerily quiet, people walking by with heads down, avoiding contact with each other. No chatting housewives, or playing children. In the market, Conner and Amelia observed the quick bustle of those few who did engage in trade, purchasing their goods with minimum conversation before hurrying on their way.

Spying a tavern, the princess walked forward, Conner shadowing her steps. A similar dynamic inside, only a few small groups of men, whispering to not be overheard by unwanted ears. Eyes surveyed the newcomers warily.

Pushing past the stares, Amelia took a seat at the closest table with her back to the room, keeping her eyes down in hopes of attracting less attention. Conner sat opposite her, at an angle where he could observe both the room and the door.

An older man, with hair more silver than brown, approached. "May I fetch you anything?"

"Wine," Conner replied, producing a piece of silver. "One for the lady as well."

"Right away," the man answered gruffly, taking the silver before turning to fetch the requested beverage.

The wine he delivered was surprisingly good, a deep red blend of blackberry, with a hint of vanilla, the blended flavors playing across Amelia's tongue as she considered her surroundings.

Her plotting on how to speak with the locals derailed when two men entered the room. Dressed in gray robes similar to her own, they distinguished themselves from the rest of the villagers with the long, silver blades at their sides, gleaming hilts protruding from black leather sheaths.

Taking a seat at a table closest to the bar, one man barked, "Ale. The good stuff, none of the cheap drivel you keep attempting to pass off as a proper drink."

"Right away, sir."

From across the room, Amelia detected the inn keeper's frantic tone, and watched as he scrambled to fulfill the order as quick as he could.

"How long does it take to get a bloody drink?"

"Coming, sir!" the innkeeper exclaimed, rushing around the bar to hand him a foaming tankard. "Apologies."

"As there should be. I don't like waiting. Makes me want to find something to do to occupy the time." His eyes moved to where a young woman, perhaps nineteen, poured water for a pair of men seated at a nearby table. "Perhaps I should visit with your pretty daughter? I'm sure she could keep me entertained."

Heat crept up the man's features. "Please, sir. She's only a girl."

"A beautiful one."

A second knight stood and approached the girl. Grasping her arm, he led her to the one speaking, forcing her to sit on the man's lap.

"You should be honored I'd show interest." He lewdly moved his hand to her stomach, spreading his fingers wide. "I could put a shifter in your belly. You'd like that, wouldn't you? To become mother to a dragon? Probably be the best thing to happen to your pathetic bloodline."

Terrified, the girl attempted to rise, but was held fast by the man's strong grip, keeping her securely in his lap.

"Calm down now." He wrapped a hand around her waist, and pressed his lips to the side of her neck. "Be plenty of time for squirming later."

"My lord, please don't harm my daughter."

"Harm her? I'm going to love her! Queen says I can take anyone of lower status as I see fit. Now go fetch some bread and soup. Need energy if I'm going to have my way with this young thing."

The girl's father stared miserably into his child's terrified eyes, before turning to fetch the requested items, leaving his daughter struggling as the crude man ran his hands all over her, circling her narrow waist before squeezing her breast through her shabby green dress.

Conner and Amelia exchanged a horrified glance as they witnessed the encounter, the girl's struggles pulling at Amelia's heart, her dragon rumbling in outrage at the man's wanton behavior.

While the man molested the younger woman, the others laughed at her occasional pleas, before boring of their game enough to glance around the room.

Spying Amelia and Conner, one of the knights nodded in their direction before rising to approach.

Exchanging another wary glance, both Amelia and Conner remained still, keeping their gaze upon each other.

"I ain't never seen you two before."

"Passing through," Conner answered, casually maintaining a hand on his goblet.

Keeping her eyes downcast, Amelia jumped as the man unexpectedly reached out and grasped her robe's hood, tossing it back to reveal her face and golden hair.

Seeing her profile, the knight let out a long whistle. "What have we here?" He turned back to his fellows. "Hey, Vinny! Look, this lass is even prettier than yours."

Amelia waited, hoping the man would have his verbal fun and leave.

A scenario that became less likely when Conner entered the conversation. "I would ask you to step back from the lady."

"The lady?" The man laughed. "I'm a member of the elite guard, boy. I can have anyone I want from these miserable villages."

"As I have stated, we are passing through and thus, are not a member of the village over which you have domain."

"She your personal whore? Must be in order to maintain this level of beauty. Look at those lips. Made to be kissed."

"I'll ask you again," Conner said, his tone tightening. "Leave the lady alone."

Amelia's skin crawled as the man stepped behind her and leaned over until his foul breath fanned the side of her face. Slipping his hand to her shoulder, his fingers crawled lower.

The undesired caress proved too much for her sensibilities. She jerked away.

He laughed, stepping in front of her. "Oh, she's going to be fun," he spoke cruelly, moving a hand to her chin, forcing her to at last meet his gaze.

"I am going…" His words died as he stared into Amelia's serpentine eyes. "You're one of us."

164

"Yes." Her voice deeper than normal as her dragon surfaced, stirred to full attention by the man's threat.

"I didn't realize…"

Conner stood up. "Remove yourself from the lady."

The other two knights rose in alarm at realizing another shifter was in the village.

"Who are you?" the one identified as Vinny demanded.

Deciding to play on a partial truth, Amelia answered, "How dare you speak in such disrespectful tones to the grandson of Lord Tyron." Referring to Conner's maternal grandfather, she had been surprised at first to hear he was descended from such a high line of nobility, but after recalling his mother's story, the relation made sense. One of the few bloodlines in the kingdom pure enough to convince Stephen's family to consider siring a child, even on a woman of non-shifter status. Additionally, Tyron had an abundance of grandchildren, and even more great-grandchildren. Enough none would question the claimed status of a man they'd never met.

"Tyron?" Vinny questioned. "As in, high advisor to the queen?"

"Yes," Conner stated. "You can be sure he will hear of your abominable behavior upon my return to court, and your attempts to impede me from carrying out the crown's orders."

"I'm sorry, my lord." Vinny dropped to a bow. "If we had known—"

"You assumed. You never bothered to inquire," Conner cut him off. "Now, leave my sight and review your deplorable actions here. Next time the person you assault may not be as forgiving. And I assure you, should you ever touch my companion again, you shall lose more than your dignity."

"Tyron is not a forgiving man," Amelia added. "Would hate to see your entire family destitute for insulting a member of his family."

"Forgive me, my lady. I…"

"Leave," Conner demanded, "and do not even think of harming the young woman either."

"The girl?"

Conner nodded. "Your behavior does not merit you the reward of the young woman. She is now under my protection. If I find any of you have violated her, I shall be expressly displeased. Am I understood?"

After a moment's hesitation, the men nodded and left the room.

When the thugs had departed, Amelia re-took her seat before asking, "Could we get a second glass of wine?"

The innkeeper nodded, fetching the wine as the girl came forth to offer water. Hands shaking, her face was flushed with a mixture of fear and embarrassment, obviously unclear as to why the lord had sought to include her in his protections.

"Don't fear," Conner assured her. "I won't harm you." He nodded toward Amelia. "This is Lady Elizabeth. As lovely as you are, she's the only woman for me." He offered a smile he hoped was comforting.

The father appeared holding the requested goblets of wine as the girl moved aside.

When Conner reached for another piece of silver, the older man shook his head. "No, my lord, please. Thank you for not letting them harm my Mandy."

"No need to thank me, but I would like some information."

Meeting Conner's gaze the man nodded, caution in his eyes. "What would you like to know?"

"If the knights' behavior is typical? And if the queen truly sanctions their vile acts?"

The man shifted uncomfortably, glancing from Conner to Amelia. He paused, entranced by her unnatural eyes.

"What we ask sounds frightening," Amelia spoke gently, "especially coming from strangers. But I assure you, on my word as a daughter of Kamar, we mean you no ill will. If wrongs are being committed in this land, I wish to know." She tilted her head, expression sad. "I can't put wrongs to right, if I don't know what is taking place."

Drawing a breath, the man nodded. "Come this way," he instructed, motioning for Amelia to follow, leading both her and Conner to the left side of the inn. Tacked onto the wall was a long piece of parchment, and at the bottom of the page, her sister's stark signature.

Amelia pulled the proclamation down, and moved to a nearby window, in order to better read the contents.

By order of her Royal Majesty, Queen Kaliyah Castel, and the High Priestess, new laws are henceforth implemented for all second-class, non-shifting members of the Kalleen Kingdom. These laws shall become effective immediately, and are issued for the welfare of the kingdom, and protection of both non-shifters and shifters alike.

1. No further marriages shall be permitted between those of shifter and non-shifter lines.

2. All non-shifters born into shifter families shall be assigned to another shifter family, in hopes of restoring the bloodline to full shifter status.

3. Non-shifters shall hereby fully submit to those of shifter lines in all instances. No request of a shifter is to be refused by those of non-shifter status.

4. Non-shifters between the ages of 18 and 26 shall report to their assigned shifter lord for work placement. Non-shifters of this age must consent to labor, in the field assigned by their given dragon lord.

5. Any non-shifter who experiences dreams of being, or witnessing, a dragon must be brought immediately to the Temples of Kamar for assessment, and possible placement within the temples.

6. Any refusal of these new rules shall be met with severe and immediate punishment, ranging from imprisonment, to the forfeit of said rebel's life.

HRM Queen Kaliyah Castel of Kalleen

AMELIA BRUSHED HER THUMB OVER the signature, mind spinning at her sister's harsh, one-sided decree.

Reading over her shoulder, Conner stilled behind her.

Renewed revulsion at her sister's cruelty washed over her, reinforcing notions of how little she actually cared. "Seeing me as a threat is one thing. But this…we are meant to protect the weaker lines, not cause them harm." Amelia shook her head. "This is wrong." She met Conner's concerned expression with wide eyes. "How could she do this?"

"There's more, my lady," these words came from the innkeeper. "With your permission?"

Apprehensively, Amelia nodded, allowing the proprietor to lead her to the back of the inn, and out a side-door.

"This way."

Emerging into full sunlight, Amelia blinked her green eyes. Following each other through a series of narrow paths between buildings, the group emerged into a shaded clearing. From the branches of strong, ancient trees, a series of bodies swayed in various stages of decay. Fat insects buzzed about the corpses, landing lazily upon the macabre banquet.

Gasping, Amelia's hand flew to her lips. The bodies were those of men and woman alike, nude, patches of skin missing from where bugs, birds, and other forest creatures had taken their pound of flesh. An overpowering stench prompted Amelia to a retching gag.

"My lady, you don't…" But Conner's words ceased as Amelia moved closer.

Stepping between a pair of hanging corpses, she spied their backs. Their skin was split as though it had been clawed through. Amelia realized these cuts were not made by an animal, but instead the slice of a crude knife, combined with the lash of a ceaseless whip.

With another gag escaping against her will, Amelia shuddered, but forced herself to continue breathing as shallowly as she dared. "What are their crimes?" she asked, fearing she knew the answer.

"Refused to obey, my lady."

"Obey what?"

He nodded toward the first of the bodies, a man who appeared to have been in his mid-twenties. "Billy refused to allow one of the queen's men to abuse his wife." He motioned toward the female hanging beside him. "They took her after he was dead, then strung her up beside him when they were done.

"One attempted to defend a friend whom the knights had decided to beat on. They bled him to death."

Amelia walked through the field, turning a corner to realize there were more bodies on additional trees. Continuing in spite of her revulsion, Amelia reached the back-most tree, where she found three men hanging not by their necks, but instead, their hands. As her foot broke a branch, one of the men opened an eye.

He's alive, she realized, her steps carrying her forward. Skin caked in blood, his back and chest were lined with hand-width cuts.

"These are the not-so-lucky ones. They're not properly hanged like the first bodies you saw. They're left to die of their injuries, and exposure."

Bugs hovered here also, one landing on an open injury as bile rose in Amelia's throat. Her gaze shifted to the other two hanging behind the man, who also managed to flutter their eyes.

"Cut them down," she ordered. "For the love of Kamar, get them down."

"We can't, my lady. The queen's knights forbid it."

Amelia drew a breath and turned to Conner, whose horror equaled her own.

Words coming through shallow breaths as she fought to contain her stomach's contents, "I'm Princess Amelia Castel of Kalleen. Cut them down."

The man's eyes widened. "You're—"

Amelia nodded. "Get help. Call your physicians; I'll deal with the men."

The older man nodded, running from the field.

Reaching into the bag where he had carried their clothes, Conner withdrew a blade. "I had hoped I wouldn't have to use this."

As Conner began cutting through the ropes, Amelia moved to assist, helping each of the mangled men to the ground as gently as possible.

"Sorry," she apologized as one moaned in pain at the jarring movements. "I know it hurts."

She was grateful when the innkeeper returned, bringing with him several men and women who rushed forward to care for the injured.

As villagers gathered, so did the so-called knights.

"What is the meaning of this?" Vinny exclaimed, eyeing Conner and Amelia with a new level of suspicion. "These rebels were condemned to die, by royal decree."

"A decree we are overturning," Amelia stated.

The three knights exchanged a glance, before turning their eyes on Amelia. "Grandson of Tyron or not, you don't have the authority to contradict a decree from the rightful sovereign."

"He may not," she answered, "but I do."

"Is that so?"

"As the princess of Kalleen, yes."

"The princess…" Vinny looked confused.

Conner cut in, "The queen's sister, you fool."

"Princess?"

Amelia stood tall, refusing to speak further as the man processed her words.

Conner stepped closer, nodding at the knight. "Bow before royalty," he ordered.

After a brief pause, Vinny did as Conner had demanded. "Forgive me, Princess. I had no idea. I…" He looked up. "I thought you had joined the temples."

Resisting the urge to look at Conner, Amelia clarified, "I've spent the past few years in the temple, yes. So by touching me against my will, not only have you offended your princess, but you have also offered grave insult to a priestess of Kamar. Would you like to add to your list of offenses by daring to contradict my orders?"

"No, my lady. I was only…"

"Proving your lewd disobedience further?"

"Forgive me, Princess. Please…"

"Like you forgave these villagers?" Amelia's anger shifted to rage, drawing forth her dragon. The creature uncurled, stretching through her as though awakening from slumber.

"My lady, please…"

"Or as you threatened this poor innkeeper's daughter? For how you've terrorized this village? Tell me, sir knight, for which acts, precisely, do you beg forgiveness?"

The dragon roared, scales erupting from Amelia's arms and legs, as Conner called, "Amelia, no!"

Her lover's plea cooled the flames pushing at her skin, but not enough to cause the partial transformation to recede.

Moving behind her, Conner lowered his head to press his lips against her ears. "Sentence them to death, if you wish. But not this way, not with the dragon's anger in control. You must embrace the creature within, my lady. But never can you allow the dragon to embrace you instead."

At his words, the scales receded, the blue color fading until her skin again sported only the textured shadow along the side of her neck and shoulder.

Once calm, Amelia considered the now kneeling men.

"It's true," the man farthest from Vinny proclaimed. "I saw the dragon princess once, blue, a color I'd never seen before on another. A child of the moon, they said."

Amelia did not register their words, instead reaching out a hand and taking the blade from Conner. Though by no means up to the skill of the brave knights who had once protected her, Amelia had been taught the basics of swordplay from a young age, her mother insisting they have another form of self-defense, other than relying solely on their dragon halves.

Grasping the blade, Amelia did not pause to consider other options, instead walking up to the first kneeling man. "Vinny," her words came more calmly than she would have expected, "for crimes against non-shifters, delivering unjust punishment, defilement, and death to those you were sent here to protect, I, Princess Amelia of Kalleen, sentence you to die."

Eyes widening at the pronouncement, Vinny did not even have time to offer protest before Amelia's borrowed blade descended, slicing through the man's throat and into his jugular, spraying himself, and Amelia's arm, with hot, sticky blood.

Without further warning, she moved the sword left, slicing the second man's throat as swiftly as the first.

Only one man remained, the time taken to kill the first two allowing him to climb to his feet.

"You claim to have seen me before," Amelia stated. "You also know what a true-blooded royal dragon is capable of. I would refrain from raising your sword unless you wish to join your companions."

Hand on the hilt of his blade, the man hesitated, glancing between Amelia and Conner, who had moved up to stand beside the princess.

"You have a choice, sir knight. In my name, you can ride to the nearby villages, order an immediate stop to the persecution of my people, and issue new orders to tend to those harmed as these men were so punished. Or you can pull that sword, and take your chances with a woman capable of fighting back, to suffer a fate far worse than these two." She gestured to the bodies of his fallen comrades. "Your choice."

The knight dropped to his knees, lowering his face to the ground before his princess. "I shall do your bidding, my lady. Please, spare my life, and I shall—"

"Go now, before my mind is turned on the matter. And know, if you betray me, or manipulate my words in any form, I shall find you, and when I do, you will not like the results of such betrayal."

"I understand, my lady. I won't betray you, I swear."

"See you don't."

With those words, the man scrambled to his feet, rushing toward the trees, and out of sight.

Turning back to Conner, she saw an odd expression on his face. "What?" The word came harsher than she'd intended.

Conner raised his hands, palms open. "No objections here, Your Highness."

Amelia nodded, glancing at the hanging bodies of those she had been unable to save. "I have to speak to my sister."

"Yes," Conner answered solemnly. "You do."

CHAPTER XLII

LATER HER ACTIONS SANK IN, the harshness she'd shown threatening to shatter all resolve. "What did I do?"

Alone in a borrowed room, provided by the grateful innkeeper, Conner drew Amelia into his arms. "You did what was necessary."

"To kill them?"

"To illustrate, without question, the threat behind your words."

Amelia shook her head. "There had to be a better way."

"In a mortal world, perhaps. But they're dragons, my lady. As are we. One cannot establish control of a dragon realm without force."

"I murdered them. In cold blood." Her words were laced with dismay, not only because of what she had witnessed, but also due to the sheer horror of her actions. "What am I becoming?"

"A queen," he answered.

"What?"

"You're becoming a queen, my lady."

"I never asked to be."

"No, you were born to be."

"Kaliyah was born the heir. Not me. I don't want her throne. I never have. Why does everyone keep assuming I do? Even my own sister. Now you."

"Amelia." Conner pulled back enough to meet her gaze. "Your sister didn't randomly decide on these changes to the kingdom overnight. These rules were well-implemented, not a rash decision on her part. This was planned for, what I would image to be, quite a long time. Tell me, my lady, would you have stood idly by and allowed Kaliyah to issue these orders?"

"Of course not!" she exclaimed. "I would never have—"

"Exactly. A fact your sister knew well."

Amelia tilted her head, incredulous. "You're saying my sister sent me to the temples to be brainwashed, because I would object to her policies?"

Conner shrugged. "Would you put it past her? She had a plan for the kingdom and, once reaching the throne, knew there was only one person who could possibly stand in her way. Tell me, Amelia, what would you have done?"

"I wouldn't have betrayed my own family!"

"But she did, Amelia. She betrayed you. Condemned you."

Amelia shook her head, mind rebelling against Conner's frank statements, even after all that had transpired. "Why?"

"Because you were the only thing stopping her."

"But why implement all of this? I don't understand."

"To protect the bloodlines. The shifter legacy."

Amelia breathed in harsh gasps as Conner again pulled her to his chest, running his hands gently up and down her back.

"It's all right," he whispered.

Meant to bring comfort, his words instead caused Amelia to draw back. "Why are you here? This isn't your fight. It has nothing to do with you. You barely know me!"

"Amelia, you're panicking."

"I'm not. I want an answer. Why are you here? What's your role in this? I don't…You've protected me, sheltered me from both physical and emotional harm, been a shoulder for me to lean on, but I don't understand why."

"Amelia—"

"I lied to you, about who I was."

"A fact for which I do not blame you, my lady. I understand why you didn't go around telling strangers you're the kingdom's lost princess."

"And you honestly want to stand by my side while I confront the sovereign queen?"

"I want…"

"What? What *do* you want?"

Conner stepped closer. Pressing a finger to her chin, he raised Amelia's head, directing her meet his gaze, which had transformed to a deep shade of amethyst, his dragon peering through primarily human eyes. "I want to follow you, my lady, wherever you may lead. To be by your side, no matter what the consequence. To be with you, at all costs."

"Why?"

"Because I never felt whole until I met you. Never have I experienced such need, such protective desire. You've burned your way into my soul, Amelia. You didn't even have to try."

She longed to believe his words, wanting them to be enough to finally put aside the harm done by another.

Stephen had never shown the intensity of the eyes now staring down as though they could pierce through flesh to see directly into her soul. Had never spoken with such demanding passion, nor stood by her side without pause or question. Had never made her feel as though she found a fresh piece of her heart every time he looked into her eyes.

Her own dragon rose up to meet his, the powerful creatures compelling the lovers forward until Conner's lips descended on her own. The kiss was primal, possessive, and undeniable. A wholeness she had never experienced with Stephen.

Without her noticing, Conner had reassembled the pieces of her shattered heart, his will making her stronger than she had been alone. Air mattered not as the dragon princess lost herself to the kiss, her soul reaching for his as their dragons echoed their possessive cries.

When Conner pulled back, he was breathless, drowning in the sweet taste of her mixed with the lilac flowers she'd used in her bath, which perfumed her skin even days later. "I don't know why my dragon led me to you, Amelia. I don't know why we have been thrown together as we have been. But you must know, I…I've never desired anything as much as I desire you. Nor considered the happiness of another as much as I do yours. Your smile melts my heart, my lady. As does your pain. I want to help you. To be whatever you have need of me to be. I don't understand all of it, other than I am utterly and completely in your power, Princess."

"And I'm in yours," she answered, moving her hand behind his head to draw him down for another kiss.

Raising her in his arms, Conner walked over to the bed and sat down with her in his lap, then extending the kiss before lying down on the bed. Dragging Amelia on top of him, Conner kissed her again, his hands running to her waist to pull her shirt from the band of her slacks.

Shirt tossed aside, Amelia raised herself enough to reach for her lover's slacks. Conner groaned as the uncomfortably tight material was pulled down, exposing him to her vision, and touch.

Amelia shifted aside, enabling her to completely remove his trousers as Conner pulled his shirt above his head, tossing it to the floor beside Amelia's. She returned to her previous position, straddling his hips as Conner belatedly realized she had managed to remove the remainder of her clothing as well.

She did not bother with foreplay, positioning herself above him and sliding down as his hands went to her breasts, brushing his thumbs simultaneously across her nipples. She gasped at his touch, causing him to smile, then groan as she lowered her velvet walls over him. Several times she paused, allowing herself to adjust to the intrusion before lowering herself further as Conner struggled to remain still, wanting to grant her complete control.

Once fully sheathed, both drew ragged breaths. Amelia leaned forward, pressing her hands against his chest to steady herself before setting an easy rhythm, which increased incrementally as the two lovers lost themselves to each other's embrace.

Nearing her peak, Amelia leaned down, and whispered, "It's okay if you want to let the dragon loose."

"What?" The sight of her gorgeous form above him, the weight of her breasts in his hands, and her inner channel wrapped around him, made it difficult to concentrate on anything but the breathtaking sensations.

"Have you ever made love to another shifter?"

Dazed, Conner shook his head. "You're the first."

Amelia nodded, pausing her movements, keeping herself pressed tight against his body. "Your dragon wants this too."

"Amelia, I don't…"

"You won't hurt me, Conner. You must have feared harming non-shifter lovers. I'm not so fragile. Let him play."

"I don't want you to think this is only the dragon. That I don't…"

"You made love to me. You alone. I know how difficult it is to struggle against our other half. You don't have to. Not with me."

Her assurance overrode his last objection, his eyes fully shifting from human to those of his dragon form. Moving his hands from her breasts, Conner grabbed Amelia, flipping her onto her back without removing himself from her. He then lifted Amelia's legs over his shoulders, granting himself deeper access to her tight sheath. A low growl rumbled from his throat, the dragon spilling forth to claim his mate.

Not caring if others heard, his dragon took full control as he slammed into her.

A deep moan escaped at the brutal claiming, Amelia's dragon answering his as her emerald eyes emanated with light, glowing in the dimly lit room.

He delivered a second full stroke, and she called his name, confirming her desires. Giving himself fully to the creature within, Conner thrust in abandonment, the punishing pace driving him to unexpected heights as he forced himself over and over again into the young beauty who gave herself so willingly.

Tension built to the breaking point as he called her name in a deep-throated growl before spilling himself, the rush of warmth coating her insides with a final deep thrust, causing her to cry out, repeating his name over and over between shaking breaths as he collapsed.

Buried inside her, Conner lay, struggling for breath. He had never known anything like this. To give himself so completely, without fear of harming himself or his lover. The act was intoxicating. Exhilarating. He pulled back enough to meet her eyes and she squirmed at the movement.

"I never knew," he stared bewildered. "I never…"

"Nor did I."

"What do you…"

"Not like that," she answered. "Not from someone who connected to my soul. I think I was fated to be with you, Conner."

He leaned down and kissed her, the man replacing the dragon as he confessed through caresses what he could not seem to find the words to express. She responded in kind before he fully withdrew, rolling to his side as he pulled her against him, holding her tight as both drifted to an exhausted sleep.

CHAPTER XLIII

RETURNING TO THE CABIN WHERE Kelsie and Chris waited, Amelia arrived to face them with a heavy heart.

"I apologize," she informed her childhood friend. "I didn't want to believe what you said was true."

"I didn't either," Kelsie replied. "I remember your sister from childhood, Amelia. Believe me when I say, I did not wish to believe she was capable of such cruelty either."

"I'll go to the palace," Amelia said, "but you must understand, I am going to attempt to avoid physical conflict. I want to try speaking with her first."

"I fear, my friend, you will find yourself disappointed. She will not listen to reason."

"That may be," Amelia agreed sadly. "Yet I must try, nevertheless. If I don't, I'll regret not doing so for the rest of my life. I love Kaliyah, no matter what evils she may have allowed to transpire, and despite the crimes she has committed against my person." Amelia drew a breath, exhaling. "For her crimes against me, I can forgive her. However, for those against the people she was meant to protect, there must be a reckoning.

"I will go forthwith to the palace tomorrow. I would go now, but exhaustion might overcome me if I do not rest."

"I understand," Kelsie answered. "I'm sorry, Amelia. Pitting the two of you against each other is the last thing I desired."

"You're not responsible," Amelia said. "Kaliyah is, for forgetting her responsibilities to our people."

"I'm sorry."

"I'll do my best to protect your daughter, Kelsie. You have my word, I shall do all in my power to help her. If I fail though, go to the palace and speak to Sir Gwain. He's a knight in my sister's guard. Tell him I said he would help you. He may be able to succeed, should I fail."

Kelsie reached for the princess, pulling Amelia into a brief embrace. "Thank you, Amelia."

"I should be thanking you, for reminding me of my responsibilities in the realm, and my duty to the people within it. I shall do my best with my sister. I can promise no more."

"Whatever you accomplish, it's enough. I wish I were capable of helping you. Being only human in a dragon's domain, I feel helpless."

"Not helpless," Amelia answered. "Differently gifted."

Amelia allowed Kelsie to draw her into a second embrace before extricating herself and leaving the room.

When she reached the bedroom, she found Conner standing with his mother before the door, the elder woman hugging her son. "I'll always be proud of you," she whispered. "No matter what."

"Thank you, Mother." He pulled back, allowing both himself and Chris to see Amelia, alerted to her presence by her footsteps along the wooden floor.

Chris smiled up at the princess and took her hand. "I am grateful you two found each other," she said. "I've spent his whole life praying Conner would find a woman such as yourself."

"Someone to lead him to his doom in a fight we can't win?"

Chris smiled, shaking her head at Amelia's sarcastic tone. "Someone who could show him not just how to exist in two worlds, but to thrive." Leaning forward, Chris placed a gentle kiss on Amelia's left cheek. "Thank you for showing him the world he was born to, Amelia. I am grateful. Now, get some rest. I'll see you both off in the morning."

With that, Chris headed out the door.

Later, as Amelia lay beside Conner, she whispered, "I would hate to think we've finally found each other, only to be torn apart."

"No matter what happens, I will never leave your side."

His words, meant to assure, instead placed a new flurry of dread in Amelia's heart as she wondered if the promise, spoken with such conviction, was one either of them would be able to keep.

CHAPTER XLIV

IT TOOK FOUR DAYS TO reach the castle grounds, Conner and Amelia abandoning their dragon forms when they reached the kingdom's inner sanctum and opting for a more stealth approach. On purchased horses, staying off the main roads, they traveled without incident, managing to avoid the majority of other travelers. No one questioned them, Amelia's dragon eyes a clear mark of her higher status among a kingdom now divided, between the blessed and unblessed children of Kamar.

Arriving at the palace, Amelia did not reveal her name, nor ask for the queen. Instead, she asked for Gwain.

"Regarding?" the gate's guardian asked.

"Tell him it's regarding Gwen. Give him this." From her inner pocket, she withdrew a rose plucked from a bush near the palace.

The guard appeared puzzled as she handed over the bedraggled flower.

"Careful of the thorns," she cautioned. "Gwain will understand."

The man nodded, turning to deliver the cryptic message while his companion kept an eye on the two travelers.

Ten minutes later, Gwain emerged, a bewildered expression on his face as he met the changed eyes of the princess he had saved years ago.

Struggling to hide his shock, Gwain slowed his approach. "Gwen," he addressed Amelia by his sister's name in an abundance of caution, "what are you doing here?"

"I need to speak with you. I wouldn't have come if I had other options."

Gwain nodded. "I understand. It's all right guys, let them through."

The men stepped aside to let the travelers through the gates.

"Keep the cloak over your face, Gwen. Lest you be mistaken for someone else."

She did as instructed, following him through the courtyard, before entering a spare room in an unused portion of the palace.

"This wing has been unoccupied for quite some time. We should be able to speak in relative safety."

Amelia pushed back the hood, pulling her golden hair from beneath the neck of her cloak as she turned to face the captain.

"What are you doing here, Princess? You swore to never return."

"Yes, I promised. And I know how much you risked helping me escape. Were you punished for doing so?" Her breath caught as she asked, afraid this man, who had already endured so much heartache, may have been subjected to additional pain because of the steps he had taken to save her.

"No," Gwain assured, easing her fears with a smile. "I was not punished, though the queen was, understandably, not happy at your escape. And I've missed Gabriel."

Amelia released the breath she had been holding. "I am glad to know you were not harmed on my account. Your stallion is well, growing lazy in my friend's care, getting too many oats from her nephew."

Gwain nodded. "I'll ask again, Princess. What are you doing here?"

"I had to come. My best friend from childhood, Kelsie, came to see me. Her daughter has been claimed by one of the lords, to be forced to bear his children in hopes they might strengthen his line. I've come to understand these actions are a result of my sister's rule. I'm here to try and reason with her."

"There is no reasoning with your sister." Gwain's frank tone took Amelia aback. "She reigns supreme, and punishes all who question her. If this Kelsie you speak of is the same woman I suspect her to be, trust me, the girl's grandparents have pleaded with the queen to reconsider. The queen hears no one except the bastard at her side."

Amelia's breath caught at the mention of Stephen, causing Gwain to bow his head, contrite. "I apologize, my lady. You loved him, and thought he loved you."

"I understand why you didn't tell me. I doubt I would have believed you if you had."

"I tucked the queen's letter, telling of their involvement, in your bag not to harm you, my lady, but in hopes that once you knew the truth of Stephen's liaison with your sister, it might allow you to one day move on. Not to wonder if he searched for you, or any other scenario where you might have held onto hope of him returning."

Amelia gave a tight smile. "You did what was best."

Gwain nodded.

"I'm trying to do the same. This isn't only about Kelsie's daughter. It's about the entire kingdom. She's directing the enslavement of the very people we are charged to protect."

"She won't hear you, Amelia. She might kill you. Or worse, send you back to the temples, and this time, no one will be able to save you."

"No one is sending Amelia anywhere." Conner stepped forward. "Queen or no."

"Who are you?"

"This is Conner," she told the knight. "He's a grandson of Lord Tyron, from a daughter who was born mortal. He was not."

"Did you bring an army?" Gwain asked.

"I don't need one," Amelia replied. "I only wish to speak with her."

"She will not be open to anything you have to say."

"Then this will be a very bad day…for both of us."

Gwain considered her. "You plan to challenge the queen."

"If I must."

"She's the most powerful dragon I've ever seen. You can't defeat her."

"I hope I don't have to, but that remains to be seen."

Gwain gave a chuckle, a harsh sound that held no trace of laughter. "You're kidding me, right?"

Her blank expression told him she was not.

"You're here on a suicide mission. Why even ask for me?"

"To ensure Kelsie's daughter is returned to her mother, no matter what."

"You have got to be kidding me. I helped you, but what makes you think I'm willing to risk so much for another?"

"Because you're a hero."

Caught off-guard by the answer, Gwain stared at the princess for a long time before shaking his head with a loud sigh. "This is ridiculous. You're going to challenge your sister, while I steal a high lord's intended."

"Not intended, Gwain. Slave. He's not going to marry the girl. He's going to defile her."

"All right. I give up. I'll do my best to save the girl. But if you engage your sister, no one can help you. Not I, nor the man at your side."

"Deliver me to the queen, Gwain. I'll take it from there."

Gwain stepped closer, lowering his voice. "You have a kind soul, my lady. Don't permit your sister to use that kindness to her advantage. Because she will, Amelia. And she'll destroy you."

Amelia took the counsel to heart, allowing the words to fully envelope her before nodding. "I understand, Sir Gwain. And thank you for the warning."

"Allow me to escort you, my lady."

"Certainly, my lord." She gave a tight smile as he formally led her from the room, Conner trailing a few paces behind.

CHAPTER XLV

HEART POUNDING, AMELIA STOOD WITH Conner beside her in the throne room, waiting her sister's entrance.

Not being told why, the queen arrived in a rush, confused by the captain's unusual urgency. "This had better be important," Kaliyah's voice reached Amelia for the first time since her sister had stripped away the only life she had known.

"I assure you, Your Majesty, this is a meeting of utmost importance."

Rounding the corner, the queen was greeted by two hooded figures.

Kaliyah looked at the captain. "What's this about?"

But the captain stepped back, not answering.

Instead the closest figure spoke, "The state of the kingdom, Your Majesty. I fear there is much of which you are unaware."

Stepping closer, the queen narrowed her eyes, attempting to better see the face of the cloaked figure who had spoken. "Of what, *exactly*, am I unaware?"

"The pain of your people," Amelia answered, chest tight at seeing her sister for the first time in so long. The queen was a vision in a deep emerald gown, the velvet material draping her body to form sharp, angled sleeves. The sister who had condemned her, wearing the same face as the one who had comforted her as a child, had held her when their mother died, and had escorted her through numerous moonlit nights, soaring into the skies before she had been old enough to venture on her own.

"Are you going to tell me, or do I have to guess?"

"I am here to address the ways in which your people suffer, under the absolute, and unjust rule of the lords to whom you have granted unlimited power."

The queen turned back to Gwain. "What is this?"

"Enlightenment," Amelia answered for him. "For surely you were unaware of the abuse, and never would have condoned such atrocities had you known."

"Atrocities?"

"Parents condemned to torture and death for attempting to protect their children from unwanted advances. Lovers tortured and murdered for attempting to protect their spouses from the same. Men mutilated for attempting to choose a line of work undesired by their lord. Shifters playing god with the lives of those who are not." Amelia shook her head, the cloak shrouding her identity. "Please, my queen, these acts cannot be an extension of your desires."

Kaliyah sighed. "You speak of non-shifters. Tell me, have you a loved one you wish to save from the newly established order? If so, such a complaint is not one I desire to hear. Those requests are forbidden, and how dare you assume I am unaware of what is taking place in my own kingdom. Of course I'm aware! The non-shifters, who continually taint our bloodline are, at last, being put in their proper place. They have lived under the protection of dragons for too long, ungrateful of the lengths the blessed go through to ensure their safety, and undisturbed livelihood. Why should they not be expected to give something in return?"

"In return? You're talking about murder, rape, enslavement! How can you possibly justify such acts?"

"Justify?" She laughed. "I don't have to *justify* anything. I am the dragon queen. It is my right to do with these people as I see fit. They are less. Little more than property, but for centuries they have acted as our equals. Well, no more.

"Gwain, take these two to the dungeons and—"

"You are not supposed to harm the weak. You're supposed to protect them! Mother would be ashamed of you, Kaliyah."

The queen froze, back straightening. She turned, heels striking the marble floor as she stepped closer.

"Amelia?"

Reaching up, the princess untied the cloak and allowed it to slip from her shoulders.

"You survived." Kaliyah stepped closer, eyes studying her sister's changed form. The unusual eyes, and diamond-shaped textured shadow on her neck. "Or, at least, your dragon did."

"It's me, big sister. Though I'm having trouble recognizing you."

"Hmm," her sister mused, a smile lifting the corner of her lips. "It's not that you don't recognize me, Amelia. You never saw me to begin with."

"You were my sister. You took care of me when I was sick. Played when I was sad. Held my hand when I was scared."

"Ah, yes. You were scared quite often, were you not?" Kaliyah's voice grew cold, her heels again echoed through the room. "Tell me, little sister, are you afraid now?"

"Not of you," Amelia answered. "Only for you."

"Ah. Well, sounds like your first mistake."

"What, by the gods, has gotten into you, Kaliyah? Why did you send me away?"

"You should have been sent away years ago!" she exclaimed. "Children of moonlight are always surrendered to the temples. But Mother would not hear of it! When she died, the temples made arrangements for you to finally be collected. However, I had to wait until I was crowned, lest some heroic fool attempt to challenge in order to save you."

Amelia stared at her sister uncomprehendingly.

"Oh don't act so surprised, Amelia. Mother always loved you above all others."

"Not true. She loved you as well."

Kaliyah scoffed. "Hardly. Mother had little illusion as to what I was, and what I intended to do with this kingdom after she was gone. That's why she called the high lords, to speak with them about seating you on the throne instead."

Amelia's lips parted involuntarily, mind reeling.

The reaction drew a cruel laugh from the sister Amelia no longer recognized. "How tragically beautiful. Here I agreed to send you away, to prevent you from usurping my throne, and all the while, you truly knew nothing of Mother's plans."

"Mother never said anything to me, Kaliyah, I swear. I never would have sought your throne."

"What *are* you doing here, Amelia? Clearly you managed to escape, in spite of my best efforts to ensure that did not come to pass. Why return? You, the only one alive who can contest my claim to the throne?"

"I came to reason with you. To tell you how your people suffer. To help you see."

"See what? How they, at last, grovel in their rightful place. If they are too weak to defend themselves, then they deserved to be slaves."

"You swore to protect them!"

"And protect them, I am. They are safe under the power of their respective lords."

"Kaliyah, what happened to you? Mother would never have—"

"I'm perfectly aware of what Mother believed, as she was aware of my own feelings on the matter. Hence the reason she could not be allowed to dethrone me for one as weak as you."

Amelia gasped, anger and confusion turning to horror. "What are you saying?"

Kaliyah did not answer, merely stared.

"You did not kill our mother." She shook her head. "Kaliyah?"

Her sister held her gaze, and Amelia's fractured heart crumbled. "No," the word escaped, causing Conner to step closer. He reached for her, but she pulled away, moving to her sister in challenge.

"This isn't true! It can't be. You didn't!" Leaning close enough she could feel her sister's breath warm her cheek, she ordered, "Tell me it's not true."

"How strange," Kaliyah observed, "that *you* should end up appearing the monster when you're the most human of all."

"And you?"

"Have always been a dragon. One not to be challenged, nor threatened, especially not by you, or our beloved mother."

The world dimmed as Amelia stared at the woman she no longer knew.

Rage radiated through every bone and, as the two royal sisters stared, their dragons roared.

CHAPTER XLVI

SCALES RIPPED THROUGH FLESH AS the dragons emerged, clothes shredding to fall in scraps along the floor.

"Amelia!" Conner called her name, but his voice was distant, his pleas not understood by the enraged creature within. "Don't let it control you!" Conner reminded as the wings expanded from her back, ripping with a speed that drew a scream of pain.

Beside her, Kaliyah transformed with the same swift ferocity, the sisters moving toward the outer balcony where the transformation would complete.

Once capable, both sisters immediately took to the air, wings spread as Conner again screamed Amelia's name.

"You can't help them now," Gwain said, appearing beside him as they watched the dragons rise. "This is a fight for the throne. No one can stop it now."

"Please," Conner prayed to the woman above, "embrace the dragon. Do not allow it to embrace you."

Above, the dragons circled, twining in an ancient dance for which they knew each step, in spite of never having performed such movements before. Screeches filled the air, causing the men below to cover their ears, more people appearing on balconies to investigate the sound.

"No one interfere!" Gwain warned.

"Our queen's being attacked!" a guard protested.

"Not attacked, challenged by her sister, as is Amelia's right."

At the pronouncement, the crowd fell to silence, all eyes upon the figures flying above, a circle of blue and silver scales.

Kaliyah initiated the first attack, sharp, jagged teeth lunging for Amelia's neck.

Jerking back, Amelia avoided snapping teeth, causing them to close on air alone.

The queen launched again, swiping a curved claw toward the tip of her sister's wing, narrowly missing cutting into the delicate membrane. With a flap of her powerful wings, Amelia rose higher, above her sister's sleek form as Kaliyah flew back in an attempt to remove herself from Amelia's immediate downward trajectory.

Folding her wings, Amelia dove to stop her sister's progress, her claws extending to bite into her sister's back. Kaliyah screamed. Amelia had managed to graze the side of her sister's wing, but the attack did not have the hoped for effect.

The silver dragon roared at the injury, causing those below to shudder at the sound as Kaliyah moved level with her sister's hovering form. The silver dragon rushed forward, claws extended. The massive creatures collided, claws locked as they spun, the weight of their bodies sending both in large circles across the otherwise clear sky.

Coming out of the spin, both dragons wheeled to again face each other, screeching their anger in a powerful display for dominance.

Amelia flew forward, tucking back her wings to increase speed as she again attempted to land on her sister's back. This time, her sister was too slow, allowing Amelia's claws to cut through the flesh.

Kaliyah roared, snapping teeth in her sister's direction, she managed to bite down into Amelia's shoulder, though not in her actual wing. Amelia screeched from the pain, Kaliyah's razor teeth biting into muscle.

The two dragons drew back, rage threatening to overwhelm all when Amelia heard a shout. Glancing down, the people appeared miniature from this height, as though figures in a painted dollhouse. Yet her dragon eyes found the source of the sound on the uppermost balcony.

Conner, the name slid through her mind, restoring her to a sense of self. She turned back to her sister, but the distraction had cost her as bright yellow flames filled the sky. Amelia managed to rise high enough to avoid direct contact, but the heat from her sister's nearly lethal attack seared her scaled flesh.

While normal flames were incapable of harming the winged beasts of the skies, the flames of a royal dragon were a different matter entirely.

She turned, facing her sister in time to witness her drawing another breath, a shower of golden flames rushing toward her.

This time, Amelia did not move, instead issuing a blast of her own internal heat, blue flames streaking forth to meet gold as those below watched in terrified fascination at their display of power.

The dragons fought, their fire coloring the sky with bands of flame and smoke. With a great beat of her powerful wings, Kaliyah surged higher. Amelia rushed to follow, but a spray of golden shards prevented her counter attack. The sparks charred the thick hide of her back, drawing a roar of pain.

Reversing direction, Amelia attempted to distance herself from her sister, but Kaliyah followed, maintaining the advantage of her higher position, again raining a stream of flames upon her retreat. This time Amelia avoided the intended attack, the tips of her wings narrowly escaping the burning slivers.

When the stream ended, Amelia took a chance, racing higher in the sky as quickly as she could. Two rapid flaps of her wings lifted her first equal with, and then above the silver dragon, before coming down on her opposite side. Her claws tore into Kaliyah's back and shoulder as Amelia flew past.

Kaliyah screeched, twisting to face her sister, but her movements were slowed by the injury. Amelia again rose higher, shifting left as another streak of golden light flashed toward her, heat from the inferno warming her as she narrowly managed to avoid the flames. Golden streams followed her movements as Amelia dodged attacks, before she managed to turn and release blue light against the gold.

When the intertwined streaks vanished, Kaliyah shifted to turn, but her body jerked as she moved her shoulder, attempting the flap the wing it controlled. Seizing her chance, Amelia dove toward her sister.

Her claws sank into Kaliyah's wings. Amelia watched the silver hide tear and, unable to support her winged form, the dragon queen fell from the sky.

CHAPTER XLVII

AMELIA PLUNGED AFTER HER SISTER'S falling form, the scream of her human heart overpowering the dragon's unholy screech. She chased her sister, Kaliyah's remaining wing flapping frantically, finding only marginal success. No longer trying to wound, but to save, Amelia grabbed her sister's back, intending to slow her fall.

Her sister's dragon screamed at the contact, twisting her neck in an attempt to bite her would-be rescuer, the woman within seemingly unable to understand Amelia's intent to save her life.

In spite of this, Amelia fought hard against their fall, managing to slow the descent, but not enough to avoid hard contact with the ground, both rolling painfully as they crashed. Stunned, both dragons lay on the ground, unable to rise.

Amelia managed to turn first, regaining her footing. One of her legs produced a sharp pain when she attempted to stand, but thankfully her wings were uninjured. Glancing at her sister, she watched the silver dragon struggle to her own feet, and hoped she had come to her senses.

But the silver dragon snarled in continued defiance. By instinct, Amelia opened her wings, rising from the ground before Kaliyah lunged, teeth snapping where Amelia had been moments before. Moving higher, out of reach, Amelia called to her sister, hoping in vain her dragon's quiet voice could reach her.

Instead Kaliyah jumped, snapping at the air. A vicious beast who knew nothing of reason. Only rage.

You're defeated, she called wordlessly to the silver dragon, knowing she could be heard, though Kaliyah was lost within her dragon's rage. *I banish you from these lands, Kaliyah. When you find yourself again, you'll understand. I'm sorry, Kaliyah. This is the last thing I ever wanted.*

Amelia rose back toward the palace. Her heart cried with every beat of her massive wings, yet her dragon eyes were incapable of forming tears.

When she reached the balcony, she landed on the ancient, cracked stone, Conner running to her as those gathered looked on in awe.

Closing her eyes, Amelia called forth her human half, and her wings immediately began to recede into her back while pale skin returned with the familiar, itching discomfort.

Transformation complete, Amelia nearly fell on her injured leg, prompting Conner to catch her before draping his cloak around her shoulders to cover her exposed form.

Shakily, she swept her gaze over the crowd. "Lord Tyron?" She searched for the high-ranking lord, hoping he would be among those gathered.

"Your Highness," a voice replied, the crowd splitting to allow an older gentleman to step forward. Garbed in a crisp silver shirt that matched his gray eyes, under a matching silk robe of state, the lord stood regally attired.

"You saw the fight. Make the pronouncement. Now."

Knowing the elder man's authority would be respected, Amelia waited while he composed himself and turned to address the crowd.

"My lords and ladies, the right to challenge for the crown, which can be issued by other members of royal blood, has on this day, been accepted, through the actions of our queen, and all those here who bore witness. Therefore, it is my duty to inform you all that Amelia is the victor of this most sacred of challenges, and stands before you now as the new queen of this kingdom."

Noting her struggle to remain upright, Conner moved an arm around the new queen, allowing her to lean against him to avoid showing her level of physical agony.

"Amelia, we must see to your leg," Conner whispered. "You're losing blood."

"Not yet."

"There's time for this later."

"No." She shook her head. "If I don't do this now, people will suffer. For every minute of delay."

Conner hesitated briefly, then nodded. "Do as you must."

"Lord Tyron," she again addressed the elder man, "this is Conner Brion Ardarg, son of your daughter, Christina."

"Christina?" Tyron's eyes widened. "Forgive me, I did not know—"

"What you did, or did not know, is irrelevant. However, what you are about to learn matters a great deal."

"My lady?"

"This is your single opportunity to claim your grandson, and restore him to the titles and birthright owed to one of your family, for I intend to name him my consort. I'm willing to do so without your agreement. However, given

190

your family's noble lineage, and connection to the crown, I assume legitimizing the one who will be consort to the new queen would be advantageous to your family."

Bewildered, but masking gracefully, Lord Tyron bowed toward Conner, whose arm was wrapped protectively around the new queen. "Consider it done, Your Highness. Conner, I look forward to getting to know you properly."

Conner nodded in acknowledgment, understanding this establishment of hierarchy was more important than the trespasses the man had committed against his mother. At least, for now.

Glancing at the crowd, Amelia was utterly exhausted, blood continuing to pour from her injured leg. "Can you dismiss them, or…" She looked again to Tyron for help, her weary expression imploring. After proclaiming a member of his family would be by her side, even a boy he had never met, she could trust him in a limited fashion.

"Let the queen pass," he ordered. "She shall address you all tomorrow with a formal explanation."

Voices rose, confused and bewildered, but Tyron held up his hands, his commanding presence bringing the crowd to silence.

"All shall be explained shortly. You have my word, and that of your new queen."

Assisting her from the balcony, Conner supported Amelia through the crowd, and down the walkway, to the room her sister had occupied an hour before. Opening the doors ahead of them, Tyron motioned for Conner to walk her through.

"Put her on the bed," Tyron ordered. "I'll call for a healer."

A few minutes later, Tyron returned with a comely woman in tow.

As she set to the task of bandaging Amelia's leg, Amelia lay still, wincing occasionally as stinging ointments were applied to the wound.

"Lord Tyron," she addressed the older man, "we don't know each other well, nothing beyond casual meetings during my sister's coronation many years ago. However, you were among my mother's trusted advisors. Whatever your faults may have been relative to the treatment of your daughter, which I am content to set aside for now, if you are willing to assist me. I—"

She hissed as the healer began binding her leg.

"I would appreciate your assistance in some immediate matters."

"What matters are those, Your Highness?"

"First, I will not lie. My sister is alive. Ancient tradition dictates one dragon should kill the other, but she's my sister…no matter what she's done."

"Family is important, my lady, even when we sometimes treat each other in an abhorrent manner."

"You understand."

"Explicitly, my lady."

191

"Thank you," she said with genuine gratitude. "Please issue a proclamation, rescinding my sister's orders that nobles may do as they wish with non-shifters. I want their protected status restored immediately, beginning with sending healers through each village in an attempt to save the lives of those recently condemned to death by exposure, or any other means which leaves them languishing in pain. I want these dispatches sent immediately."

"As you wish, my lady. Though it will likely upset a great number of the lords."

Amelia nodded. "So noted. The high lord of every province is to be called to the palace. I wish to address them all at once. Together we will right the wrongs committed in this land.

"Also, locate the daughter of my friend, Kelsie. Conner will help you find and identify her."

Lord Tyron nodded. "Is there anything else for which I might be able to provide immediate attention?"

"Yes, one other." She paused. "I wish to speak to the high priestess on a private matter of great importance. Please send for her at once."

Tyron bowed, before turning to carry out Amelia's orders, but paused at a commotion on the other side of the doors. Struggling to the bed's edge, the new queen forced her bandaged leg down, wincing as she rose, keeping as much of her weight as possible on the uninjured one.

"My lady, you ought to stay off the leg," the healer warned.

She ignored her, using a hand on the bed to transfer her weight to her arm. The voices grew in volume, though their words remained indistinguishable as Conner stepped closer to the threshold.

"Open the door," Amelia directed, watching as Tyron moved to follow her orders.

But before he could get there, the door flew ajar, and Stephen emerged. She stared blankly, disarmed by the sight of her former lover, appearing regal in a golden shirt that matched his captivating eyes.

Conner attempted to step between the newcomer and Amelia, but Tyron shook his head, a subtle signal to wait for her command. Reluctantly, Conner drew back, deferring to the elder lord, and permitting Stephen a clear view of the new queen.

"It's true," Stephen exclaimed as he progressed toward the bed.

Bewildered, Amelia stared at the man who had once held her heart. She attempted to speak, but coherent words refused to form. At her wide-eyed expression, Stephen moved closer, opening his arms to embrace her.

Amelia jerked back, falling on the bed as a startled cry escaped her lips.

The distressed sound prompted Conner to leap forward, wrenching Stephen across the room.

Unprepared for Conner's protective reaction, Stephen glared at the unfamiliar man before turning back to the queen.

"What is this, Amelia? I find, after all these years, that you're alive, and you run from me as though a stranger?"

"Not a stranger," Amelia found her voice as she again rose. "A liar. A thief!"

"Thief?"

"You stole my heart, and betrayed it. You said you loved me. You didn't. What does that make you, Stephen, if not guilty of both charges?"

"What?" Stephen shook his head. "Amelia, you vanished! I spent months, no—years—searching."

Amelia met his expressive golden eyes. *Could it be true?* "You searched for me?"

"I did."

"And the day they took me away?"

"I wasn't here. Your sister sent me from the palace on business. Said she'd let you know where I was going. By the time I returned, you were gone."

His claims rolled through Amelia's mind. While she grappled for a response, her gaze traveled the room. She avoided Conner's eyes, but paused as she met those of Lord Tyron. Staring intently, Tryon gave a shake of his head so slight she would have missed the motion had she been less focused. His stern expression, along with the insight, centered her.

"Tell me, Stephen—and do not lie, for if nothing else, on this the truth is owed—how much time did you spend searching before falling into my sister's bed?"

Stephen drew a breath. "She was the queen, Amelia. She had the right to choose her consort."

"How long did you mourn my loss, Stephen, before deciding to bed your new sovereign? My own sister!" Anger strengthened her resolve, and she straightened as much as she could with the injured leg.

"I didn't have a choice, Amelia. Any more than you had a choice in going to the temples."

"But I did not go to the temples. I refused her command. My love for you prompted me to fight for my freedom."

Stephen moved closer, and this time Conner allowed it. "Amelia, had I known you were alive..."

"Kelsie found me. Too easily for comfort, in fact. How is it, Stephen, that a non-shifter with no resources uncovered my whereabouts, when you, a dragon shifter named consort to the queen, with all the kingdom's authority at your disposal, was unable?"

"Amelia, I swear—"

"You stood by my sister's side while she enslaved her own people—your people. While her edicts terrorized the provinces."

"I advised against her actions," Stephen defended.

"Yet did nothing when she continued."

"What should I have done, Amelia? No one was permitted to challenge her, except you."

"You should have done your duty to the realm. You should have helped them."

"Such acts were the queen's decree, not mine."

"I *never* would have stood by and allowed such atrocities to take place. You should have left her."

"What good would that have done? The orders were issued, with or without my approval."

"You could have searched for me. You could have argued with the council against her proclamations."

"I tried—"

"Never," Tyron's voice cut through Stephen's protests. "And when those on the council did offer objections, Stephen advised the queen to imprison all who dared to question her actions."

Stephen glared at the elder lord before returning his eyes to her. "Tell me, Amelia, who are you going to believe. A man you know nothing of, or the one who holds your heart?"

After an uncomfortably long pause, Amelia answered harshly, "You don't hold my heart. You broke it into so many pieces, the fragments slipped right through your deceptive fingers."

Only then did Stephen fully acknowledge Conner, standing to the right of Amelia, close enough to step between them if required. Stephen's voice took on a low, grumbling tone, his dragon saturating his words with an implied threat of violence. "Let me guess," he drew the word into a hiss, "this stranger was kind enough to reassemble the pieces?"

"No." Amelia drew a breath, shaking her head. "I slowly repaired it, piece by piece, and once finished, I chose to give my heart to one who proved far more worthy than you ever were."

A deep growl emanated from Stephen's throat as he stared at Conner.

"Eyes on me, Stephen," Amelia ordered, her voice deepened to match his, her dragon shining through elongated pupils. A light blue tinge came to her permanently imprinted scales. "I am banishing you, from this court, and my sight."

"Banishing?" He gave a gruff laugh. "What makes you think you have the power to do so?"

Her dragon roared at the challenge, but she focused, cautioning the beast to patience. "You are a dragon of Kalleen, and I am your queen. You will obey, or my dragon will incinerate the heart in your chest, before it stops beating."

Amelia's eyes glowed brighter, the threat not an expression of anger, or loss of control, but a lethal pronouncement of truth.

Stephen's beast receded, surrendering to the ancient power of the royal flame. He stepped back, lowering himself into a submissive bow, remaining in this position until Tyron called for guards to escort him from the palace.

Once Stephen was removed, Amelia collapsed to the bed. The healer came forth, enough blood having spilled she had to redress the injured leg.

Fresh bandages in place, the healer offered a low bow, winked, and left the room. Lord Tyron followed her out the doorway.

Adrenaline fading to new awareness, Amelia faced her love. "I'm sorry, Conner. I..."

"No need to apologize. I'm aware he hurt you."

Amelia nodded, grateful for his understanding. "Because I loved him once, I couldn't order him harmed, though he deserves to be."

"Banishment will be punishment enough for one such as he."

A shudder ran through Amelia, then another. "And my sister..." Amelia struggled with unsteady words. "She killed our mother. But, Kaliyah..."

"Is your sister," Conner repeated.

"I loved her. I didn't want to harm her."

"You did what was required, to defend your kingdom, and life, Amelia. Even in your anger, you controlled the dragon enough to spare her life."

"I heard you. I don't know how. What you said about not letting the dragon embrace me. I heard."

Conner nodded, pulling her to him. "It's all right, my lady. You didn't kill her, though the dragon would have had you do so. You should be proud of how you stood up for your people."

"It all feels so wrong."

"I'm sorry, my lady."

"Will you hold me?"

"Every night," he answered. "For as long as you'll have me."

CHAPTER XLVIII

1 MONTH LATER

AMELIA STOOD ON THE BALCONY. The transition over the past weeks had been a difficult one, with many high-ranking lords unhappy to find their absolute power roughly revoked. Scattered reports had come in describing continued ill behavior of certain lords, but Amelia was quick to intervene, often dispatching the palace guard to reinforce the safety of all her people, including the non-shifters.

The most problematic obstacle was proving to be the temples, who had defended their right to continue taking young girls as they saw fit. So far, the priestesses were the one entity Amelia had been unable to move to compassion, nor control with outright strength.

However, today was different. A tiny victory, which she achieved after much negotiation with high lords and the temples alike. Though many believed she risked a great price for what they considered to be an insignificant prize.

Enjoying the cool breeze of the familiar ice-tipped mountains, Amelia's heart silently called to Conner, who had embarked upon a short trip back to the northern mountains. Along with retrieving Gabriel, he would bring his mother back to the palace with him, to become an advisor to the new queen.

While unprecedented to have a non-shifter on the dragon queen's council, Amelia had argued it to be appropriate, given not only her implicit trust of Christina, but also the benefit of allowing non-shifters a voice, the consequences of this absence demonstrated by her sister's unchecked actions.

Noting Gwain's approach, Amelia smiled at the man she had recently named her personal captain and advisor. A promotion he had accepted graciously.

"You requested to see me?"

"I did." She drew a breath. "I have a gift for you, my lord. Though one that may be difficult to receive."

Shifting his shoulders in an act of uncertainty, Gwain glanced at the young queen, a multitude of possibilities spinning in his mind. "What is it, Your Majesty?"

"Come with me."

Traveling along a series of hallways, Amelia led Gwain to the castle's east wing, and a door where two guardsmen stood. At the sight of their queen, both men stepped aside.

Amelia opened the door to the chamber, crossing the threshold with Gwain beside her. Inside sat two elderly women, speaking quietly.

Turning to face her friend and knight, Amelia inhaled sharply. "It took time to find her, my lord, and even more time to convince the priestess to surrender her to the crown. But…"

Gwain's eyes slid past Amelia to the bed. There lay a girl who, even in her unconscious state, could be mistaken for none other. Quickly stepping across the room, Gwain fell to his knees beside the bed, shaking as he reached a hand to brush a stray strand of golden hair from the side of her face.

"Gwen," he spoke softly. "Oh gods, Gwen." Up close, her hollow, pale cheeks, and the dark circles under her eyes, broke his heart anew. And she was so small, as tiny as she'd been the last time he'd seen her.

"She's in bad shape," Amelia spoke solemnly. "I'm afraid the temples have kept her in this state for quite some time. I don't know if we can, or what it will take to free her mind from whatever prison they have created. I'm sorry. I…"

"You found her." He turned, tears falling from his eyes, voice shaking. "You found my sister. Oh my gods."

"You risked your life to save me," Amelia answered. "It's the least I could do."

"Gwen. Gwen, it's me. Your brother. Listen to me. I'm going to take care of you. Do you hear me? I'm going to take care of you, little sister. I promise."

He spoke his next words for the queen, but did not remove his eyes from Gwen's still form. "Thank you, Amelia. I'll find a way to help her. Do you hear me, Gwen? It's Gwain. It's your brother." He reached out and clasped her hand in his. "You're safe now, little sister. You're safe."

CHAPTER XLIX

TO THE NORTH, CONNER VENTURED into the coldest part of the Kalleen Mountains, to a place so barren and frigid the land was all but uninhabitable. Yet for a dragon, the cold was a minor annoyance.

Over the mountain peaks, Conner flew, maneuvering through icy winds until he spied the deep cave. He knew the location by heart, even when sight failed, the enclosure hidden by thick blankets of snow.

Diving down between the flurries, Conner landed, stepping into the cave before allowing the transformation to take place, shifting back to his human form. Walking to the cave's side, he rummaged through a pile of clothes kept there for such an occasion, pulling on a pair of gray pants and a deep green sweater, before venturing farther in.

Carved long ago by shifters, the massive structure could easily hold multiple fully transformed dragons, the ceiling towering over Conner's head as he trudged past stone walls into the cave's inner sanctum.

Rounding a wide corner to enter a second chamber, Conner spied the dragon he sought.

Hovering in the air on feathery wings, the deep purple beast was immune to even the coldest of winter nights. Glowing embers burned within the wings, like the hot coals of a forge, lighted within the plumes, yet visible from the outside. Two wings extend into additional curved claws, while its hooved feet pawed the air.

At Conner's approach, the creature tucked its wings, hooves clattering to the ground as it landed. A shudder began at its snout, traveled down its back, to finally reach the wings and tail. As its feathered wings slid back, the creature's neck shrunk, and the dragon's facial features took on a more human appearance.

But the transformation didn't complete. Silver eyes maintained their reptilian shape, elongated pupils refusing to change form. Hard, purple scales remained embedded in the skin on the left side of his neck and shoulders, down the arm, and lining the man's nose.

Glancing at the man's half-formed features, Conner stepped closer to meet his slate gaze.

More beast than human, the man who had long ago lost his ability to fully transform directed his attention to Conner's lilac eyes.

"Hello, brother."

BONUS MATERIAL

The story will continue in...

RELEASING THE DRAGON

Expected 2018

Read on for a preview.

CHAPTER I

PRESENT AGE

ACROSS THE ICE-TIPPED MOUNTAINS, a lone dragon flew. The rhythmic beat of her wings the only disturbance to the silent night, shadows rippling over the barren land until she reached the sought valley.

Upon landing, talons sinking into soft dirt, the creature twisted her slender neck, gazing at the recently full moon through emerald eyes. Nostrils flaring, enjoying the frigid air against heated flesh, the dragon walked through the valley undisturbed, basking in a rare moment of solitude, far from the troubles her other half would be forced to face once the creature surrendered control.

When she reached the forest's edge, the dragon paused, moving to a large pond for a drink of cold water, further soothing her internal flames.

As she rested between the water and tree line, the creature again looked to the sky. Having flown most of the night, dawn was soon to come and she selfishly wanted to enjoy the first splash of the sun's rays before embarking upon the return journey.

Dawn's hour flew by, chittering birds and scampering small wildlife providing nature's accompaniment to the growing rays of light. Lying quietly so as not to startle this valley's furry inhabitants, the dragon moved only her eyes as the sky flickered with various colors, from deep blues with hints of purple, to lighter pinks, splashes of orange, and streaks in various shades of red and yellow. When the sun eventually crept over the mountain, the dragon suppressed the urge to release a bellowing roar, mindful again of not wanting to frighten nearby animals.

As the sun fully ascended, the dragon closed her eyes, enjoying the warmth with the same pleasure as she had welcomed the previous cold. With a satisfied sigh, she moved to the water, again partaking of the refreshing liquid, and the resulting ripple disrupted the reflection of blue scales framing jeweled eyes.

As the dragon quenched her thirst, a shadow fell over her form, dimming the sunlight. Presuming it merely a stray cloud, the dragon was unprepared when an ear-splitting screech filled the air.

Turning with a spray of unswallowed water, she found an immense beast above her. Holding an ebony body aloft, deep purple wings, with a feathered appearance, glowed with visible golden flames, though they did not burn. It had hooved back feet, but its front arms were clawed, similar to a bird, with talons protruding from the outer tips.

The menacing creature glared down upon the grounded dragon, silver eyes glinting as its nostrils framed fire within. Each methodical beat of its wings caused the prey's heart to leap, as the normally stoic creature tasted a very human fear.

Rushing backward, into the shallow pool, the grounded dragon attempted to avoid the inevitable, all the while knowing there would be no escape.

The purple dragon's jaws opened, flames spilling to engulf the creature below before she could utter a single scream.

Amelia awoke with the shriek her dragon had been unable to complete. Body trembling upon the expansive bed, she clutched the sheet against her chest, pressing the edge to her lips to suppress her fear.

It had been the same dream, yet...not. She had never experienced the dream in her dragon form before.

What does it mean?

Before she had always watched the dragon from afar, frozen and unable to move. Unable to help. This time she had attempted to run, but suffered the same fate despite her efforts.

Knowing she'd not return to slumber after the recurring nightmare, Amelia rose and pulled a warm cloak over her gown before stepping into a pair of slippers. Not wanting to disturb the servants at such a late hour, she'd fetch herself a goblet of wine.

Walking down a series of hallways she had wandered since birth, her blood ran cold at the sound of a high-pitched scream. Freezing, she waited until a second shriek shattered the cold air. Heart pounding, she rushed down various corridors, fearing the worst, a foreboding which only increased as the sounds led her to a familiar door.

"Gwain!" she called, announcing her presence as she opened the door without waiting for an invitation.

"My lady," the knight answered. "I'm sorry, she's having a bad night. I've called for a healer to give her a calming tonic, but she has not yet arrived. I'm trying to calm her, but..." The normally capable knight appeared utterly helpless.

Amelia's eyes took in the sight of his sister writhing on the bed, screaming gibberish between incoherent shrieks. She stepped forward, speaking softly, "Gwen, you're safe."

At the sound of Amelia's voice, Gwen's eyes opened, her eyes meeting her queen's with abrupt clarity. "Cerulean," the girl whispered, "burns."

Gwain stepped back, allowing the queen to reach his sister.

"What do you mean?" Amelia asked gently.

"Burns," she repeated. Gwen's head tilted, enabling her to view both captain and queen. "They come."

"Who?"

"Amethystine," she answered, and Amelia's blood ran cold. "Amethystine comes. The Cerulean will burn."

The girl's eyes widened, seeing horrors beyond other's sight. "No," she whimpered, the pathetic sound pulling at Amelia's heart.

"Gwen," Gwain's voice echoed Amelia's helplessness as he pushed past the queen and grasped his sister's hand.

She shrank from his touch.

Watching the scene, Amelia's dragon stirred unexpectedly, but unlike her normally rough emergence, she arose gently, more of a request than a demand. At its unspoken prompting, Amelia took a knee beside the bed, and reached for the same hand Gwain had attempted to grasp. The distraught girl flinched, but did not push Amelia away.

The royal dragon pushed her way to the surface of Amelia's mind, the permanent etching in her skin transforming to pale blue as her emerald pupils took on an increasingly florescent light, becoming green flames in the darkness.

"My lady," Gwain said in alarm.

"She means no harm," Amelia spoke of her dragon half with unexpected certainty, motioning him to silence. "I promise."

Meeting the young girl's eyes, Amelia reached out her other hand and pressed her blue fingers gently against Gwen's cheek. "A dream," she soothed in tones deeper than her normal voice. "It can't harm you, Guinevere."

The royal dragon's strong, confident tones reached her on a level where human attempts had failed. Amelia studied her, appeasing her dragon by allowing the creature freedom to guide her actions.

"Safe," the dragon spoke through her twisted voice. "Safe."

Gwen's eyes narrowed, her pupils constricting and elongating, forming a familiar diamond shape with a silver gleam that masked all hints of color. In shock, Amelia leaned forward to better view the transformation. But no sooner had it begun, the mutation vanished, the child's eyes retreating to the same rounded lavender they had always been.

Amelia turned to Gwain, her dragon receding as swiftly as the apparition. "Did you see that?"

"You reassured her," he said. "Thank you."

Amelia turned back, intending to study the girl's eyes, but they were closed. Her breathing had calmed to the gentle rhythm of a dreamless sleep.

"Thank you," Gwain said again.

"No need. Your sister is not the only one who awoke from troubled dreams this night."

"What?"

Amelia shook her head, and stood, returning her gaze to the knight, the deep circles under his eyes visible even in the dim light. "Nothing to worry about right now. Why don't you get some rest? I'll sit with her."

"Her words, I don't understand them. I don't know how to help her."

"The mumbling of nightmares. And even if it were more, you are in no condition to solve this mystery tonight. You're no good to anyone this exhausted."

Gwain hesitated, as though he considered arguing, then thought better of it, instead asking, "Are you certain you wish to stay with her yourself, Your Majesty? I would be happy to have one of my fellow knights—"

"You have done the same for me, many times over." She offered a bittersweet smile. "If not for you, I would share your sister's fate. 'Tis the least I can do."

After a brief bow, he walked toward the door, pausing at the threshold. "It goes without saying—"

"I'll call you, if needed."

Amelia watched him leave, standing until the heavy thud of his boots faded before sinking into a plush chair.

Pressing a palm to her forehead, Amelia closed her eyes, allowing the girl's prophetic words to replay against the backdrop of her nightmare.

Amethystine comes. The Cerulean will burn.

THE DRAGONS

DRAGON OF KALLEEN

AMETHYSTINE DRAGON

©2018 RAVEN QUINN

AN INTERVIEW WITH
K.L. BONE AND RAVEN QUINN

Over the past few years, I have been thrilled to work with incredibly talented illustrator, Raven Quinn. We met years ago over a fun-filled Halloween weekend, when we were both invited to New Orleans by bestselling author Anne Rice for the Vampire Lestat Fan Club Ball. The event, now in its thirtieth year, is a celebration of not only my favorite vampire and the author who created him, but of friendship, as friends both new and old gather to celebrate and enjoy the city of New Orleans.

In 2014, I had the added privilege of meeting Raven, when we were placed on an author panel together. Introduced by Becket, Rice's long-time personal assistant and a bestselling author in his own right, I had fallen in love with Raven's work after seeing her drawings in Becket's YA series, *Key the Steampunk Vampire Girl*. In addition, she is also an incredible singer and songwriter, with several albums including a self-titled one and her most recent release, *Not in Vain*.

After meeting Raven and spending several days getting to know each other, I inquired if she would consider drawing a map for my fantasy series, *Rise of the Temple Gods*. In response, Raven informed me she had never drawn a map before. I asked if she would like to try. Three maps and two dragons later, I gained more from that fated trip to New Orleans than I had dared hope. I gained an illustrator, wonderful memories, and an incredible friendship.

Now, I am happy to announce Raven has agreed to speak about her art and creative process in this joint interview, in hopes of giving readers a brief insight into our creative worlds.

— K.L. Bone

INTERVIEW QUESTIONS

Tell us a little about yourself.

RAVEN: I am a singer/songwriter and a recording artist, as well as a fantasy illustrator for several bestselling children's/YA books. My music is a blend of rock/hard rock/alternative rock/and alternative pop. I've released two full length studio albums (my self-titled debut album, *Raven Quinn,* and my sophomore album, *Not in Vain*) and an all-acoustic album entitled *The Acoustic*

EP. Currently, I'm working on my third studio album entitled *Alchemy* with Juno award-winning producer Dan Brodbeck (Dolores O'Riordan, Landon Pigg.)

I've been writing and recording music since my teens—but have been singing, performing, and drawing since my very early childhood. Some of the prouder moments in my music career include having the number one fastest selling album on Amazon (number one on the Movers and Shakers chart, as well as holding top ten positions in all albums, and in the rock and pop charts), being included on the official Grammy Awards Ballot across several categories including Album of the Year, and having three of my songs included in the Rock Band videogame series via their Rock Band Network store.

As for my illustrations - I've been drawing since I was old enough to hold a crayon, but it was actually through my music that my drawings found an audience. Having developed a following on social media after releasing my first album, I began posting some of my drawings for fun. Eventually, I was contacted by bestselling author Becket (also long-time personal assistant to Anne Rice). He had listened to my music online, which lead him to browsing through my artwork on my website. Serendipitously, my artistic style happened to be exactly what he had envisioned for a forthcoming children's series he was working on! It was shortly thereafter that he offered me my very first book illustration job, and I became the illustrator for his entire Steampunk Sorcery Series of children's novels.

I will forever be grateful to Becket for believing I could illustrate books, and for his amazing friendship and support over the years. Since working on the Steampunk Sorcery series, I've had the opportunity to work with several other incredible authors (who also became wonderful friends!) including K.L. Bone, Sarah M. Cradit, and Alys Arden.

In my personal life, I'm a huge rock music fan and I love going to concerts. I'm also an animal lover (my better half and I have four dogs, two lizards, a cat, a rabbit, and a bird!), a bookworm, a gamer (primarily World of Warcraft), and a homebody who loves to spend time with my family and friends.

K.L.: I am a bestselling author of paranormal romance and dark fantasy. I currently have 3 stories available in the Rise of the Temple Gods series, 6 in the Black Rose series, and several novellas. I spent five years living in England and Ireland where I have been studying with the hope of obtaining a PhD in Creative Writing.

I love to travel! I've been to many countries in Europe, such as England, France, Greece, Romania, and the Czech Republic, just to name a few and recently traveled to Australia and New Zealand. I am also a great lover of all things gothic, having earned my MA in English by writing a dissertation of the evolution of the American vampire, focusing on the works of Anne Rice.

I also have two cats, Mojave Leia and Guinevere, who love to keep me company as I write. I am also a Star Wars girl.

Are there any artists, styles, or genres which influence your style of art?

RAVEN: Absolutely. As far as my illustration work goes, I've long been inspired by the works of Arthur Rackham, Brian Froud, Trina Schart Hyman, and Dirk Zimmer. I've always been fascinated with fairytales and fantasy— whether it be books or films. The movies *Labyrinth* and *The Dark Crystal* captured my imagination as a very small child, and have arguably influenced and inspired me more deeply artistically than anything else.

Musically, I love many genres—but my heart will always belong to rock (particularly of the nineties alternative variety.) My favorite bands/artists are Garbage, David Bowie, The Smashing Pumpkins, Poe, The Cranberries, Nine Inch Nails, and most recently Ghost.

K.L.: I love epic fantasy, specially the work of J.R.R. Tolkien. I also love Gothic texts such as *Wuthering Heights* by Emily Brontë, Bram Stoker's *Dracula*, John Milton's *Paradise Lost*, and Anne Rice's *Vampire Chronicles*.

My dark fantasy series, *Black Rose*, was specifically influenced by the legend of Tristan and Isolde. This arthurian tragedy of an Irish Princess and a knight of Cornwall, destined to become star-crossed lovers, had a strong impact on my writing for my own dark fantasy series. The first time I heard a version of the tale, the narrator spoke of the death of these lovers, and from their graves came a vine and a rose. No matter how many times these were cut back, they would always return, intwining the lovers' graves. This story stayed with me, providing the influence to the enchanted roses found in the black rose world.

As for the *Flames of Kallen* series, I had always wanted to write a dragon book. From *The Hobbit* to *Game of Thrones* to the film *Dragonheart*, I have been in love with these mythical creatures and am very excited to be able to write my own story featuring these magnificent myths.

What is your creative process when bringing characters or worlds to life?

RAVEN: My process (if you can call it that) is very organic. I always like to begin by having a verbal conversation with the author I'm working with, so that we can discuss what they're hoping to see in the finished product and so

I can bounce some of my initial ideas off of them. I also ask for a document that outlines their wishes after we've spoken, so I can refer back to it as I work. I will often ask follow-up questions to fill in any blanks.

Once I have those specifics in hand, I set up my materials (pencils, pens, water color pencils, and sometimes markers), light a candle, put on some favorite music or an inspiring movie, clear my mind, and I just start to sketch. Every so often, I'll look down and realize that I don't love the direction I'm heading and I'll start again—but most of the time, what begins to form on the page intuitively is what I like to keep. Once my pencil sketch is complete, I'll send a photo of the sketch to the author for approval (at this stage they can still ask for changes). After the author has approved the pencil sketch, I begin the ink and color phases.

You have depicted worlds based on both fantasy lands and real locations. Which do you prefer and why?

RAVEN: I ALWAYS prefer fantasy, because it opens up countless options for artistic interpretation. When I am illustrating something that only exists in the mind, I am free to interpret that image in whichever way I am most inspired to. Having that freedom to roam within my own imagination is one of my favorite feelings in life.

K.L.: I personally tend to prefer worlds of pure fantasy, as I can build them from the ground up. I love crafting magical castles, describing lands which exist only in my mind, and designing my own rules for the different societies I create. In Flames of Kallen, I particularly enjoyed getting to consider how a land ruled by dragons should appear, from the society to the icy mountains upon which they thrive.

I also strongly prefer writing in medieval lands, when kings won what a sword could win, or in the case of Kalleen, a fire-breathing dragon could win. I enjoy crafting scenes involving swords particularly and investigating aspects such as what clothing people would have worn, what they would have eaten, or how they might have lived, in a medieval era.

In your point of view, what should writers consider when commissioning an artist?

RAVEN: Hmmn. I think the main thing to consider would be artistic style. What do you want to see? Be aware of the style of art you want first, and *then* try to find an artist that speaks to that style. All artists have different strengths. For example: my art has a very specific look and feel—it's fantastical and very whimsical. So, if an author were looking for hyper realism, I wouldn't be the right fit. (But if it's "fairytale" they'd like, I'd be the girl for the job.) I also think it helps to verbally visit with the artist first to make sure that you get along and communicate well. Just like any relationship, good communication is essential. (On that note, every author I've worked with has ended up being a dear friend because we truly have fun talking and working together—BONUS!)

K.L.: I would have to say it is important to ensure that the author and artist have a similar vision of what they hope to create together. I would strongly encourage writers to examine an artist's previous work, as well as maintaining an open and honest dialogue between both parties, to ensure the vision of the artist and author remain similar though the process.

For *Embracing the Dragon*, Raven drew two illustrations, one for the Amethystine Dragons and one for the Dragons of Kalleen. What type of research was involved or influences used when decided how to create these mythical creatures?

RAVEN: I've been very lucky. So far, I've been blessed to work with authors who understand my artistic style and who have been incredibly supportive about me interpreting their work in my own way. I don't like to do *too* much outside research, because I don't want my work to look like someone else's vision apart from the author's and my own. My main source is the author. Their work (and any additional materials they may choose to provide me with) is what inspires my imagination and I create based on that. I think that's probably how I developed a distinctive style of my own. Although I am very inspired overall by the artists that I grew up loving, I don't actually refer too much to anything outside of the source material and my own imagination when I draw.

K.L: I spent some time examining other films and books which referenced dragons. Stories such as *Game of Throne, The Hobbit,* and *Beowulf* were at the top of the list. I also looked at different drawings and depictions of dragons by other artists from modern to medieval times. These helped to inspire and gave me various ideas on how I might both honor dragons of the past, while still creating a unique character within the story.

Tell us what your desk typically looks like on a creative day. Are there any rituals or traditions required to let you enter a creative zone?

214

RAVEN: I gave away most of my rituals earlier, but one additional (perhaps odd?) thing I do is to tidy EVERYTHING up before I create. I love to sit in a clean/organized workspace, with a candle lit and my materials lined up in front of me. And as I mentioned before, I absolutely always listen to music or have a favorite movie on while I draw.

K.L.: A moderately organized mess! Stacks of papers, generally separated between current writes and current edits. Tons of pens scattered about and several folders worth of both research, generally with a cat sprawled in the center, wondering why I'm staring at a screen instead of paying attention to her.

As to rituals, I must have music to write. Different books normally require different playlists, and even these tend to change based on specific events taking place. For example, fight scenes often require different music than more romantic chapters. For *Embracing the Dragon*, the list frequently included music by Celine Dion, Evanescence, and of course, Raven Quinn.

If you could visit a place you have drawn or created, would you? And if so, where?

RAVEN: YES. Every author I've illustrated for has also been responsible for creating some of my very favorite worlds! I would love to wander through the many Gothic castles on the maps I've created for K.L. I've dreamt many times of exploring Key's Floating Mansion and adventure with the Goblins in Becket's Steampunk Sorcery Series, and I'd love spending endless nights prowling the streets of New Orleans with Sarah M. Cradit's and Alys Arden's characters.

K.L: I would love to see Lethia Castle from the *Black Rose* series, which is described as an ancient seat of gothic architecture, surrounded by roses. Or the castle Amelia calls home in Flames of Kalleen, overlooking eternally ice-tipped mountains. I love medieval structures, and have visited castles all over Europe to gain inspiration from the Tower of London to Bran Castle in Romania. Each trip has inspired my work in various ways, as I often go to these structures taking both extensive notes and photographs which I refer to later during the writing and creative process.

How about the world of another artist or writer?

RAVEN: Absolutely! I'd live at Hogwarts if I could! But I'd spend my summers in Rivendell. ☺

K.L.: Probably Middle Earth to see Rivendell or anywhere else which was a home to elves! I traveled to New Zealand last year and visited several of the Lord of the Rings filming locations and truly loved the experience!

What is the latest news? Do you have any recent or upcoming projects you would like to share?

RAVEN: I do! On the illustration front, I'm currently working on several illustration projects (none of which I can announce yet—but I always make sure to update my social media regularly so watch for announcements forthcoming!) On the music front (as I mentioned earlier), I am in the midst of recording new music and planning some very special extras to accompany the release. The lead single and title track "Alchemy" from this new record features guitar legend George Lynch (Dokken, KXM, Lynch Mob) —and I'm over the moon to have him back for this track! George also played on my debut album, and it's always surreal to have him involved.

K.L.: Last week I had a short story release titled "Lamia's Tower," in the anthology, *Mirror*. The story is a retelling of the fairytale, Rapunzel, with a dark, gothic twist. My next release will be this fall, titled *Releasing the Dragon*, the second novel in the *Flames of Kallleen* paranormal romance series. I'm also preparing to resume my studies for a PhD and am very excited to be continuing my studies!

Find Raven Quinn online at www.ravenquinn.com

CLAIMING THE DRAGON KING

THE ELITE GUARDS

Read on for a preview...

CHAPTER ONE

Several figures stood bathed in the moon's light as their leader decided their course of action. Centuries had passed since that fateful night so long ago, a night he had never forgotten and never would. Revenge brought them to this point in time, to this place of horrors. He would never forgive what they'd done, or forget it. That course of action and chaos had molded him into a fighter, a survivor. He'd become driven by the need for revenge, to take from them what they had taken from his people. Tonight he would do the unthinkable: he would become no better than they were. Tonight he would steal the infant children of the newly-crowned Horde King.

Blane lifted his head, staring up at the starless sky. He sent a silent prayer that it wouldn't be in vain; that this mission wouldn't go askew and that his people wouldn't suffer more for this valiant play to secure peace for his kind. Life for his kind was in turmoil, never-ending suffering as they remained in the shadows, in lands that not even the Horde would walk through and yet they couldn't return home, not without securing peace or taking down the Horde's most powerful creature, their king.

A noise sounded from the mouth of the cave they waited in front of, bringing Blane back to the here and now.

Sadie pranced out, swaying her hips as she licked her lips as she held his line of sight. She was younger than he, easily manipulated. He'd almost felt bad for what he had done, seducing the young maid to feed him information. Blane hadn't wanted to use her, but the more he learned about her and her brothers, the less guilt he felt at his actions. She was also what he hated most, Horde to her core.

"They're holding court," she announced as the blood dripped from a dainty fang. "The guards are down, never to wake again," she laughed musically. "Now pay me."

Blane had promised her dragon tears, a priceless commodity considering the world thought them extinct. He held out a vial, and her fingers jerked and twitched with longing as she held her hand out to accept her payment.

"And tell me, Sadie, what will you do with them?" he asked softly, carefully. He gazed at the cold marble features that hours ago had been screaming in pleasure as she'd rode his cock.

"I will use them to lure children to me," she purred. "The blood of the innocent is…exotic," she sighed huskily as if the thought of helpless children turned her on. Blane stepped closer, his hands itching to wrap around her dainty throat.

"You'd kill innocent children for fun?" he asked angrily, not shocked in the least. She was one hundred percent Horde and thrived on the pain of others. He watched as she tipped her dark head back and laughed as if the ire in his tone amused her. Anger pulsed through him, red-hot; rage filled his soul and lightning fast, his sword cut through the air soundlessly and effortlessly, as he'd been trained to do from birth. Her gaze met his as her head left her body, separating from it. No sound reached their ears other than her head as it hit the sand beneath their feet.

"Hide the corpse," he growled.

"You didn't have to kill her," Fyra said in a bored tone. "She could have been fun."

"We're not here for fun," Blane snapped. "We are here to take the king's children."

"You think he will bow to us once we have them?" she argued. "You're a fool, Blane, if you think they will even care that they are gone. They are Horde; they hold no love for their spawns, not when they can make an endless supply of them now."

"He's different," Blane retorted crisply. "He protects them, which means they can be used against him. He'll trade his life for them, and once he has, he will die for what he has done to our kind. After we've ended his reign, we will move to take the castle, and with it, we will rule the Horde."

"Is that what you really want? To rule a murderous, monstrous bunch that dragons have never cared to claim or be a part of?" she asked as her ice blue gaze searched his. "No, you don't want to be king; you want to end them for what they have done to us. If we kill the head, the body doesn't follow. You and I both know that isn't how this works. Once he dies, another one will rise. I understand your position, but this is a war we won't win, Blane."

"We are not trying to win a war," he said coldly. "They slaughtered my sister inside these walls, as well as my father. Fury was the rightful

219

dragon king, and Alazander murdered him simply because he could, as a warning to any who thought to rise against him. No one intervened, not one royal house stepped in to defend us after they'd given us their word that they would fight beside us. Instead, they let the Horde attack us until no dragon was left."

"But they fucked up, didn't they?" she laughed softly. "They left a young boy alive, and hundreds more who were hidden from them. And now we will rise, Blane. Let's hope this plan works, or they'll have slaughtered another dragon king inside these walls."

"The Goddess is on our side," he uttered as he nodded towards the headless corpse. "Get rid of her before the next patrol comes on and discovers it. I won't have this plan thwarted before it begins."

"Rumor has it they have an *actual* Goddess," Wren grumbled, bending down to blow on the corpse. Flames ignited from Wren's hands, and dragon flames of red and green hues consumed the corpse, leaving nothing but ashes as the fire burned out. The wind heaved, blowing them onto the sand and into the waters behind the castle.

"Does anyone have anything useful to say? Or do you all just want to fucking hold your dicks and whine a little longer?" Blane snapped. He knew they worried; hell, he was worried. He could be walking his best friends to their deaths. This was their chance, though, their time. The Horde had kept them down, kept them running from fear of being discovered. His people couldn't hide much longer, not with the creatures of the forest attacking more and more.

No, he had to move now to secure peace. His people needed a home, a place they could call their own. They'd hidden in the mountains, in the marshes, and in the deserts of Faery for long enough. The Mages were out there, preparing to fight the Horde, and everyone knew they couldn't fight two wars, not at the same time. Not with the damage done to Faery, where they pulled their strength from. It was now or never.

"Let's move," he growled as he started towards the cave's mouth, the forgotten entrance into the Horde stronghold. It had been built when the castle itself was created, a bolt-hole to escape if the Horde ever turned on the royal family. It consisted of low-hanging caverns and winding, twisting passageways that led deep beneath the castle. "The wards are down, the guards are changing so be watchful. If we are discovered, you know what to do."

"It takes time to open the portal, remember that," Fyra grumbled as they entered the pitch-black cave. There would be no escape if they were discovered before Fyra could open the portal; they'd go out fighting, which was more than his father had been able to do.

He trudged through the darkened tunnels for what felt like hours until they reached a false wall, one Sadie had discovered long ago when she'd been sleeping with a guard. He spared a moment for the vampire he'd dispatched, and then a cold smile played across his lips. She couldn't hurt any more children. Her days of feeding on them and leaving corpses in her wake were a thing of the past.

Blane pushed against the door and hesitated as the wall gave a loud creak and moved, revealing the dungeon of the Horde. Inside was damp, cold, and as dark as the tunnel they'd just exited. It looked unused, empty as far as his eyes could see. His chest tightened with pain as he imagined his sister and father locked in the tiny cells.

He pushed the pain away, pushed the memories of them to the back of his mind as he emerged into the room and made his way to the staircase that led deeper into the stronghold. Once there, he pulled the armor from the bag that rested on his hip. They made quick work of changing into the uniform of the Elite Guard, praying no one noticed the difference in craftsmanship.

"From here on out, silence. Not another word until we reach the living quarters."

It took everything he had inside him not to cut down the Fae who moved through the larger rooms they walked in. No one spoke to them, not even the other guards who were positioned everywhere inside the castle. Every exit or door held armed guards, an added precaution for the lack of wards. His small group looked and moved just like them, but then he'd watched them closely for over a century as they moved around the land of Faery.

They started up a grand staircase, never stopping until they reached the furthest hallway. They split off from the others who moved about the halls, going to and from the guards living quarters and the royal family's. No one noticed a group of guards lingering inside the hallway where the Elite Guard lived, not when they looked as if they belonged there.

Once they were at the end, Blane opened the door leading to the royal family's rooms. His gaze scanned the hallway with relief at finding it empty. They slowly entered it, moving along the wall as he searched the wards to be sure Sadie's information about them being down was correct. Once he was sure, he removed his hood and placed his hands on the wall closest to his position.

"They're down, fully down," he mumbled absently, wondering why they'd done it. Why remove wards in this part of the castle without quickly replacing them? Stupid, but it was working to their advantage tonight. He passed several doors before finding one that was elder oak, crafted from the ancient wood, just as Sadie had said it would be.

His hand touched the knob as a musical voice sounded down the hallway. He tensed and turned to the men who all stood in a line as if they were protecting what lay inside the room. He slipped his hood up as two women moved briskly down the hallway to his location.

His heart sped up as they neared. Neither female paid them any heed as they stepped between the guards to enter the room. The rich and enticing scent of freshly plucked night flowers followed them. Blane remained erect until they'd closed the door behind them.

"What the fuck do we do now?" Fyra demanded in a hissed tone as her blonde brow furrowed and creased.

"It's two girls," Wren shrugged. "We can use more women anyway. Not a problem."

Blane scrubbed his hand down his face as he turned and looked both ways down the hall before he opened the door and stepped inside.

CHAPTER TWO

Ciara laughed at Darynda's lips as they pouted at the empty cribs. She'd felt the same way; seeing them empty had been a hard blow. She'd offered to be in the rotation for a chance to see them, to play their pretend nanny until they were back. Everyone had a part to play here, and with the war with the Mages looming on the horizon, she'd made sure to put her best foot forward.

Of course, at night, she was free to do as she wanted, which normally ended up with her hanging at the two nightclubs she'd been approved to visit by the king, her brother. Her hand absently touched the charm that hung around her wrist on the platinum bracelet Ryder had given her.

She'd known it wasn't just a regular bracelet, but today it itched. She pulled on the beautiful charm until the bracelet snapped off. Holding it in her hand so that whatever it did wouldn't alert her brothers to the fact she'd removed it, she bent over the crib and brought Zander's blanket up to her nose, inhaling his scent. She missed the little monsters; their perky smiles and endless laughter had made her life here a little less challenging to endure lately.

The door opened, and she turned around, watching as the guards piled into the room. Her eyes narrowed at them and waited for the charge guard to speak; when he didn't, she did.

"What are you doing in here?" she asked, examining the physique of the tallest one. "I asked you a question, you will answer it." It wasn't her brothers, and most of the Elite Guard was made up of her brothers, or other kin. She stepped a little closer and watched in horror as he withdrew his sword.

Instantly she summoned her own swords to her hands as Zahruk had trained her to do. She body checked Darynda, who didn't respond to the threat in the room. Her mouth opened and closed even as she hit the ground, hard.

"You're not Elite Guards," Ciara seethed as she took in the differences in their armor. It was close, but the actual armor of the guards contoured to their bodies; it had iridescent fabric that made them able to move around undetected. Ciara watched as he removed his hood, revealing piercing blue eyes that never left hers. He had high chiseled cheekbones, with a full mouth that lifted in the corners, giving her a dangerous smirk. His hair was a mixture of light brown with dark tips that reached his shoulders. He was striking, almost beautiful. Yet there was roughness in his face that spoke of harsh climates and sun. Not that it took from the beauty; in fact, it added to it.

"No, we're not, woman," he said thickly with an accent Ciara couldn't place. She took another step back, giving herself enough room to fight him, them. Her heart leapt to her throat, and her hands grew sweaty against the hilts of her blades as fear crept up her spine. "Do you really think you can fight me?" he asked and she smirked at his naiveté.

Ciara lunged, catching him off guard as she took an offensive attack against him, ignoring Darynda's scared cries as blade crashed against blade. He met her attacks with skill, deflecting blow after blow as she continued to assault him. Her arms burned from the blades she'd called to her, too heavy, not the slim ones she'd been using to practice with only a few hours earlier. Today's training had been grueling, meant to drain her until she couldn't fight anymore. It was how every training course had gone in the last few weeks. It was how the Elite Guard trained for war, and she'd begged Zahruk to push her past her limits. However, she hadn't planned on fighting off attackers that day, either.

He parried her attack and then slammed his blade hard against one of hers, sending it crashing to the floor. Ciara looked at it as her lungs burned, her chest heaved with exhaustion, and the reality of the situation took hold. Her eyes lowered to the bracelet on the floor, and then back up just as he forced her to move into defensive attacks. He calculated each attack, carefully backing her up to the wall and out of room to move.

She was slowing, her body exhausted from the rigorous workout she'd done after training today. No doubt Zahruk had pushed her twice as hard today so no one would be forced to trail her at the clubs tonight. Metal clashed against metal until Ciara felt Darynda at her back where she'd risen to stand and watch the fight. She shivered and tried to push forward again, only for him to force her right back to where he wanted her. She thrust her blade at him with everything she had, ignoring the pain that shot up her arms with each clash of their metal. Sweat trickled down her spine as a sense of foreboding settled in.

Sweat dripped down her forehead as she realized the wards were not responding, and her brothers weren't coming. Somehow these men had known the wards were down, and then she realized why they were. These men had come to take the babes, and a sense of relief washed through her that Ryder and Synthia had been smart enough to hide them.

"Put it down, little girl," he ordered.

"You first, asshole," she seethed.

"Put it down, and you won't get hurt," he amended.

"I'll die before I put it down," she growled. She'd heard horror tales of what happened to women when the fighting ended. She'd been forced to endure endless hours of screaming as her father took his women to bed. She had no interest in what would happen if she stopped fighting.

"So be it," he warned as he lunged, sending her blade sailing from her hands before she knew what he intended to do. He raised his blade to strike again, and Darynda screamed.

"She's the princess! She's worth more alive to you, please. Don't kill her!"

Ciara's blood ran cold as she turned horrified eyes on Darynda. Betrayal stung, and her eyes watered as the reality of what Darynda had said registered. She knew Darynda didn't do it out of any malice; she was trying to save Ciara from certain death.

"No, no...no," she whispered as she turned wide, horrified eyes back to the male. His sword was raised, his eyes narrowed. Ciara kicked him right between the legs, landed an uppercut, and dropped, kicking out her foot in a move Synthia taught her. He fell to his knees with a muffled growl as the female behind him jumped in to take his place.

Ciara backed up, pushing Darynda with her. The blonde looked as if she'd relish the kill. Ciara focused her mind, pushing away everything else, and brought forth her reserved powers. Her brands ignited, giving proof to Darynda's claim of who she was. She pushed a burst of energy at the group and grabbed Darynda's hand, making a beeline towards the door. Something caught her foot, and she stumbled, taking Darynda down with her.

She spun on her derriere and kicked out, hitting him square in the nose with her booted foot. He ignored it as if he hadn't felt the kick and pulled her to him. His hand wrapped around her throat. He held her there, trapped beneath the heavy weight of his body as her labored breathing forced her chest to rise and fall.

"Open the fucking portal," he snarled.

"On it," the girl said as she got to her feet, staring at Ciara with hatred. "Get the babes," he ordered. Ciara turned her head as the men rushed to the cribs, tossing the blankets and toys about.

She laughed even though it came out choked and distorted from where his hand held her throat. "You fool, you risked your lives for nothing," she cried out as his hand applied more pressure. "You'll die for this."

"I don't think so," he whispered as his eyes searched hers. "Where are they?" he demanded icily.

"They're with the Gods who they share blood with," she snapped and watched the color drained from his face. "The same ones that will hunt you down and destroy you. You have no idea what you have done, do you?" she laughed and then winced as he sat back, holding her down with the weight of his body.

"Get that fucking portal open now," he snarled.

Darynda lunged, taking him off of Ciara long enough for her to gain her feet and rush towards the door. A sickening noise stopped her, and she turned, staring at Darynda's bloody head before lifting her chin as a blade was placed against her throat.

Her eyes didn't leave Darynda's motionless body. Blood pooled around her head, and Ciara screamed with anguish and anger, which caused the wards to ripple. The hum of danger intensified, the wards began to glow, and Ciara closed her eyes as her sense of hopelessness began to diminish as the wards alerted the guard.

"Thirty seconds," the female announced.

"Don't try it," the male said as Ciara turned to look at the door, and then back at the bracelet that sat beside Darynda. The blade pierced her flesh as she moved and she lifted her hands, pushing it away. Her lips parted as a hiss expelled from her lungs and her palms burned with pain from being sliced open. Blood pooled at her feet as they bled openly. "Stupid female," he snapped as he pushed his sword away and grabbed her hair. He tugged her with him as a portal opened up inside the nursery.

"We have nothing to barter with," a male with emerald green eyes said.

"On the contrary, we have the only daughter of Alazander in our possession," the male she'd been fighting replied as he pulled her body close to his and pulled her through the portal.

THANKS &
ACKNOWLEDGEMENTS

I WOULD LIKE TO OFFER a special thanks to a few people who both assisted and supported me throughout the creation of this novel.

To my family for their never-ending love and support. This never would have been completed without them.

I would also like to thank my longtime writing mentors, Kate, Pam, and Mike for instilling within me a passion for writing.

To the friends and fellow artists who have listened patiently while I ranted, raved and driven them crazy as I went through the writing process, and who understand, because they have had similar stories writing their own characters—Becket, Greg, Raven, Christine, and Stina. Also thanks to my PA, Gladys, for her time and dedication.

To my fabulous editor, Tara, your willingness to work with me, challenge me, and passionately debate the various aspects of this story has helped me to become a better writer. Thank you also for the many discussions on the intricacies of fire, and how best to remove soot. I appreciate all that you do!

Finally, to my cover designer, copyeditor, and formatter, Skyla, who takes the jumbled pictures in my head and consistently turns them into beautiful covers. Your work is nothing short of marvelous! Thank you for being my friend and mentor on this journey.

ABOUT THE AUTHOR

K.L. BONE IS A BESTSELLING author of dark and romantic fantasy. Her work includes the Black Rose Guard series, the Rise of the Temple Gods series, The Flames of Kalleen series, and a stand-alone science fiction novel, *The Indoctrination.*

Bone has a Master's degree in modern literary cultures and is working toward her PhD. She wrote her first short story at the age of fifteen, and grew up with an equally great love of both classical literature and speculative fiction. Bone has spent the last few years as a bit of a world traveler, living in California, London, and most recently, Dublin. When not immersed in words, of her own creation or studies, you'll find her traveling to mythical sites and *Game of Thrones* filming locations.

Bone has a master's degree in modern literary cultures and is working toward her PhD in literature. She wrote her first short story at the age of fifteen and grew up with an equally great love of both classical literature and speculative fiction. Bone has spent the last few years as a bit of a world traveler, living in California, London, and most recently, Dublin. When not immersed in words, of her own creation or studies, you'll find her traveling to mythical sites and *Game of Thrones* filming locations.

Follow her at: www.klbone.com
On Twitter: @kl_bone
Or on Facebook: https://www.facebook.com/klboneauthor

25450340R00127

Made in the USA
Columbia, SC
09 September 2018